Praise for *The Patient One*

"Gray tells a beautiful story of friendship, love, and truth born out of pain and grief. This story reminds us to hold those we love close."

—Rachel Hauck, *New York Times* bestselling author of *The Wedding Dress*

"A pleasing story about recovering from grief and a solid beginning for a new series."

—*Publishers Weekly*

"Gray has created an endearing cast of characters . . . that both delights and surprises—and kept me thinking about the story long after I turned the last page. Bravo!"

—Leslie Gould, #1 bestselling and Christy Award–winning author of more than thirty novels

"Like sunshine breaking through clouds . . . Readers who love Amish stories and/or Christian fiction are sure to take pleasure in following the saga of this wonderful group of friends [who] learn to support each other and follow their hearts as they attempt to discern God's will in their lives."

—*Fresh Fiction*

"This is a four-star book that everyone should read."

—*Cover to Cover Cafe*

Dear Reader,

About ten years ago, right when I first started writing Amish fiction, my friend Celesta told me about Clara, her two daughters' first babysitter. Clara is Old Order Amish. The details are a little hazy now, but I do recall Celesta sharing how Clara sat for her in Sugarcreek, and the arrangement worked out great because both she and Clara had daughters about the same age and they could play together. Over time, Clara and Celesta became very good friends and their daughters did, too. Much more recently, Clara's family attended Tracie's wedding and everyone had a great time.

These ladies' long friendship made a true impression for me. I've always loved visiting Holmes County because whether I'm in the local library, the markets, or a neighborhood restaurant, everyone just goes about their business. Buggies share the road with cars, everyone shops at the same stores, lives near each other, and helps each other out. It doesn't matter if they are Mennonite, Amish, or English.

All that—together with a fondness for two movies from the 80s, *The Big Chill* and *St. Elmo's Fire*—inspired this series.

I hope you enjoy getting to know The Eight and that one or two of the members connect with you. I especially love the romance in *The Patient One*—but then, who could resist a former homecoming queen falling in love (at last!) with her secret crush, the very admirable, very Amish John B.?

Thank you for taking this journey with me, and thank you for giving this book—which is dedicated to Celesta, Clara, and their daughters—a try. I hope you like it!

With my blessings,
Shelley Shepard Gray

Also available from
Shelley Shepard Gray and Gallery Books

THE WALNUT CREEK SERIES

The Loyal One
*Friends to the End**

*ebook only

The PATIENT ONE

Shelley Shepard Gray

POCKET BOOKS
New York London Toronto Sydney New Delhi

Pocket Books
An Imprint of Simon & Schuster, Inc.
1230 Avenue of the Americas
New York, NY 10020

This Pocket Books paperback edition October 2019

Interior design by Erika Genova

Manufactured in the United States of America

10 9 8 7 6 5 4 3 2 1

ISBN 978-1-9821-2181-5
ISBN 978-1-9821-0088-9 (ebook)

For Celesta and Clara and their daughters: Stephanie, Tracie, Miriam, and Mary. Your lifelong friendship inspired me long before I wrote this series. I hope I did y'all proud.

Some friends may ruin you, but a real friend will be more loyal than a brother.

—Proverbs 18:24

Our eyes are placed in front because it is more important to look forward than to look back.

—Amish Proverb

PROLOGUE

WALNUT CREEK, OHIO
JULY

"Thank you for coming. I'm so glad you could make it," Mrs. Warner said as she clasped Katie Steury's hand between her own. "Andy . . . well, Andy would have been pleased to see you here."

"*Jah*," Katie mumbled as she tried not to cry or yank her hand from Andy's *mamm*'s grasp. There were times when *Englischer*'s customs felt so strange and awkward that she never knew how to respond. This funeral reception was one of those instances.

She didn't want to be thanked for attending Andy's funeral. She didn't understand why Mrs. Warner acted so surprised that she'd dropped everything to go. But most of all, Katie didn't ever want to think of Andy looking down from Heaven and being pleased to see her standing in his dining room after watching him get laid to rest in the ground.

Nee, she didn't want to think about that at all.

Mrs. Warner tried again. "It was a beautiful

service, don't you think? Pastor Douglas did a nice job describing Andy."

Somehow she found the words to reply. "It was a beautiful service, Mrs. Warner. *Jah.*"

She didn't lie. But had the pastor described the Andy Warner she'd known?

As far as she was concerned, he hadn't even come close.

Obviously out of words as well, Mrs. Warner ran her hands down her tailored black wool skirt.

Smiling awkwardly again, Katie scanned the room. The crowded room felt stifling. Drops of sweat trickled down her back, making the heavy black fabric of her dress and apron feel like it weighed twice as much. Even the black *kapp* covering her head made her uncomfortable. She needed some fresh air.

When she spied five familiar faces standing on the lawn just outside the front door, she started to take a step away.

Mrs. Warner noticed. Dismay appeared in her eyes before she regained her composure again. "Well . . ."

Ack, *but this was so hard!* Steeling her shoulders, Katie forced herself to do the right thing, which was staying put. "Mrs. Warner, I'm mighty sorry for your loss. I . . . I loved Andy. I will miss him always." Though those words were heartfelt, they didn't begin to convey the depth of her grief. She opened her mouth to finish her speech, to pull something out of her to try to comfort Andy's mother, but she couldn't seem to form any more words.

After the briefest of pauses, Mrs. Warner nodded, her expression tight. "Yes, of course." She smiled wanly before turning away.

Shame burned a path down Katie's throat. Mrs. Warner was hurting. She'd lost her son. Katie should've said more. Should've said something comforting and meaningful right at that moment.

It felt like she'd failed Andy once again.

The air conditioner clicked on, sending a frosty blast that didn't do much to cool down the crowded room. Standing next to the vent, Katie shivered as goose bumps prickled her arms. Yet, perversely, the heat in her body reached a new height. She was sure her cheeks were burning bright red.

It was too much.

Feeling dizzy, Katie turned and awkwardly weaved through the throng of mourners. Most were holding clear plastic plates heaped high with croissant sandwiches and heavy-looking potato and macaroni salads. Someone had four or five meatballs rolling around on a plate, each one stuck with a bright blue plastic toothpick. Andy, who'd become a vegetarian when he was twelve, would've hated this meal.

The front door loomed like an invitation. Katie

kept her head down as she rushed toward it, then pulled it open with too much force. It snapped back and caused the terrier resting on the stairs to bark in annoyance.

Feeling like she was almost out of breath, she stepped onto the stoop and then firmly closed the door behind her, panting in relief as the warm July breeze fanned her face.

"Katie, there you are," John B. said as he waved her over. "We were wondering if you were ever going to come out here. Come join us."

"I only just now looked out the window and saw you all," she replied. Though she'd seen them during the service and had stood by their sides when Andy had been lowered into the ground, she'd been in too much of a cloud of grief to look at them closely.

Now, in the bright light in the space of the Warner's front yard, she was able to study them. In spite of the circumstances, they looked good. Familiar and comforting, like her favorite terry cloth bathrobe at home. "Hiya."

"Hi to you, too," Marie returned with a watery smile.

Somehow, even though she was dressed in black, Marie still managed to look beautiful. Perhaps it had something to do with her long golden hair, perfect skin, and luminescent green eyes.

"Katie, I was going to ask if you wanted to sit with me during the funeral," Marie continued, "but the church was so crowded I wasn't sure if I could hold you a spot. Then, I wasn't sure if you would have wanted to sit with me and my parents."

Katie knew why she'd said that. Marie was English, and Katie was Old Order Amish. Though it didn't used to, for some reason that mattered now. "Don't worry about it. I came a little late and was glad to find a pew in the back." She smiled, then scanned their group. The remains of the Eight.

She, Marie, and John B. Then there was Logan, Harley, Elizabeth Anne, and Will Kurtz, whose mother used to watch over them in the summers while some of their mothers worked.

"I just spoke with Mrs. Warner. She thanked me for coming here today." Only this group would understand how that affected her.

Marie winced. "She thanked me, too. I didn't know how to respond."

"I don't think there is a right way," John murmured. "The majority of me feels so bad and empty, it's all I can do to stand here in Andy's front yard."

"I don't feel good about things, either," Elizabeth Anne said. "But it isn't all our fault. I mean, we didn't know Andy was depressed." She looked each of them in the eye. "At least, I didn't."

"I didn't, either," Will said. "But does that even matter? Andy used to be one of our best friends, and he hanged himself four days ago."

Harley, always the quietest of the group, sighed. "To my shame, I even have excuses. I've been working on the farm and Andy worked for some computer company. It wasn't like we had much opportunity to see each other anymore."

"Yeah. I mean, I stayed in Walnut Creek and am seeing Andy's sister, Trish, but that didn't mean I was privy to all of Andy's thoughts," Logan murmured.

"How is Tricia?" Marie asked. "I thought she might have been out here with us."

Logan eyed the front door like it was more of a barrier rather than the entrance to a home he was once so familiar with. "I don't know. She's devastated, of course. I think she's pretty confused, too. She's been trying to find a way to tell her parents that she wants to become Amish but hasn't gotten up the nerve yet."

"I think she was hoping Andy would clear the way for her," Elizabeth Anne said.

Logan nodded. "I think you're right." Glancing at the closed door again, he murmured, "Sometimes I wish I could simply pull her out of that house. There's a lot of pressure on her inside. And now with Andy gone?" His voice lowered. "I just don't know."

"I still can't believe he's gone." Katie shook her head. "I feel like I let Andy down. Back when we were little, he was our ringleader."

"Even in our twenties, he still was our leader," Will said. "Remember last year, how he tried to get us all together at Christmas? No one could agree on a date."

Marie wiped her eyes. "I told him I was much too busy at work to drive here from Cleveland. Why did I act like seeing my best friends in the world was too much trouble?"

"You can't do that to yourself, Marie," Logan said. "I didn't take the time either."

Looking at each member, Katie knew they were all suffering from guilt and regret. But she was enough of a realist to admit that it wasn't as much of a surprise that they weren't *still* friends. The surprise was that they'd ever become so close in the first place. Three of them were Amish, three—including Andy—were English, and two were Mennonite.

On paper, they should have had their own circle of friends with their own kind. Instead, they'd found deep friendships based on things outside of their religions. Each of them had believed in loyalty and friendship. They'd each possessed a small amount of rebelliousness, too. That rebelliousness had cemented a bond among them and had allowed friendships to grow, even when other people had said their group was odd.

John B. exhaled. "It won't bring Andy back, but I'd like us to make an effort to see each other more often. Does anyone want to do that?"

"Of course," Marie said.

Her sweet, instant response triggered a memory. Without thinking, Katie met Elizabeth Anne's gaze and smiled. John B. had always been shy, and Marie, their very own homecoming queen, had always been sweet on him. Andy used to joke that the two of them were going to have to be stuck somewhere in a blizzard for them to finally get together.

But maybe it wasn't going to take a blizzard. Maybe it was a funeral.

Mr. Warner poked his head out, and his expression softened when he saw the group of them before it hardened into grief again. "A couple of people wanted to share a few stories about Andy," he said slowly. "I thought maybe one of you would like to share, too?"

"Of course, Mr. Warner," Marie said with a polite smile. When he closed the door and they were alone again, she turned to Katie. "You were always the best at telling stories. Would you do that for us?"

Would she mind sharing a story about the Andy she'd known? For the first time since Katie woke up that day, a sense of calm filled her. "I've got a story in mind and would be happy to share it . . . if everyone is sure they want me to do the talking?"

"I do," Logan said.

"*Jah*. Tell us all a *gut* one," John B. said. "Something to make us remember what we used to be like when we were all together."

Katie knew what John B. meant. He wanted a story about back when they used to be closer and had shared every hope and dream together.

Back when they used to think anything was possible.

Back when instead of just seven, they'd been a group of eight.

ONE

"The first thing you all should remember about Andy was that he was afraid of snakes," Katie said with a grin, her voice cracking slightly. "He was also really embarrassed by that. Which, of course, is why one afternoon, back when we were fourteen, all eight of us decided to go for a walk in the woods."

THREE MONTHS LATER—OCTOBER

"This little house isn't much, and I can't say I'm real thrilled about its location, but I suppose it has a certain amount of charm," Marie's mother said as she ran one manicured nail along the granite kitchen countertops. "These are sure pretty."

Marie smiled with pride. "Thanks, Mom. The kitchen is the reason I snapped the place up. That, and the amazing amount of closet space."

"It really does look better on the inside than on the outside." Mom looked out the window, frowning at the chain-link fence surrounding the yard. "Are you sure this area is perfectly safe?"

"Mom, it's Walnut Creek. Of course it's safe. This place is going to be just fine. I'll be fine."

"Well, you're right, I suppose. Most of Walnut Creek is perfectly safe, almost like something out of Mayberry." Still staring out the window, she added, "This street doesn't have a real good look to it, though. Be sure you lock your doors at night."

"I'll do that." Like she didn't already.

After giving the weed-filled yard one last glance, her mother turned back to her. "I hate to bring it up again, but I still don't understand why you transferred over to that branch out in New Philly and elected to drive there from Walnut Creek. You had a nice life in Cleveland."

"You're right. I did." Her mother wasn't wrong. After going to college and majoring in English, she'd had a hard time finding work. She'd finally landed a job as a teller at Champion Banks and discovered she loved it. One thing led to another, and by the end of her first year, she'd been promoted and was actually making pretty good money.

Good enough that she'd leased a lovely loft in picturesque Chagrin Falls, a well-to-do suburb east of Cleveland. She'd decorated it pretty and met a nice group of girlfriends. Just a couple of months ago, she'd started dating. Many of her customers were single, eligible men who her parents would have been thrilled to meet.

It was all good. All things she knew she should be happy about. Her parents were proud of her, too. Not only was she living on her own and supporting herself, but they were also sure she was eventually going to bring home a nice man who was a lot like them, i.e., wealthy and good-mannered. Then, in no time, she would settle down, get married, have her two children, and eventually raise her own homecoming queen.

Though all of that hadn't been exactly her goals in life, Marie knew it was a possibility. Maybe she would have done all that, too, if she hadn't begun to realize that everything she had wasn't actually everything she'd ever wanted.

After Andy died, she'd decided to stop contemplating change and actually make one.

Three months ago, when John B. had asked them all to make a promise to reconnect, she had agreed immediately, knowing that both her heart and her soul needed these friends of hers. Needed them more than a fancy future or even making her mother's dreams a reality.

And then, of course, there was John B.

After living most of her life in his periphery, wanting to be more than just his friend, but feeling sure that he would never want the same thing, she'd decided to give things between them one more try.

It might be a pipe dream. John might never look beyond their differences or want to put her in front of his family's wishes. But Marie knew that if she didn't finally make her desire known to him, to simply lay it all out there and hope for the best, she would always regret it.

Treating her to the intense look Marie was oh so familiar with, Mom said, "Are you ready to tell me the truth about why you moved back to Walnut Creek?" She suddenly frowned. "You aren't having bad dreams again, are you?"

Her mother was referring to the same reoccurring dream she'd had since childhood. She used to wake her parents up at least once a week with her cries. "Some, but they haven't been too bad."

"Are you sure? I bet I could call around and see if Miss Flemming is still in practice."

Miss Flemming had been her therapist for two years back when she'd been in middle school. She was a nice lady, but she'd been old even then. "I hope she's still not practicing, Mom. I saw her years ago. She needs to be sitting on a beach somewhere instead of listening to everyone else's problems, don't you think?" she joked.

Her mother didn't crack a smile. "She helped you learn to relax, Marie."

No, Miss Flemming had helped her learn how to cope when things happened that were out of her control. "I've been doing my breathing exercises. I'll get better. It's just been a really difficult time, Mom."

"I know. I still worry about you. Dad and I love you."

"I know. And I love you, too. That's one of the reasons I'm glad I'll be here in Walnut Creek. It will be nice to see you both more often. I also have a really good group of friends here. I want to live near them. The rest of the Eight feel the same way."

Her mother's expression softened. "They were good friends to you. Good kids, too."

"We're all adults now, Mom."

"I know that. It's just that when I think of the Eight, I can't help but remember the way you all would run around together." Her lips twitched. "My goodness. You all were so loud! Always laughing. Always in a hurry. Dad used to call you guys a pack of hounds. Practically inseparable."

That comment should've made her feel better. Instead, it only served to remind her that they'd drifted apart . . . and they'd suffered for it, too. Especially Andy.

Not wanting to start crying again, she cleared her throat. "See? Relationships like that don't come along more than once in a lifetime. They need to be nurtured, don't you think?"

"Dear, you're only twenty-four. You've got years and years to make more really good friends."

"I made new friends in college and in Chagrin Falls, but they weren't the same as the Eight."

"Marie . . ."

Hating that her mother was likely to launch into a well-meaning but misguided lecture, Marie hardened her voice. "Mom, I don't want to make more new, good friends. I want to work on keeping the ones that I have."

Her mother's expression softened. "I'm not saying that you shouldn't all still be friends, Marie. It's just that sometimes you have to accept the fact that people change and they choose their own path. Just because they were a part of your childhood doesn't mean they need to be a part of the rest of your life."

Before she could interrupt, her mother continued. "Then, too, there's the fact that while you might be grown up, none of you have married yet. Things change when you get married."

"I know that."

A pair of lines formed in between her mother's brows. "Then there's the fact that some of you simply don't have anything in common anymore. You've each gone down your own paths."

"We do, though. We talked a lot at Andy's funeral."

Her voice gentled. "Marie, I'm very sorry about Andy. He was a wonderful person. I know you're heartbroken about his death. Dad and I have been keeping his parents and Tricia in our prayers. But I'm also talking about how some of those ah, *adults*, now live a completely different lifestyle from you."

"Because some of the Eight are Amish?"

"Well, yes." Her gaze hardened. "And don't go acting like it doesn't matter. It does. If your Amish friends haven't been baptized yet, they soon will be. Then their paths will be set. I know it's hard, but it's a fact of life. Sometimes childhood friendships are best left as good memories."

She shook her head. "Mom, as much as it makes me feel like I'm sixteen again, I'm going to have to tell you that you don't understand."

Her mom chuckled. "I actually do recall you telling me that a time or two, back in the day."

"And?"

"And, at the risk of repeating what *I* used to tell *you*, I'm going to have to say that I might understand more than you think."

"I love you, Mom." She reached out and gently squeezed her mother's hand, hoping the words and the gesture would ease her obstinate tone.

After giving her a squeeze back, her mother dropped her hand. "I love you, too, Marie. And unlike when you were sixteen, you're a grown woman now. I'll try to keep my opinions to a minimum."

"Thanks."

Seeming to come to grips with herself, her mother said, "All right then. I told your father I wouldn't be home until close to seven. That means we've got all afternoon to turn this place into a little home for you. What do you want to do first?"

"Can we work on my living room? I think I need something to store things in. And maybe a new lamp."

"I saw some cute shelving units we can put together over at the Walmart in Millersburg. Want to head over there?"

Before her mother reached for her purse, Marie flung her arms around her. "Thanks, Mom."

Her mom wrapped her arms around her, too. "For what?"

"For not arguing with me."

After pressing her lips to her brow, her mother started chuckling. "You might know the Eight the best, but I know you pretty well, too. And you always were as stubborn as all get out."

Thinking that her stubbornness might finally get John B. to notice her, Marie smiled. After all, that was what she was counting on.

TWO

Katie continued, her eyes bright with humor. "So there we were, all traipsing through the woods at the back of the Kurtz house, when Will and John B. started pointing to the creek that ran along the ravine on the edge of the property. John B. told us all that just the day before he saw four snakes sunning along the banks. So, of course, we had to head down there to catch a glimpse of them. As you might imagine, it wasn't our best idea."

"We should feel on top of the world," Will said to John B. with a grin as they walked down Maple Street. "Our team got another trailer built today."

John B. smiled. "*Jah*, we did. It's a beauty, too."

"I couldn't believe it when I heard that the buyer wanted it painted yellow and black, but I think it turned out right nice."

John still thought it looked like an overgrown bumblebee, but it was eye-catching, he'd give it that. "Mr. Kerrigan said it's going to some famous country western singer. I guess when he's not touring the country being rich and famous, he wants to pull his little trailer and go camping in style."

"And why wouldn't he? They're great little trailers."

"That they are." John hadn't ever imagined that he'd enjoy working in a camper factory, but he surely did. Part of the reason was that it was family owned. Mr. Kerrigan was a good man who always put his faith, his wife, and his children first. He expected his employees to do the same.

That meant that they started early but always stopped for the day at four o'clock during the week and at noon on Saturdays. No one was ever expected to work on Sundays, not even when some of their more demanding customers offered to pay extra for a rush job.

Furthermore, the little trailers were so popular because each one was custom-built. Some of their customers were famous; some lived nearby. The vast majority of them, however, were just regular men and women who enjoyed the outdoors. They called Mr. Kerrigan and placed their orders from all over the country, then came into Walnut Creek when their trailer was done.

When they arrived, Mr. Kerrigan would take them into the warehouse so they could meet all of the men and women who had worked on it. That made the job even more special to John. He liked the idea of looking at their customers in the eye.

When he'd first gotten hired, John B. had thought maybe he'd work there only until something better came along. Now he was of the mind that there wasn't anyplace better for him. Will, who'd just started working there eight months ago, had quickly come to the same conclusion.

Whenever they worked the same days, they walked home together, sometimes even stopping for an early supper along the way. John, who had always been on the quiet side, liked how Will was always full of news and didn't mind sharing it.

"So, guess what I learned last night?" Will asked when they got to the top of the ridge and turned left into town. "Kendra Troyer is moving here next month."

"Really? I'm surprised." Though Kendra wasn't technically a part of the Eight, she might as well have been. They all knew her well. Especially him, since her family was also New Order Amish.

"Are ya? Huh. Did you not get a chance to speak with her at the funeral?"

"*Nee*, but it was crowded. Unlike you, I stayed outside as much as possible."

"You missed a good spread. Those meatballs were tasty."

He chuckled. "Only you would be eating well at Andy's funeral."

"And only you would have gone home hungry in order to avoid half of Walnut Creek."

"True." Unlike himself, Will was never bothered by crowds and noise. He could work a room like an experienced politician. Realizing that he didn't sound pleased, he quickly added, "Don't get me wrong, I'm glad Kendra's coming back. I was just surprised. She seemed real settled in Columbus."

As was his way, Will thought about that for a good block before replying. "Maybe she was . . . or maybe not. She had a tough time about four years ago, remember?"

"I remember."

Kendra had gotten real sick her freshman year. So sick she'd had to quit college. Then John B. had heard that she was so disappointed that she'd started drinking. That bad habit had soon gotten out of control and had led her down a dark path. She'd ended up getting help for that, too.

He'd written her a couple of letters, but she'd never responded. He'd felt helpless but hadn't known what else he could do, not without any encouragement from her. "We'll have to make sure she gets moved in okay," he said, glad he could finally be of some use to her. "Kendra's parents were never a lot of help."

"That's one way of saying it. One could also say

that they were the root of her problems." Frowning, he continued. "Ever since I can remember, they were distant."

"Even on their best days," John agreed, remembering how Kendra was always the last to be picked up when they were little, and they were never around once she got old enough to look after herself.

"My *mamm* once said Mr. and Mrs. Troyer were the complete opposite of Marie's parents. Now *they* were doting."

Unable to help himself, he smiled. "*Jah*, they were."

"It used to drive Kendra crazy, the way Mr. and Mrs. Hartman acted like the sun rose and set on Marie."

Before he could stop himself, John blurted, "Well, she was pretty special, even when she was just a little thing."

Will laughed. "Are you ever going to do anything about what's been brewing between the two of you?"

With anyone else, John would've pretended he didn't know what he was talking about. "*Nee*."

"Why not?"

They were almost at the pizza place that had just opened up. "She's English. I'm not."

Marie Hartman was also a lot of other things. Beautiful. Vibrant. Rich. Popular with most everyone. What could a man like him ever offer her?

"You haven't joined the church yet."

"I know. But I intend to."

"But you haven't . . ."

John shook his head, not wanting to go down that path, not even with Will. "Whether I've been baptized in the church or not ain't the point. Marie most likely has a boyfriend." From the time she was fifteen or so, he couldn't ever remember her not having some guy by her side.

"I know for a fact that she doesn't . . . and that she is living in one of those run-down houses near Folsom Road."

Everything inside of him froze. "What? Who's she living there with?"

"No one." Will raised his eyebrows as they walked into the restaurant.

John B. felt himself fuming as he digested the news. That unexpected flare in temper made him keep his mouth shut while the hostess seated them.

Only after they had ordered a large pizza with pepperoni, mushrooms, and peppers did he feel like he had himself under control enough to talk about Marie again.

"Folsom Road ain't the place for Marie. It's dangerous around there. Doesn't she know that?"

"Well—"

"And, come to think of it, why is she even there

in the first place?" Though Will opened his mouth to speak, John kept on talking. "I thought her parents looked out for her. They certainly did when she was in high school. Don't you remember when they wouldn't let her go camping with us?"

Will nodded. "Marie was real upset."

Marie had started crying so hard, he'd had to pull her into his arms and hug her tight.

Feeling even more frustrated, he threw out a hand. "What has happened since then? They should've forbidden her to move there. She's going to get hurt. Then what—" He stopped himself just in time from revealing far too much about his secret feelings for her.

Looking bemused, Will took a long sip of his Sprite. "John, I'm thinkin' her parents knew better than to forbid Marie to do anything. Because she likely told them she was too old to be told what to do."

"What about Logan? I thought they were close."

"They are, but I never thought she was any closer to Logan than the rest of us."

"But still, Logan should've said something."

"Maybe he did and she didn't listen." Leaning back against the bright red pleather, he added, "I think you should go check on her, John B. She might listen to you."

"She might." Thinking about the fact that she was

a grown woman with a good job and now her own home, he started thinking that Will might be right. Marie might not appreciate him sharing his opinions about how she should run her life. "Or she might not."

Will stared at him intently. "Didn't Andy's death teach you anything?" he asked after the server deposited their pizza in the middle of the table. "Stop stalling, John B. Even if you don't think she and you are ever going to be a couple, you're her friend. Maybe her best one."

All of the reasons he had to stay away from Marie fell away. Will was right. It was time to stop stalling. "You know what? I think I might stop by her *haus* real soon."

Will grinned. "Oh yeah? How soon?"

Realizing Will was practically daring him, John gathered his courage. "Tomorrow afternoon. I'm going to bring her a chocolate cake from Mount Hope when I go talk to her about her safety."

"Oh, you're going whole hog, bringing a *kacha* to sweeten your cause."

"I ain't ashamed to use bribery. Marie has a much kinder disposition when she is eating chocolate."

"That cake should at least get you in the door and encourage her to listen to you."

"Not at first. But Marie has always been pretty practical. She'll come around to my way of thinking . . . eventually."

Pulling off the first slice of pizza, Will chuckled. "For once, I'm real glad I'm working Monday morning. I can't wait to hear how this visit turns out."

John B. groaned as he set his own piece on the plate in front of him. Will had just played him well. Now he had no choice but to go see Marie on Saturday, after he drove his buggy all the way over to Mount Hope tonight to place the order and then again tomorrow to pick up Marie's favorite chocolate four-layer cake with coconut filling.

Just thinking about being alone with her in her home made his cheeks heat with embarrassment. He'd spent many a night going to sleep just imagining such a thing.

When Will laughed again, John glared. "You'd better not tell anyone about me calling on Marie."

"Don't worry, buddy. From the way you're already blushing, everyone's gonna already know."

THREE

"Down we went. All eight of us descended in some kind of haphazard line, with John B. in the front with none other than Marie right beside him." Katie paused. "I still *canna* figure that out."

"I liked snakes back then!" Marie called out.

"Huh," Katie said, "and here I always thought it was because you liked something else."

It was a fact. She had way too many cookbooks. Marie had unpacked only half of them and was already out of space in the hutch she'd bought to stand along the back wall of the kitchen.

Taking another sip of coffee that she shouldn't be drinking at six at night, Marie knew what she should do. She needed to get rid of ten or twelve. But even thinking about that made her wince.

"Marie, you are being ridiculous," she chided herself out loud. "Think of E.A. She'd tell you to stop being so silly and learn to live with less."

But even thinking of Elizabeth Anne's plain and simple lifestyle didn't make much of an impression on her love of the cookbooks.

Or for most of the things in her life, she supposed. She liked shoes and purses and clothes and coffee cups. No, there really wasn't anything either "plain" or "simple" about her. E.A. would probably tease Marie for even *imagining* she could be like her.

Thirty minutes later when the doorbell rang, Marie couldn't reach the door fast enough. Anything would be better than continuing this charade of sorting books.

But she realized she was wrong when she opened the door. Because there was John B., holding a white cardboard bakery box.

"What are you doing here?" Nothing would have surprised her more, except maybe if both of her parents had shown up in jeans and said they wanted to go for a hike.

His half-smile slowly faded as the seconds passed. "I'm sorry, Marie. Is this a bad time?"

"No." Finally getting out of her fog, she shook her head and ushered him in. "I mean, of course not, John. Come inside."

After entering her tiny foyer, she closed the door behind him and turned the dead bolt. She startled as he said, "I brought you a cake."

Reaching for it, she read the stamp on the top of the white box. "It's from Mount Hope Bakery."

"Chocolate with coconut filling," he said, humor lighting his expression.

She almost gasped. Okay, maybe she actually did. "John, that's my favorite." What she almost added but didn't was that she knew from experience that it wasn't an easy cake to get.

The ladies at Mt. Hope made a lot of things daily. Cinnamon rolls, snickerdoodle cookies, apple and cherry pies, even plain chocolate cakes. But this one? It had to be special ordered.

But the difficulties didn't end there. One couldn't simply pick up the phone and place an order. Mt. Hope Bakery was Amish owned, so no one there had anything to do with the phone or the computer. That meant in order to ask for this cake, one had to stop by the bakery and place the order in person. Then one was at the ladies' mercy for when they would make it. Marie knew this from experience. The last time she'd ordered one, she'd been dismayed to learn that they had two wedding cakes on their schedule and wouldn't have time to make "her" cake for at least two weeks.

Smiling at her, he chuckled. "*Jah.* I know that, Marie."

"How did you ever manage to find it? Did you simply get lucky?"

"I did, in the sense that the ladies took pity on me, yes. They made it for me in a day." He sighed. "And I wasn't going to tell you that."

She had so many questions bouncing around in her head, Marie didn't know where to start. Why had John gone all the way to the bakery in the first place? Why had he ordered her a cake? And why had he brought it here, by himself?

Could it be that maybe . . . *maybe* he was finally going to see her as something more than just one member of the Eight?

But, of course, she couldn't pepper him with questions. That would be rude.

Or maybe it was rather that she was too tentative around him. John B. could be pretty sensitive. The last thing she wanted to do was embarrass or offend him and send him on his way.

Walking him into her kitchen, she set it on the counter. Then, unable to help herself, she lifted the lid and peered inside. And there, in all its splendor, was one of her favorite things in the world, the chocolate cake from the tiny bakery. If she had been alone, she would've stuck a finger in the icing and taken a swipe.

However, she was her mother's daughter. Looking John directly in the eye, she smiled and said, "This looks delicious. Thank you so much."

He gave a little bow. "You're welcome."

"Would you like to have a piece with me?"

Looking around the room, he murmured, "I would, but not yet."

"Oh? What do you want to do first?" Though the words didn't mean anything, she realized they might come across as suggestive. Or maybe that's just because where John B. was concerned, almost everything about him made her think of romance.

Hazel eyes flashed back to her. They almost seemed to read her mind. "Maybe you could give me a tour of your new home?"

Like a difficult jigsaw puzzle, everything finally clicked into place. John B. had come over to give her a housewarming present.

It didn't really matter that he'd come alone. Or had brought her a cake that wasn't easy to get.

"All right." Pinning another smile on her face, she said, "As you can see, this is my kitchen."

"Looks like you're getting ready to do some cooking."

"More like I'm trying to get ready to do some cleaning. I have too many cookbooks." Pointing to the hutch, she said, "I had high hopes of putting them all there, but obviously that isn't going to happen."

"I'm afraid you're right about that."

Comments like that were why she practically melted around him. He was kind. He never criticized, never tried to change her. Instead, he simply accepted her as herself. And though most people in her life would have never imagined that she had such a need, it seemed she did.

"It's a mess in here. Come on, I'll show you the rest of it." She walked into the living room, which was actually right next to the kitchen.

"I like your fireplace. Does it work?" he asked.

"I hope so. The inspector said it did." She walked to the small bathroom just off the living room. "Here's the powder room. I think it's kind of in a bad place, don't you?"

"Why is that?"

"Well, if there's a lot of people in the room and someone has to go, everyone will know."

"You're worried that everyone will know that a person has to go to the bathroom?" His lips twitched.

Put that way, she supposed that her worry was kind of silly. After all, everyone had to go to the bathroom sooner or later. "Anyway, at least it's an extra bathroom so people won't have to use mine. I'm glad about that."

Pointing down the hall, he said, "And down that way?"

She walked down the narrow hallway, which was painted a worn-looking vanilla. "This here is the extra bedroom." Of course there wasn't a bed in it. "I can't decide what to do with it. Maybe I'll get a twin bed and a chair? Maybe a desk, though I don't want to work at home." She paused, waiting for him to offer a suggestion.

But of course he didn't. Instead, with his hands firmly clasped behind his back, he looked at everything carefully. "Is that a closet?"

She opened it. "Yes. I'm using it as a linen closet." The explanation was unnecessary, since it was loaded with sheets and towels, all stacked haphazardly. Boy, she really needed to become a better housekeeper.

"Ah."

Becoming embarrassed by her mess, she turned on her heel. "Come on. Let's finish this up." She opened up the next door. "Here's my bathroom. It's a good size, I think."

"I think so, too."

Unable to help herself, Marie walked into the room and wrapped a hand around the bathtub's rim. "It has a really pretty old-fashioned bathtub, which I love." While John studied it, she chuckled. While some might have called it a monstrosity, she thought it was perfect. It really did look like it had been pulled out of one of the interior design magazines her mother loved so much. The tub was cast iron and had claw-feet. She felt like a princess every time she filled it with water.

"I like its feet," John said.

"It's a great bathtub. I've taken a long bath in it every night since I've moved in."

He glanced at her before looking away again. "I'm glad it works."

Suddenly realizing they were talking about her bathing, she rushed to her bedroom and threw open the door. And bit back a moan. Because, of course, her bed was unmade, and there were pillows and shoes everywhere. And a lacy, light purple nightgown had been thrown in the middle of the floor.

"I usually make my bed. Sorry," she said before ushering him out, hoping, really hoping that he hadn't spotted it.

But judging from the blush on his cheeks, he hadn't missed a single thing.

Marie closed the door tightly behind her, like she was afraid that the nightgown was going to exit the room on its own.

"So, that's the house. What do you think?" she asked as she led him back to the kitchen.

"I think you seem happy here."

"I am. I mean, I will be once I clean up everything and get settled in." She realized then that instead of looking pleased for her he seemed distracted. "Is anything wrong?"

"*Nee*. Well, not beyond that I came over here to persuade you to move."

His blunt statement felt like a slap. "Is there a certain reason you don't want me around?"

"It's not that I don't want you around, I don't want you here."

"Because?"

"Because this ain't a safe place for a girl like you."

She was a team leader at the bank. She had several people, both men and women, who reported to her. She wore suits and took conference calls and was busy enough to have to schedule most meetings a week or two out at a time. No one at Champion Banks made the mistake of acting like she was a naive, clueless girl more than once or twice.

So while with pretty much everyone else in her life she would have jumped all over the use of that term to describe herself, she focused on his solemn expression.

He was really worried. "Why don't you think I'll be safe? Everyone around here seems nice enough."

"Most of the people who live in this neighborhood aren't like you."

Marie supposed there was a compliment in there somewhere. "So far, my neighbors have been just fine."

"You know what I mean. You are a pretty woman with a good job. People here are a little rougher. I've heard that there are even some men living in this neighborhood who've spent time in jail. They might be desperate and see you as someone they could take advantage of."

"I came here from Cleveland, remember? I'm used to living in a big city. I know how to take precautions."

A muscle in his jaw clenched. "Do you even have a security system?"

She was just about to tell him that she didn't, but there was something about his stance that made her say something else. "Maybe."

"What does that mean?"

Unable to hold her joke back, her lips twitched. "It means that you are acting a whole lot like a Rottweiler, so maybe I do, absolutely, have my own security system. You."

FOUR

While the chuckles subsided, Katie glanced over at Mr. and Mrs. Warner. When she noticed they were smiling, too, she continued.

"I guess you all have a good idea of who was at the very end of our little line. It was our formerly fearless leader, Andy. Turns out when snakes are involved, he was our leader no more."

Just before John left work, Mr. Kerrigan had called him into his office. He'd just gotten off the phone with a client out in Idaho who'd had a special request. The man not only wanted a few more bells and whistles in his trailer but also a unique paint job. He wanted the entire outside to look like a sunrise. Lots of grays, oranges, yellows, and blues.

"I'm hoping you can be the lead designer on this one, John. I don't know of another person in the company who would have the patience to bring this client's dreams to life," Mr. Kerrigan had said. "What do you think?"

John thought that the question was the opportunity he'd been hoping and praying for. From the time he'd started at the trailer company, John had been working late and arriving early. Doing as much as he could to impress his boss and let him know that he was a man who was worth investing in.

Once he and Mr. Kerrigan had developed a good rapport, John had gotten even braver. Little by little, he had started offering more opinions regarding the designs on the trailers. He enjoyed both planning and applying the artwork and loved seeing how the finished product illustrated months of careful consideration and hard work. Just last month, his boss had asked him to work side by side with Job, their company's lead builder.

"I think I'd like to take the lead on this one. I have lots of ideas already," he said. "*Danke*, Mr. Kerrigan."

His boss held out his hand. "No, thank you, John B. Your eye for design and steady hand have put the company's reputation on the map. I'm glad you're willing to do even more."

The hard-earned praise had felt good, and after taking his boss's notes, he'd ridden his bike home and had played with the customer's wants in his head while showering.

Now he was at his desk, eager to put a pencil to paper and start sketching out his ideas. Before long, his rudimentary scratches began to take form, and the hour he'd intended to spend on the project slid into two. Wanting to get as much done as he possibly could, he pulled out his colored pencils and began shading in the drawing.

"Hey, John?" his youngest sister called out from the doorway. "Mamm wants to know if you want supper. Do ya?"

Startled, John turned to look at Molly, who was parked outside his bedroom in her wheelchair. Molly had been thrown from a horse when she was nine and it had injured one of the lower vertebrae in her spine. Ever since, her legs had been paralyzed, though she had some small amount of feeling in her thighs.

That accident had been a dark moment for his family, but Molly's determination and bright spirit had shined through. She'd never felt sorry for herself and hardly ever complained about her circumstances.

Sometimes John felt like the rest of the family had taken her injury harder than she had. It was difficult knowing his pretty sixteen-year-old sister was always going to have a handicap that might limit her future choices.

"I'm sorry, Molly. Have you been sitting there long?"

"Only a minute or two. I was kind of worrying about disturbing you. It must be a big project."

"It is, but I didn't hear you approach down the hall. Did your chair get a tune-up?"

She rolled her eyes, proving that she might have lost the use of her legs but her sarcasm wasn't hurt. "*Nee*. You were concentrating so hard on your sketchbook, you wouldn't have noticed a herd of cattle if they'd charged down the hall."

"You might be right." He stood up and stretched. "I've been working on a new design for a client."

"So, are ya?" Her voice was thick with impatience now.

He ran a hand through his hair. "Am I what?"

She lifted her chin. "John, are ya going to sit at the table with us or not? Mamm wants to know. And I need to know, too, 'cause it's my turn to help with supper."

"What are we having?"

"Pizza pie."

He didn't even try to hide his dismay. "Again?"

Molly looked almost stoic. "I'm afraid so."

"I'll pass." Their mother, who did a great many things right, rarely made a meal that didn't go wrong. Her pizza pie, a jumbled-up casserole with hamburger, mozzarella, noodles, and assorted vegetables, was one of her worst.

Molly grunted. "You made a *gut* choice. Mamm discovered old cauliflower in the refrigerator." Before he could comment on that, she'd deftly turned her chair and rolled back down the hall.

He'd intended to get back to work but now was feeling a little guilty. He decided to follow Molly. Even if he didn't want pizza pie, he didn't have to make Molly be the deliverer of bad news.

When he heard the echo of everyone's voices drifting his way, he was tempted to turn back around and close his door. He might not want to make his sister do his dirty work, but he wanted to deal with everyone else even less.

Because there were a lot of them in the Byler family. Ten, in fact. His parents, his father's parents, Molly, James, Anton, Amanda, Ezra, and him. All together in their big, sprawling, mixed-up house.

And the house truly resembled a rabbit warren. Parts of it had been originally built by his great-grandfather in the 1930s. He'd added on a wing when his brother came to live with him after his wife's passing, then another section was added after his grandparents had gotten married and had seven *kinner* of their own. More changes and additions had also taken place, including a long hallway connecting the *dawdi haus*. The homestead was now near seven thousand square feet of housing headaches.

Though the house didn't have to be passed down

to the oldest son, that was how it happened in their family. Which was why James was already feeling the pressure of one day owning the monstrosity. More than once, James had hinted that he would gladly let John inherit the house.

Every single time, John had lightly refused the offer. The fact was, he was pretty sure he'd rather live in a one-room log cabin than be responsible for the family home—and all of its inhabitants—for the rest of his days. Though a lot of Amish families he knew got along splendidly, his did not. Everyone seemed to have their own opinions, and not a one seemed to think it was a problem to share those opinions loudly and with pride.

Yep, there was always too much commotion, too much talking, too much conflict.

At least once a day he found himself being envious of Marie's single-living situation.

No, he supposed he should at least be honest with himself. Whenever he thought about being at her home, the last thing he found himself thinking about were her four walls. The only thing he ever thought about when it came to Marie Hartman was Marie. And she'd just about killed him tonight, what with her talking about taking hot baths, leaving purple nightgowns on her floor, and comparing him to a protective guard dog.

He had it bad for her, and that was a fact. The problem was he didn't know what to do about this infatuation. Did he finally move forward and actually do something about the feelings he'd had for her for, well, forever?

Or did he do the right thing and face the fact that the only way he could have a future with her was if he left everything that he had in this house?

Just as he was about to turn the final corner and enter the main living space, he practically ran into his youngest sibling, Ezra.

"Oh *gut*. I didn't have to run all the way down to your room," Ezra said.

"I already told Molly that I wasn't joining everyone for supper."

"Mamm heard. This ain't about that." Ezra's freckles seemed to light up as he grinned.

Unlike him, his fourteen-year-old brother loved commotion. "What is it about?" he asked impatiently.

His grin widened. "Mommi and Dawdi want to see you."

His grandparents wanted him at the table, too? A dozen reasons flew through his head, none of them good. "Why?"

Ezra's humor vanished with a shrug. "I don't know. But I think you'd better come join us and be quick about it."

"Because?" he asked, though he was already following Ezra down the hall.

"Because Daed's in a mood today. I think he's about to tell Dawdi to stop bossing everyone around."

He bit back a sigh. "Really?"

"I wouldn't lie about that, John."

"I know you wouldn't," he murmured as he mentally prepared himself to sit at the long table with a giant spoonful of pizza pie on his plate and deal with the lot of them.

He loved them all, but he could have gone another year without it, mainly because the conversations were going to be exhausting and happened often. Though everything inside him was aching to tell Ezra that neither Dawdi's requests, nor their father's perpetual grumpy mood were his problems, he knew they were.

He was prepared to do the right thing, even if it cost him his sanity.

FIVE

"When we finally got to the creek bed, we all scattered about. Most of us ended up sitting on the banks, glad for the break. Except Andy. He hung back, saying he was bored. 'Course, we all knew the real reason he stayed away. Snakes were known to sun themselves in the trees along the banks."

"Now that supper is finished, perhaps you would care to visit with Mommi and me in our *haus*, John?" Dawdi asked.

His grandfather's voice was quiet and polite. It was also as formal as ever—and as forthright. John had never been brave enough to refuse a direct request from his grandfather. He doubted he ever would.

Though supper had felt like an eternity and he wanted nothing more than to go back to working on his designs, John nodded. "Of course, Dawdi."

"You are such a *gut* boy, John." Mommi smiled as she wrapped a hand around his elbow and tugged.

An outsider might simply think his grandmother was both affectionate and enjoyed a bit of support while walking, but John knew better. There was a bit of iron in that grip. He was not going anywhere until she was done with him.

Walking slowly by her side, he looked over his shoulder and saw both Anton and Amanda watching him with wide smiles. James was sitting on a chair in front of the fireplace, actively looking like he was trying not to laugh. Even sweet Molly looked amused.

John didn't blame any of them. Being pulled to the *dawdi haus* for a heart-to-heart was not exactly an uncommon experience for him or his siblings. At least once a week, his grandparents would commandeer one of them and escort him or her to their small house, which was attached to the back of the main one.

From the time he was a little boy, he'd been both excited and fearful of these visits. Sometimes his grandmother would have baked him something special. Once, his grandparents had invited him to their house to praise his good grades in school.

But just as often, one or the other would have decided that he needed a talking-to. That was a rather painful experience. Dawdi loved to talk and pound a point into the ground.

As soon as he escorted his grandmother into her kitchen, Dawdi pointed to the kitchen table. "Do sit down, John. Mommi and I thought maybe you'd like to have a cup of *kaffi* and a slice of apple pie?"

As the words registered, a burst of relief ran through him. Perhaps this was one of the "good" visits that he and his siblings were so fond of. "*Danke*, Dawdi. I would love some pie and coffee."

Looking pleased, his grandfather sat down next to John with a hearty sigh. "Best make that a big slice, Esther. Supper wasn't *gut* tonight."

John bit his lip. He didn't want to disrespect his mother, but his grandfather had been exactly right. Cauliflower Pizza Pie had been an especially bad idea.

"Did you see Ezra ask for seconds?" Mommi asked as she opened a cabinet door.

"I think he did. He cleaned his plate. Twice." Dawdi ran a hand down his beard. "That boy is growing."

Mommi shook her head as she scooped a large ball of vanilla ice cream on a slice of pie. "He ain't growing that much. Ezra wants something. Mark my words."

"Hmm. John, what do you think?" Dawdi asked.

"I couldn't say."

"You can't or won't?" Mommi asked as she delivered both his plate and his grandfather's to the table.

Uh-oh. They were tag-teaming him. Maybe this visit wasn't going to be all "good" after all. "I honestly don't know why Ezra ate so much," he replied slowly. "Could be he liked supper."

Mommi shook her head as she joined them with a much smaller slice. "*Nee*, that couldn't be it."

Unable to help himself any longer, John chuckled. "It wasn't that bad."

"I love my daughter-in-law, I surely do. But it wasn't good either." After she put a napkin in her lap, she said, "Let us bow our heads and give thanks."

John said a quick prayer, thanking the Lord for his grandmother's apple pie—and asking for patience to get through the next hour.

After they lifted their heads again, John took a large bite and almost moaned. As bad as his mother's casserole was, his grandmother's pie was perfection. The apples were sweetly tart and still slightly firm. The crumb topping was tasty and filled with spices. The ice cream on top only added to his enjoyment. "Mommi, this is wonderful-*gut*."

"*Danke*, John." She smiled, looking pleased.

After they'd taken another couple of bites and John had poured coffee for all three of them, his grandfather crossed his legs and looked at him directly.

Uh-oh. Here we go.

"John, your grandmother and I wanted to talk to you about your baptism."

A sinking feeling settled in his formerly very happy stomach. This was much worse than he'd anticipated. He'd been dodging a discussion with his parents about scheduling his baptism for the last two months. "What about it?"

A line formed in between Dawdi's brows. "What do you think, boy? It has not happened."

He couldn't deny that. "*Nee*, it hasn't."

"John, why not?" Mommi asked. "James was baptized years ago. And your younger siblings Anton and Amanda made the decision just seven months ago."

Seven months ago. They'd been counting. "I realize that. I'm also happy for them. You know that."

His grandfather grunted. "Don't see how your happiness for them matters a whole lot when your own future is in jeopardy."

He might have been twenty-four, and on the late side for making a decision, but he doubted the Lord was all that concerned. "It ain't hardly in jeopardy, Dawdi."

"Well then, what are you waiting for?"

Now, that was the real question, wasn't it?

Four months ago he would have said he wasn't sure. Now he knew. But coming to the realization in his grandparents' kitchen and actually saying the words felt like two far different things.

He studied them both. Rested upon his grandmother's blue eyes, bright white hair, and lovely skin. Eyed his grandfather's scarred face, the remnants from a bout with teenage acne. Examined the many wrinkles around his eyes, the result of having spent most of his life farming in the hot sun with only his hat protecting him.

Both of their expressions were so dear and familiar.

In many ways, he valued their opinions even more than his parents'. They'd always been thoughtful and caring and far less concerned than his parents about managing a big household. Just as importantly, he hated to disappoint them.

Feeling like he was ripping off a Band-Aid, he said, "I've been praying and stewing about my baptism for a while now. Something was holding me back. At first, I wasn't sure if I needed more time, or that it simply felt like a permanent step."

"Which was it?" Dawdi asked.

"What I'm trying to tell ya, is that it wasn't either of those things." Looking at them both, he said, "The truth is, I don't want to be baptized in the Amish faith."

The moment the words were out, he inwardly flinched. He'd never dreamed of making this decision, and certainly would have never wanted to tell his grandparents the news at their kitchen table. "I'm sorry," he added. No simple apology was going to make his words easier to bear, though. He knew that.

His grandfather sighed. Dropped his hands to his sides. In contrast, Mommi hardly moved. Simply stared at him.

It took everything he had not to bow his head in shame. He wanted to always make them proud. Or, at the very least, never go out of his way to disappoint them on purpose. "I didn't plan on making this decision tonight."

"Child, you only just decided it?" Mommi asked. Her voice was blatantly skeptical.

"Kind of. I mean, I've been thinking about it for some time. But, it wasn't until just now that I said the words that I knew it was the right decision."

"How do you feel?" Mommi asked.

"Sad and embarrassed because I've upset you."

"Ah." She picked up her cup. Took a long sip of her coffee.

What did that mean? John glanced at his grandfather. To his surprise, he had a small smile on his lips. "Dawdi?"

"I'm not upset, John-Boy."

John-Boy. His grandparents were so formal in public, so well, so *traditional*, it sometimes took him by surprise that they had ever done anything that varied from their strict codes of conduct.

But once they'd shared that they'd gone on a Pioneer Bus trip to Florida and stayed in a motel. When it rained for three days straight and Mommi contracted a sore throat and fever, they ended up sitting in bed and watching hours of television. And somehow, in the middle of all that, his grandfather became a huge fan of some show called *The Waltons*.

In it, there was a character called John-Boy who Dawdi was mighty fond of. And because of that, when John was born, Dawdi would often call him that, especially during times when Dawdi was especially pleased with him.

Never in a million years would he have imagined that this was one of those times.

"Dawdi, I'm going to be real honest with ya. I don't know what you're thinking right now."

He sighed. "John, your Mommi and I have known for some time that you weren't going to join the church."

"How would you know that? I didn't."

Mommi chuckled. "The Eight, child."

Sometimes people thought his English friends encouraged him to be like them. What was true was that it wasn't like that at all. The reason they were so close was because they were all so different. Their differences had made them stronger.

Thinking of Andy, his heart clenched. Well, he'd always thought that, but now he wondered if that was a naive way to see the world.

"No one tried to convince me to be different, Mommi. My English friends wouldn't do that."

"Not even Marie?"

Though he tried to hide it, everything in his body tensed up. "Marie?"

Dawdi's half smile turned wider. "*Jah*, John-Boy, and don't play dumb. You know exactly who we are talking about. Golden-haired Marie. Your Marie. The girl who's had your heart for all this time."

John swallowed. "She and I aren't a couple. I mean, she ain't mine."

"Of course she is, John," Mommi said. "I remember when you all were eighteen or nineteen, she came over when she was on break from college. Every time she looked at you, she had stars in her eyes."

John felt himself blush. "I don't know what to say."

"That's why we have you in here, John," Dawdi said. "You need to tell your parents, and stop dithering around."

"It's not that easy."

"It's not that hard. Have you been praying?"

"*Jah*."

"With an open mind and an honest heart?" Mommi prodded.

"Yes."

After studying him a moment longer, his grandfather nodded. "If you have been doing those things, then the Lord has already helped you make your decision. You are not going to be my Amish grandson John."

"Then what will I be?" An immediate feeling of loss sliced right through him. Maybe his grandfather was going to disown him after all?

His grandfather stood up, walked around the table, and kissed him on the brow. "You will simply be our John."

"Is that enough?" Even though he had already made his decision, he still hated the thought of not being as close to them as he once was.

"It always was enough, child," Mommi murmured. "Always."

Standing up, he hugged his grandmother, loving how small and fragile she felt in his arms. Loved that she patted him on his back. Just like she used to do when he was small.

Just like she always had.

SIX

Katie paused. "Actually, I think all of us were finding our little journey boring as well—until Logan screamed."

"Excuse me, miss," a woman in a bright teal dress called out. "Could you help me? Oh! Sorry, I thought you worked here."

Before Molly could correct the *Englischer* and say that she actually did work at the library and most certainly could help her, the woman had scurried off to Mrs. Laramie's side.

Seriously irritated, Molly wheeled her chair down the aisle so she could watch the woman ask Mrs. Laramie, her boss at the Walnut Creek Library.

Mrs. Laramie leaned close, nodded twice, and then pointed her toward the next room.

If Molly had to guess, she'd say that the woman wanted to check out either movies or audiobooks. After the woman disappeared through the doorway,

Mrs. Laramie glanced over at her and shook her head in mock dismay.

That was a game they had developed over the last two years, ever since Molly had started helping out there. At first, she'd only volunteered. Both she and Mrs. Laramie had wanted to take things slowly, wanting to see how the job and the responsibilities fit her. Being a librarian was harder than it looked. One had to be organized, well read, and quick-thinking. It was also helpful, she'd quickly discovered, to have the patience of a saint.

After six months, Molly had shown enough aptitude for the job that the librarian began asking her to fill in from time to time when they were shorthanded. Six months after that, Mrs. Laramie had offered Molly a full-time position.

Obtaining this job had been a source of pride for not only Molly but her whole extended family, too. It had proven to them all that Molly's accident might have limited her choices but it hadn't cost her everything. She could still have an independent job and earn her own money. Just two months ago, Mrs. Laramie had given her a raise, telling Molly that even though she was only sixteen, she was one of her library's best employees.

Unfortunately, there were still some patrons who avoided her at all costs.

To be fair, Molly knew it wasn't just her wheelchair that made people give her a wide berth—it was the fact that she was Amish, too. It seemed a white *kapp* on her head and a set of metal wheels under her feet made a lot of people think that Molly couldn't find books or information all that well.

Remembering something her brother John often told her, about how it wasn't possible to please everyone all the time, Molly placed a stack of books on her lap and headed toward the adult fiction section. She had an hour left of her day and she'd love nothing more than to be able to tell Mrs. Laramie that she'd taken care of all the books that had come in that afternoon.

Picking up the top book, a mystery by James Patterson, she wheeled down the aisle.

And almost ran over Danny Eberly.

Danny stepped to the side just before her front wheels knocked into his shin. "Watch out, speedy," he teased.

"Danny! I'm so sorry!" Why couldn't she have watched where she was going? And if she had to run into someone, why did it have to be *him*?

Danny, all five feet nine inches of good looks and perfection, looked down at her and shrugged. "Don't worry about it, Mol. I'm all right."

She felt herself blush. Which, unfortunately, made

her feel even more flustered. "I don't know what I was thinking. Are you truly okay?"

He held out his arms. "Good enough to still help out this weekend at Newman's Farm."

With effort, she tried not to notice just how big his biceps were or how broad his chest seemed under his dark blue shirt. Keeping her eyes firmly on his light blue ones so they wouldn't drift, she swallowed. "I didn't know you were working there now."

"I've been working there for eight months, but this is the busy season, of course."

He was looking at her like she should know why. She didn't. "Really? What are you doing there?"

"This month I'm helping out with the annual Fall Festival. Are you going?"

"To the festival? Um, probably not." From anyone else, she would assume he was teasing her, or maybe even being sarcastic. But Danny wasn't like that. He wasn't sneaky and didn't play games. If he liked you, he was nice. And if he didn't like a person? Well, they usually realized that real fast, too.

"You sure? You don't even want to go on *Samshdawk*?"

"What's going on Saturday?" She knew she shouldn't even ask, but she was willing to talk about almost anything to delay him walking away.

"It's when all the locals are going. Believe me, it's a much better time than on Friday."

She smiled at him. "It would be nice to avoid all the tourists."

Looking put upon, he widened his light blue eyes. "You don't even know what chaos they cause."

Unable to help herself, she giggled. "I think maybe I'm glad about that."

He leaned down. "Think about going Saturday night, Molly. We're gonna have hayrides and a bonfire, and we're opening up the corn maze."

It all sounded like a lot of fun—and almost impossible to do while in a wheelchair. "I'll be sure to tell my family about it. Maybe Anton and Amanda could take Ezra or something."

"I'm sure your little *broodah* would have a *gut* time, but it's for people of all ages, Molly. Everyone is going to have a great time."

It was like he was forgetting that she couldn't walk. Hoping that her voice didn't sound too strained, she said, "It's too bad you have to work."

He laughed. "*Jah*, I've gotta work, but I'll be over at the corn maze. And I've already been warned to be on the lookout for couples taking advantage of the rows of corn."

He was talking about kids kissing, of course. Though she might have been only sixteen, Molly wasn't shocked. She had four older siblings, after all. "James used to say if kids got caught it was their own fault." Their own fault for not being sneakier, that was.

Danny grinned. "I'm already planning on not looking too hard at too many shadows among the rows. Last thing I want to do is embarrass one of our friends."

She chuckled, just thinking about how awful it would be to run into a couple in the middle of a passionate embrace. Of course, it would even be worse to be the one getting caught. "Next Sunday at church, you'll have to let me know what happens. I have a feeling you're going to have more than a couple of stories."

His smile faded. "You're really not going to go?"

It seemed he was going to make her say it after all. "I'm stuck in a wheelchair, Danny. No offense, but I don't think Mr. Newman's corn field is exactly wheelchair accessible."

His face went blank. "I guess you're right. Sorry, I wasn't even thinking. Sometimes I completely forget you're in that chair."

He would never know how much that meant to her. "No reason to apologize," she said lightly. "I really will want to hear about how Friday night goes, though. I'll be thinking of you."

"All right, next time we see each other I'll let you know."

"And I'll be sure to listen."

"Excuse me, miss?"

She turned her chair toward the voice. "Yes?"

"The manager told me that you work here." The woman looked her up and down like she found that hard to believe. "Is that true?"

"I work here, yes. How may I help you?"

"I need help finding a book. But with you being handicapped, I just don't know."

Her patience almost used up, Molly took a deep breath, ready to explain that she had lost the use of her legs in her accident, not her brain.

But then Danny stepped forward. "She ain't handicapped," he said, his voice quiet and sure.

The woman's forehead wrinkled. "Pardon me, but she is in a wheelchair. I didn't mean anything by it."

"What do you need, ma'am?" Molly asked quickly. What he didn't realize was that she received comments like this at least once a day. She'd learned not to let them bother her.

"I need a book that's out of my reach. And no offense, but I don't see how you can reach it either." She blew out an irritated sigh. "I guess—"

"I'll help ya," Danny interjected.

"Oh! Well, that's nice of you." She pointed to the top shelf of a nearby bookshelf. "It's right here."

Face void of all expression, Danny walked to where she pointed and pulled down the book she wanted and handed it to her without a word.

"Thank you, son," she said, her voice sweet like syrup.

"You're welcome, but I ain't your son."

After staring at him for a moment, the woman glanced at Molly again, sighed, and walked off.

"Uh-oh. I think you made her mad," Molly said.

"Good. Because she made me mad. She shouldn't talk to you like that."

"I work here, Danny. It's only right that she expects the employees' help."

He shrugged, like the woman's wants or expectations meant little to him. "She should be glad that I didn't tell her what I thought about her rudeness. She shouldn't be speaking to anyone that way, especially not a girl like you."

Molly was flummoxed. Ever since her accident and the Lord had decided that she would lose the use of her legs, she'd encountered a range of attitudes. Some talked to her in a voice full of pity. Others acted as if she'd had a brain injury instead of a leg one. They spoke in simple, short sentences, almost as if they were sure she couldn't understand the smallest bit of instructions.

Still others acted as if she weren't there.

She did have girlfriends who saw her. And her family did, too. But ever since they'd all graduated from eighth grade, she'd felt different. Her girlfriends were boy crazy and couldn't wait for the next singing or gathering. After going to a couple last year, she'd elected to not go to any more. It had been obvious that her circumstances were too different. None of the boys saw her as a prospective sweetheart, and none of her girlfriends wanted her by their side when they got together with the boys.

At first she'd been hurt. No, she actually was still hurt. But her sister and mom had assured her that everyone would come back once all this running around was out of their system.

"Thanks for standing up for me," she said at last. "It was really kind of you."

"I wasn't being kind," he said before he looked a little embarrassed himself. After running his fingers through his light blond hair, he continued. "Look, I've got to go. I've got a meeting with a lady about a job. But, Molly?"

"*Jah?*"

"Even though it won't be easy, think about coming on Saturday night, okay? At the very least, you could keep me company at the corn maze."

"All right," she said softly before thinking the better of it.

After treating her to a grin, he walked away.

Unable to stop herself, Molly watched Danny weave his way through the crowded room, all the while looking straight ahead and not seeming to notice the appreciative looks more than one girl was sending his way.

After he disappeared from sight, Molly turned her chair and quickly wheeled down the aisle to get back on track. She had a lot of books to shelve and straighten by four o'clock, and she didn't want Mrs. Laramie to think she was slacking off too much.

But as she finally placed the Patterson book on the shelf before wheeling down the row to straighten an Anne Perry book, Molly couldn't help but smile.

What had just happened had felt like a turning point in her life. Maybe she didn't always have to step back and say no to things that sounded like fun.

She had a feeling that if she didn't go to the Fall Festival she was going to miss out on something special. Oh, not hayrides and bonfires—but something more important.

She would miss out on being like everyone else. Being a teenager having plans on a Saturday night.

On taking a chance to be more than just Danny Eberly's shy friend.

And that?

Well, that was something she wasn't sure she could ever say no to.

SEVEN

"I didn't exactly scream," Logan interrupted. "It was more like a manly grunt."

"No, it was definitely a girlish cry," John B. said. "You frightened birds overhead."

"I had good reason, you know."

Looking around the room, Katie nodded. "He did. Not only were there snakes lying about, but a great number of leeches." Looking across the room at Marie, she added softly, "There was also an old pillowcase with a knot at the end."

It was becoming kind of hard for Danny Eberly to keep from smiling. The *Englischer* woman kept pointing out obvious things that were wrong with her sorry-looking yard and explaining in great detail what the problem was. As if anyone with two good eyes couldn't see it for himself.

Fact was, Marie Hartman's front yard was a weed-ridden mess in need of a good dose of weed killer, a shovel, a few yards of dirt, and a whole lot of elbow grease.

And prayers. The yard needed lots and lots of prayers.

At last, after teetering on the tips of her high heels for another couple of minutes, Miss Hartman walked to the sidewalk and took a breath. "So, what do you think, Danny? Can this yard be saved?"

Since "saved" was a pretty broad description, he nodded. "I reckon so."

"Really?" Hope entered her expression before she looked him over again. "Now, tell me honestly, do you think you can handle this project?" Before he could answer, she added, "I mean, it's going to be a lot of work. A ton, actually."

Since he was fairly sure she'd said the last part to herself, Danny rocked back on his heels and stuffed his hands in his back pockets. He'd learned from experience that doing this helped him look like he was contemplating something real seriously.

And just like it had worked with other clients, little by little, Marie Hartman looked more at ease and like she was finally ready to listen.

"Well now. Miss Hartman, can I be real honest with ya?"

"Only if you call me Marie." She smiled at him.

"I'm older than you by a few years but I'm not old yet."

He smiled back at her. "All right then, Marie. I think all your front yard needs is some time and attention. I can do both of those things. I'll be happy to take care of the weeds, clean out the flower beds and the thicket on the side, and plant some mums and a couple dozen perennials."

"You can do all that?"

"I can. And I'll mow the lawn for you every week until winter comes."

"You sound so sure about your plans."

"That's 'cause I am sure." After quickly adding up the costs, he named a price to charge.

Her smile widened. "That is far more reasonable than I'd anticipated. I'm so glad I called you."

"Me, too." Once he got rid of the weeds, it wasn't going to take that much time and would bring in a good amount of extra money.

"When can you start?"

"Well, I work at Newman's Farm most of the time, and this is the busiest weekend. It's the harvest festival, you see."

"Oh! I forgot that was already."

"You've heard of the Newman's Fall Festival?"

"Of course! I know about the festival—I grew up here in Walnut Creek."

He was surprised. She looked like a city girl. "Oh. Well, then you know how busy I am right now. I'm going to be manning the corn maze booth."

"Boy, I haven't been to Newman's in ages." Eyes sparkling, she said, "However, I do remember it being quite the spot for teenagers. Boys used to conveniently get lost with their girlfriends in the middle of the maze." She chuckled. "Boy, I bet kids don't do things like that anymore."

There was no way he was going to share that he'd "gotten lost" among the cornstalks a time or two. "I'm not sure, but I bet that happens from time to time. I guess I'll find out when I man the ticket booth."

She laughed. "Good answer. Very diplomatic."

He wasn't sure what she was getting at, but he figured it didn't matter. "As far as my schedule goes, I could get started on your yard on Monday morning. Then, I'll work on it as much as I can when I'm not at Newman's. How does that sound?"

"Perfect. How long do you think it will take you? A month?"

"*Nee*. I'll have the job done within two weeks."

Her green eyes widened. "Two weeks? Are you sure?"

This time he didn't even try to hide his amusement. "I'm guessin' you haven't been on too many

Amish farms. I'm used to working hard. *Mei daed* wouldn't have it no other way."

She blinked. Then, to his surprise, her expression warmed. Almost like she was hiding a secret or two. "Well, as a matter of fact, I actually have been to an Amish farm once or twice."

Thinking of some of the families in the area that catered to tourists, he said, "Did you go for a meal? Maybe some shoofly pie?" He didn't know why, but all the tourists seemed to love that.

"Well, as a matter of fact, I've never had shoofly pie." Looking just beyond him, her voice changed tone, warming like fresh syrup on the back of his grandmother's stove. "John B., how come you've never served me shoofly pie?"

Danny turned around to see John Byler walking up Marie's driveway. John was staring intently at Marie, like she'd just asked him something really important.

"If I had known you wanted shoofly pie, I would've made sure you had it, Marie," John said as he joined them. "You want me to bring you a pie tomorrow evening?"

She rolled her eyes. "Definitely not. I just finished the cake you brought me." She gestured to him. "John, have you met Danny?"

"*Jah*. Danny Eberly, right? Rupert is your father?"

Danny nodded, feeling the burst of unease whenever anyone mentioned his father. His father wasn't a bad man, just a mighty unhappy one. "I'm his oldest."

"Your name sounds familiar. Do you have older siblings?"

"*Nee*. Just a little *broodah* named Sam. But you might know my name from Molly. She and I were in *shool* together."

And just like that, John B.'s friendly gaze sharpened. "Is that right? I don't remember her mentioning you."

He didn't know what to say to that. "There were a lot of students in the school when we were there." But even to his ears, the excuse seemed hard to believe. After all, they hadn't gone to the public school like a lot of Amish kids in the area did. They'd gone to the Amish schoolhouse. It had been one room, with maybe forty students during its most crowded year.

"How well did you know her?"

"John, what does it matter?" Marie asked, breaking the tension that was starting to simmer in the air. "And why would you expect your sister to tell you everything? I mean, I certainly didn't come home every day with stories about all of my classmates."

"Molly tells me all sorts of things."

"She doesn't tell you everything. I can assure you that."

After staring hard at Danny again, John B. blinked. "It doesn't really matter," he said as he turned to Marie again. "I'm just glad I found you here at home."

"I told you last night that I'd be home right after work."

John stepped closer to Marie. "And so you did."

As Danny watched Marie smile softly at him, he realized two things. One was that they were sweet on each other.

And the second? His presence was definitely not wanted or needed any longer.

"I'm going to go ahead and leave, Marie."

She turned to him in surprise, like she'd forgotten he was there. "Oh? Okay. I'll see you on Monday, Danny. I mean I will if you're still here when I come home."

"If you're not, maybe I'll see you the next day."

"That sounds real good. Thanks," she murmured, looking back at John B. again.

Feeling like the air was practically alive, the sparks passing between the two were so strong, Danny started walking. He'd just about made it to the street when he heard John B. call his name again.

"Danny?"

"*Jah?*"

"Are you good friends with my little sister now?" John was looking at him intently.

"*Jah.*" He certainly intended to be.

"Then I expect we'll be seeing each other again."

"For sure." He smiled and waved a hand goodbye before he started walking again. Thinking all the while that it was mighty coincidental that he would have conversations with both Molly Byler and her big brother all in the same day.

And since he was planning to be spending more time in Marie's front yard, he had a feeling that one day he and John were going to have more to say to each other.

EIGHT

"None of us wanted to find out what was inside that pillowcase. But all of us also knew that we had to do the right thing."

Marie didn't even try to hide her amusement. John B. had come over to visit again. Moreover, he was all cleaned up, and he didn't look surprised to see her still in her suit from work. No, it was like he knew when she'd be coming home and had been waiting for her to arrive.

That was interesting.

What was surprising, though, was that John did not look pleased to see her standing in the front yard with Danny. Actually, she would bet the day's deposit at the bank that his glower wasn't just about Danny's friendship with his little sister. It seemed a lot more personal, maybe he was even jealous.

But maybe she was imagining things?

Maybe . . . or maybe not. All she knew was that even the thought of John Byler acting like a possessive boyfriend was pretty amusing.

Once Danny was firmly out of sight, and out of earshot, she giggled.

John folded his arms across his chest and glared at her. "What is so funny, Marie?"

"Oh, nothing. I'm just surprised to see you."

"Surely you aren't that surprised. I've stopped by before."

"That's true." But only once before. This time, however, he looked a little more polished. He'd taken time to put on a fresh shirt. And he was freshly shaved, too.

Still looking irritated, he said, "You know what? It's *gut* I came by. You didn't need to ask that kid to do work around here."

Looking pointedly at the proliferation of weeds surrounding her feet, she said, "Um, yes I did. It needs a lot of help, and I have my hands full with the inside of the house." There was also the fact that she liked flowers but definitely did not enjoy the hard work that went into planting them.

"I don't remember you telling me you were upset about the yard."

"I thought it was a given. I mean, it's all weeds. I doubt anyone has spent any time on it in years."

She was starting to feel like he was trying to pick a fight. Maybe it was better to go inside and get him a drink to cool off. "John B., what's going on?" she asked as she approached the front door.

"Nothing." Before she could touch the handle, he turned the knob and guided her inside. Their clothes brushed as she stepped beside him.

Taken by surprise, she inhaled sharply then called herself ten times the fool for being caught off guard by something she shouldn't have noticed in the first place.

But, judging by the way John had stilled, she knew she wasn't the only one to be aware that things between them were different than how they used to be. His expression was strained as he closed her door firmly and locked it.

Focusing on that action, Marie began to wonder if John was upset with her—or maybe one of their friends? "John B., talk to me." When still he hesitated, she smiled. "Come on. This is me you're talking to."

Hazel eyes met hers before looking away quickly. "That's the point."

The point of what? "You're speaking in riddles."

"Not so much. I would think it would be pretty obvious. You are a *gut freind* of mine and need a helping hand. You shouldn't have to pay some stranger to help you out. You should have asked me."

"First, I'm a grown woman. I can hire someone to work for me if I want to."

His voice softened. "Marie, of course I know you

can do just about anything you want. All I'm thinking of is your safety."

"I promise I'm going to be safe around Danny. He's a friend of Molly's, after all."

"Maybe he is. I'll have to ask her about that."

Unable to help herself, she started giggling. "Boy, you're in a crabby mood!"

"Is that some kind of grass and lawn joke?"

It took her a second to realize he was referring to crabgrass. Not wanting to touch that one, she said lightly, "John, how about something to drink?"

"*Jah.* Sure." After accepting a glass of iced tea, John sighed. "I guess I've been acting a little out of sorts, hmm?"

"Just a little." Or a lot.

"Well, um, besides the fact that you didn't ask me to help ya, my mood has to do with Molly."

"Because Danny acted like he was a special friend of hers?"

He nodded. "You know I'm protective of my little sister. Her being in that wheelchair makes her a target at times. Especially from kids her age."

"Even Amish kids who she'd gone to school with?" That surprised her. Marie didn't know her well, but she'd certainly seen Molly from time to time over the years, and John's little sister had always been a pretty, sweet girl.

Then there was the fact that Molly most likely always had at least one of her siblings in school with her. She couldn't even imagine Ezra, who was two years younger than Molly, putting up with anyone being mean to her.

"As much as it pains me to say it, even Amish *kinner* aren't perfect all the time."

The familiar light was back in his eyes. Reaching out, she curved a palm around his shoulder. "Ah. There you are again."

He smiled at her before it faded yet again. "Um, Marie, if I'm confessing things, I guess I should tell you something else."

"Okay . . ."

"I wasn't happy about Danny speaking with ya alone."

It took her a second to get the gist of what he meant. "John, he's just a kid."

"Not a kid. He's seventeen."

"He is still just a boy, John."

"He was also staring." When she started chuckling, he said, "Hush, now. You have to know what you look like in your . . ." He waved a hand. "Outfit."

"My suit?"

"It ain't just that. You've got heels on and your skirt don't even reach your knees." A line formed in between his brows. "Your legs . . ." His voice drifted off.

She looked down. Her skirt was slim fitting. It skimmed the tops of her knees. She knew it was flattering, but it was a far cry from risqué.

With anyone else, she would've burst out laughing. Maybe even pointed out how silly he was being just before she mentioned that her calves were certainly nothing for a teenaged boy to get all excited about.

But she couldn't do that to him. He looked so earnest, as if each word was being pulled out of somewhere deep inside of him, and not by choice either.

"John, as attractive as you are making me sound, I have to tell you that I don't think Danny noticed my outfit." Just to tease him, she winked. "Or my legs."

But John didn't crack a smile. "Marie, he noticed. I watched him noticing plenty when I walked up."

"Care to tell me why you are acting jealous of a teenager I hired to do yard work?"

"I ain't jealous."

"Are you sure about that?"

His cheeks turned red. "I might be feeling some *gneid*."

He actually was feeling jealous? Now they were getting somewhere! Well, they would be, if everything he was doing and saying didn't sound like such a surprise. "You know what? Instead of getting annoyed, I'm going to take it as a compliment."

His worried expression deepened. "Marie, I don't

know how to tell you this, but I . . . well, the truth is that I've had feelings for you for some time."

"You have?"

He nodded. "*Jah*. Years, now."

Years. He'd had feelings for her for *years*. "Oh," she murmured, because even though everything inside her was screaming with glee, her lips didn't seem able to form a coherent word.

After a pause, John spoke again. "At first I assumed it was because of your looks. You are *shay*, you know."

She knew *shay* meant pretty. "But it's not just my looks that you are fond of?"

He shook his head. "It's a lot of things about you. The spark in your eyes. The way that you got yourself a good job and a promotion, too. The way that you've been so loyal to all of us. The way you are always the first to send people birthday cards or to reach out when we're having a difficult time."

Everything he said was beautiful and sweet. Words that she would no doubt play over and over in her head when she was calming down after another bad dream.

"John, thank you for all the sweet words. And . . . well, you know I care about you, too."

Relief filled his eyes. "That's good, don't you think?"

She nodded. It really was. She and John were finally moving forward, finally acting on the pull that had existed between them for years. Even though they still had to figure out what to do about the differences in their lifestyles, she knew she should be ecstatic.

Unfortunately, she still didn't quite feel like herself.

"Marie, talk to me. What did I say?"

She hesitated, then said, "I think I'm still having a hard time dealing with Andy's death. I'm sorry. I guess every time I think about having a future, I remember that Andy isn't going to have the future that he hoped for." She pressed a palm to her cheek. "Sorry. Way to ruin the mood, huh?"

Pain laced with sweet concern that entered his expression as he reached for her hands. "Oh, Marie."

She liked how her hands felt in his. How his rough, warm palms made her feel secure and taken care of. Feeling like she could share even more, she murmured, "I wish I would have been a better friend to him. He needed me to be better. I should have called him more."

He gently squeezed her hands. "At first, I didn't think any of us did enough for Andy, but now I sometimes wonder if there was anything that we could have done."

"Even if there wasn't, I still think I could've tried

harder. To make sure he knew he had friends who cared."

"He knew."

"Do you really think so?"

"The eight of us haven't just been good friends. We've been best friends for most of our lives." Releasing her hands, he pressed one palm flat on his chest. "I know it in my heart. Don't you?"

"But back when I was working in Cleveland, it wasn't the same. Distance matters."

"Not that much."

"I disagree. John, I never called any of you when I was feeling sad or lonely."

He looked stunned. "You should have. If you had called and said you needed something, I, or um, we would have been there for you."

"Calling all of you would've made me feel weak." Though it was hard to admit, she continued. "We can tell each other that we care about each other and will be there for each other no matter what, but it might not be the truth."

His expression darkened. "It is true."

"John, even if you love someone, that doesn't mean you trust that person with all your secrets." When he opened his mouth to protest, she stepped closer. Close enough to smell the soap he'd used when he'd showered before coming to see her.

Close enough to feel the heat emanating from him, to hear the difference in his breathing.

Close enough that hardly any space existed between them. "And don't say you don't, John Byler," she whispered as she looked up at him. "Because you just admitted that you've kept a secret or two from me."

He gazed down at her. His heated look skittered over her face before settling on her lips.

She licked her bottom lip. His eyes flared.

She was ready. Ready for him to bend down a little farther. Ready to finally do what they'd been teasing each other about for years. Ready to lift her hands, fold them around his neck, to lean close. To kiss him at last.

"Marie." He groaned, just before he dropped her hands and jerked back, as if he'd been stung. "We can't do this."

"Why not?"

"Because it ain't right. We haven't even talked about our relationship."

"I thought we just did."

"Not enough. And actually, all that really happened was that I admitted I've been besotted with you forever. I have no idea how you feel about me. I need to know."

Marie didn't know what was going to happen between them. She didn't even know what could happen in their future.

But she knew enough about how she felt to tell him the truth. "Not only have I always known my best friends were the Eight, but I also knew that there was only one of you who claimed my heart. And that was *you*, John B. I've loved you forever, too."

"Marie." His voice was strained.

Panic set in. Was he surprised? Disappointed? Had she just really messed things up between the two of them? "Don't start telling me that I don't—"

But she couldn't have been more wrong about his reaction. Because in two seconds flat, John pressed two work-roughened palms against her cheeks and kissed her.

His touch, his kiss, it was so intense, so perfect, so everything . . . well, all Marie could do was close her eyes, and wholeheartedly kiss him right back.

NINE

"Even though we were fourteen and thought we knew so much, we were really just kids. Sweet kids who were all half-afraid to see what was inside that knotted pillowcase. Just as someone suggested we draw straws to see who was going to have to do the deed, Andy announced that he would."

Katie shook her head. "Patience never was Andy's best quality."

Her scent was on his clothes. Taking advantage of being alone while he walked home through the alfalfa fields, John lifted his forearm to his face. Breathed in deep like a teenaged girl.

And yes, smelled Marie's perfume on his skin, too.

He had no experience with such flowery scents, but he was fairly certain that no flower in his grandmother's garden smelled like that. No, this scent was purely feminine, expensive, almost tangible. All Marie.

For years, it had haunted him whenever she'd been

near, when they were in the same room together, and it would make him turn, looking for her. Or lingering in the room long after she was gone, making him long for things that could never be.

But those faint hints had been nothing compared to its strength when he'd held her in his arms just now. For a moment, he'd simply wanted to hold her close and appreciate the feel of her in his arms and savor the moment.

Of course, he'd gone one step further and kissed her. He shouldn't have. He knew it. But did he regret it? He couldn't say he did, even in the slightest.

When they'd broken apart, Marie had looked dazed. And, yes, thoroughly kissed.

Though he knew he probably shouldn't, he'd felt a burst of pure masculine pride. He might not be able to do a great many things, but it seemed he could do one thing rather well, and that was putting a dreamy expression on Marie Hartman's face.

But now his clothes were wearing the evidence of their embrace, and it was a very real possibility that more than one member of his family was going to notice. And it went without saying that if they noticed they weren't going to keep it to themselves either.

Especially not James. He would probably point out the fact that John smelled like Marie. Which would cause quite the discussion and no less than a few pointed comments about how he had no business being so close to an *Englischer* girl who he had no intention of having a future with.

Except that wasn't really true. If he was honest, John would admit that he most certainly did have intentions toward a future with her. The dream went beyond their pasts, their differences, and maybe even common sense. Where Marie was concerned, he never saw her in a category.

She was simply Marie.

His only hope was to go in through a side door, circle back toward the rear stairs, and quickly change his clothes before any of them saw him.

But all of his hopes were dashed when he reached the yard and saw the twins, Amanda and Anton, half-heartedly weeding the front flower beds. The moment they saw him, they got to their feet. It was obvious that they were pleased to have something else to do besides dig in the dirt.

"John, you're back!" Amanda called out. "Come join us."

"With your weeding? I think not."

"We won't make you weed," Anton said. "I wanted to tell you about who I saw today at the market."

Realizing there was no way he could get out of it, John approached. At least the scent of freshly dug dirt was in the air. Surely it would permeate any lingering scent wafting off his shirt.

"Who did you see?"

"Micah Troyer." Anton waggled his eyebrows. "Do you remember him?"

John couldn't resist grinning. "I remember he was the bane of your existence for years."

"Well, he was . . . before he moved away," Amanda added.

"Don't make me wait. Has Micah come back?"

"I guess so," Amanda replied. "But that ain't the important news, John." Smiling broadly, she continued. "Guess what? He jumped the fence."

This news was startling enough to push all his worries about Marie's perfume away.

Micah Troyer had been a strange stickler for rules when it came to being Amish. He had constantly tried to correct Anton during school, calling him out if he ever bent any rules of the Ordnung or even acted like he was entering his *rumspringa* early.

He'd actually tried to start this foolishness with John once, but John had put an end to that. He had five siblings and two sets of adults to answer to all the time. He'd had no intention of answering to a kid who was two years younger. Especially not when it came to defending decisions as personal as *rumspringa*.

"Wow. I didn't see that coming," John admitted.

"I didn't either," Anton said. "It took me off guard."

"We didn't even recognize him at first," Amanda added, her voice filled with glee. "John, you should see his hair! He shaved it so close one would think he joined the army."

That made him smile. Micah had always worn his hair long and slightly curved around his face, what he and his siblings had always derisively described as a cereal bowl haircut. It had been yet another example of the boy's strange adherence to his perception of being "really Amish."

"Was he any nicer?"

"*Nee*. But he did approach the two of us. Wearing jeans with holes in them and a T-shirt," Anton replied.

"And a swagger that would have made Miss Annalee blush," Amanda added, naming their former schoolteacher. Now thoroughly entertained, John knelt down next to them and pulled a weed. "Well, now you have me curious. What happened to make him jump the fence?" When both twins looked as if they were attempting not to laugh, he added, "Did he say?"

"Micah did eventually tell us," Amanda murmured as she pulled a dandelion. "But that was after Anton asked him why he was dressed like an *Englischer*."

Looking smug, Anton said, "He told me that he'd finally had enough of his parents overseeing every bit of his life."

"What?"

Anton nodded. "*Jah.* It turns out as bad as Micah was, his parents were worse. He needed some freedom in a bad way."

Amanda continued, tag-teaming the story the way they'd done their whole lives. "I guess Micah tried to talk to them about his need for space, but that did no good."

"Yep. When they wouldn't back off even a little bit he decided to take things into his own hands," Anton added with a grin. "In a big way."

John pulled another weed as he stared at the twins. "So bossy Micah Troyer gave up everything he had always said was so important to him because he was mad at his parents?"

Anton shrugged. "I guess so. It's a puzzle, truly. Not a bit of it makes a lick of sense to me. Well, besides needing to get away from his parents. I wouldn't have lasted as long as he did."

"Me neither," Amanda said. "Mrs. Troyer was always bossy and mean when she helped out at school."

Starting to feel guilty about their gossiping, John shook his head in disbelief as he stood up. "I guess it just goes to show you that one never knows what will happen in one's future. Anything is possible."

Anton smiled in midnod. "Why, John. You certainly just said a mouthful."

A prickle began to buzz along the back of John's neck. "What is that supposed to mean?"

"It means that I never would have guessed you'd be spending so much time with Marie Hartman, but you are."

Realizing the dirt wasn't as pungent as he'd hoped, he took a step backward. "I don't know what you're talking about."

"Oh?" Anton smirked. "I find that surprising, seeing as if I closed my eyes I would think she was standing in the garden with us."

Amanda stood up and sniffed the air. "Oh, don't worry about him none, John."

Anton raised his eyebrows. "Really? You can't smell Marie's perfume?"

"Oh, I can smell it, all right. But I wouldn't say I would imagine that she was here with us. More like that John had been with her." Her lips twitched. "Standing mighty close to her, that is."

Anton folded his arms across his chest. "Care to tell us a story of your own, *broodah*? Just how close have you been standing next to Marie?"

There was only one answer that needed to be given. Even though he'd heeded his grandfather's words, he still hadn't found the right opportunity to talk to his parents and tell them what he'd decided.

Which he was kind of horrified about.

"*Nee*. I need to go inside anyway."

"What's your hurry?"

John considered lying but because he couldn't deny it any longer, he smirked. "I need to take a shower."

Their laughter carried him into the house. Along the way, he passed Molly, which brought to mind yet another thing he had to do.

"Hiya, John," she said from her room.

"Hey. Remind me to ask you something after supper."

"All right." A small line had formed in between her light blond brows, but she didn't say anything more.

He hoped that this might be one rumor that wasn't actually a hint of something far deeper.

TEN

"Andy pulled out four tiny gray and white kittens. They'd been left there to die, you see."

John kept Molly in suspense until later that night. Before they talked, Molly had to help Ezra and Anton clear the table and wash and dry the dishes. After Amanda finally said the kitchen was clean enough, Molly wheeled out of the kitchen in search of John. She finally found him sitting on a chair in the hearth room.

"I'm all done with the dishes, John."

He looked up from the book he'd been reading. "That's good timing. I just finished a chapter."

"What did you want to talk about?"

"It's nothing important." Looking uncomfortable, he pulled at his collar. "I mean, I don't think it is."

She was starting to get pretty worried. Maneuvering her chair closer, she lowered her voice. "What is wrong?"

"Wrong? Oh, nothing. I only wanted to ask you about a boy I met earlier today."

A boy? "Who might that be?"

"Danny Eberly."

"Danny?" All at once, she was thankful for the lack of electric light in the room, because she was sure her cheeks were bright red.

But maybe the battery-powered floor lamp John had been using to read wasn't all that dim because her brother's expression sharpened. "*Jah*. Do you know him?"

"Well, yes." A thousand questions were running through her mind, all revolving around how he'd met Danny and how John had learned that she and Danny were friends. Deciding to play things safe, she said, "Danny Eberly and I went to school together." Not quite liking how that sounded, she hastily added, "Ezra knows him, too, of course."

"I guess he would." He rubbed the back of his neck. "I had forgotten that."

How could he have forgotten? "Why are you asking me about Danny?"

"Well, he mentioned that he went to school with you. Not Ezra, now that I think of it."

"There were a lot of us in Miss Annalee's schoolhouse, John. You know that."

"That's true." Looking at her intently, he said, "I told Danny that I had never heard you talk about him."

Of course she would never talk to her big brother about her secret crush! A little irritated, she said, "I graduated the eighth grade almost two years ago, John. I don't recall if I ever talked about him to you or not. I'd be surprised if you remembered."

"I guess you have a point." When she raised her brows, he said, "So, have you seen him lately?"

"*Jah.* I saw him at the library today. We talked."

"He was at the library? Did he go there to see you?"

"I'm fairly sure he went there for a book. We've got a lot of them there, you know."

"You don't have to be so snippy."

"Well, you don't have to be so nosy." Before John could get in another word, Molly glared at him. "Just so you know, I'm getting pretty tired of playing *tsvansich* questions. I don't understand the point of this conversation, either."

"I'm not getting at anything. I just want to know more about your relationship with Danny."

"I don't have a *relationship* with him." At all. "We are friends." Well, kind of. "Why are you so concerned, anyway?"

"Yeah, John," Amanda said from the doorway. "What are you getting at?"

He turned to glare at his other sister. "Go on out, Amanda. This ain't any of your concern."

Amanda propped a hand on one of her hips. "Sorry, but I'm thinking it maybe is. You're making Molly upset."

"I'm not upset," Molly said. She was actually angry and irritated. There was a big difference. But more importantly, she hated her siblings acting like she was fragile and couldn't stand up for herself.

"If you ain't upset, then answer my questions," John said.

Molly crossed her arms over her chest. "*Nee*. Danny and I aren't any of your business."

"You're my sister."

"So?"

He groaned. "Mol—"

Amanda interrupted. "I think you should share with us where you happened to run into Danny Eberly, John. Was it when you just *happened* to be calling on Marie Hartman?"

"Are you finally courting her, John?" James asked as he entered the room. "When did that happen?"

"I'm not courting anyone, James," John snapped before turning to Amanda. "And where I was is neither here nor there, and you know it."

"I think it is," Molly interjected, happy to talk about his business instead of hers. "You had no problem sticking your nose into my business."

John glared. "Watch your tone, Molly."

"You better watch your tone, too. You aren't my father."

"Just because I'm looking after you—"

Her voice rose. "You aren't looking after me. You're being bossy and prying into my personal business."

"You shouldn't even have personal business," John retorted, his tone matching hers.

"What is everyone arguing about?" Mamm asked as she joined them all.

Great. Shooting daggers at John, Molly said, "Nothing, Mamm. John is just being nosy."

"I'm not being nosy, I just don't want some boy taking advantage of you."

"How could Danny take advantage of me?"

"Because." John waved a hand at her chair. "You know."

She shook her head. "*Nee*. I don't."

"Molly, you are my baby sister and you're in a wheelchair. Of course I don't want some kid treating you badly."

His statement hurt. No matter what she did or said, John always seemed to think of her as a handicapped child. She raised her voice. "Do you think Marie's parents are talking to her right now, warning her about John Byler?"

"Molly!" Mamm said, just as Amanda sucked in a shocked breath and James stared at her in shock.

"What?" Glaring at the four of them, Molly shook her head. "Mamm, you and Daed have never coddled me. You've never made me feel like I couldn't help out around the house or should expect my five siblings to serve me or wait on me."

"Of course not."

"Then why does everyone have no problem treating me like a regular sixteen-year-old woman when it comes to work around the house, but when it comes to the rest of the world I'm suddenly supposed to be fragile and addle-brained?"

"Did you just call yourself a woman?" James murmured.

Mamm looked shocked. "Molly, no one in this *haus* treats you that way."

"Are you sure about that?" she asked all of them. "Are all of you positive you don't ever wish I lived the rest of my life in this house being surrounded by all of your advice and good intentions?" She wasn't surprised when both John and Amanda looked away. "You know, I get this attitude a lot at the library. People ignore me or talk to me really slowly, like I'm only pretending to work at the library. I don't need you acting like I can't handle a relationship."

"Do you have a boyfriend, Molly?" Mamm asked. "Have you been seeing this, this . . ."

"Danny," Amanda supplied.

"Have you been seeing this Danny in secret?" Mamm asked.

Good grief! "*Nee.* But I do know I'm never going

to get to spend any time with any boy if my *broodah* doesn't back off."

"I just want to make sure that you know I talked to him."

"*Danke*. I think you pounded that point in."

"We never did hear about when you actually did talk to Danny," Amanda said with a sly smile. "Or why you were over at Marie's *haus*."

John stood up. "That is none of your business."

Amanda propped one hand on her hip. "I see. Well, next time I see Marie, I'll be sure to ask where the two of you talked."

"*Kinner*, all of you are giving me a headache," their mother said with an aggrieved expression. "James, John, and Amanda, leave Molly and me, if you please."

For the first time ever, the three of them obeyed their mother without hesitation and walked right out. Molly wanted to throw something at them.

Instead, she watched her mother compose herself and sit down in John's chair.

"Do I even want to know what was going on?" Mamm asked after a few seconds passed.

"If I say no, will that be the end of it?"

"Probably not."

"Fine. Somehow John talked to Danny Eberly today, and Danny said that we were friends. For some reason John decided that meant he needed to tell me to look out for Danny. He makes me so mad."

"Do you think we coddle you too much in the real world?"

"I don't know. Not usually. But if I have more 'discussions' like this, then yes."

"You know we all just want to look out for you."

"When I was little, you said it was because you were afraid I'd hurt myself."

"That's true."

"Well, I think it's gone from that to a bad habit. Everyone thinks that I don't realize that things are different for me because I'm in a chair. Don't you think I realize that?"

"I guess you would know better about that than any of us."

"I do. I love you but I don't want to live here with you and Daed for the rest of my life, Mamm. I want to be independent. And I want to date, too. And make mistakes."

Her mother's eyes lit up. "So you want to be like everyone else."

"Yep."

"We'll do our best. So, when are you going to see Danny again?"

"I don't know. He said I should go to the Fall Festival on Saturday night, but I told him that wasn't the place for me. It's too hard to get around the grounds in a chair."

"Hmm. We'll have to see about that. I seem to remember Newman's farm having some pretty good paths."

"Really?"

Mamm smiled softly. "Let me do some thinking. Maybe there's a way for you to still be able to go—without me or one of your siblings walking by your side."

"*Danke.*"

"No, thank you, dear. I can't say that I'm glad that you and John and Amanda got into a little tiff, but I am glad to know the reason behind it."

"Mamm, about Daed . . ." She really didn't want to go over all of this with him.

"I'll fill your father in. You might be surprised, but I think he's going to be your biggest supporter."

"Really?"

Her mother smiled broadly. "Oh, *jah.* You see, I remind Daed all the time that my father once had to be convinced that I was safe with him."

Later that night, when it was close to midnight, John picked up his flashlight from his bedside table and went into the kitchen to eat a bowl of cereal.

Usually he fell asleep the moment he closed his eyes, but sleep was escaping him that evening. Every time he'd tried to get comfortable and relax, he'd find himself replaying one of the day's conversations in his head.

He'd been so silly about Danny Eberly with Marie and far too nosy and bossy with his little sister.

Then there was that kiss . . . and that they'd at last shared their true feelings about each other. All of that had been wonderful and amazing. It had been a long time coming, and it should have made him feel like he was on top of the world.

Except he still hadn't completely made a decision about his faith.

Or had he?

"You've already made up your mind, man," he muttered to himself around a mouthful of cereal. "The only person you're fooling is yourself."

Chomping on another bite, he let that little tidbit sink in. Tried to figure out what to do next.

"I was just telling myself that getting a midnight snack was a bad idea," his father said as he walked into the kitchen, his muscular body illuminated by his own flashlight. "I guess I was wrong. What are you eating, John?"

"Frosted Flakes. Don't tell Mamm." His mother

had always hated any of them eating the sugary cereals.

"I won't . . . if I can have a bowl, too." Daed looked over at the bare countertops. "Where did you hide the box?"

"Behind Amanda's tin of granola."

His eyes lit up. "Good idea. Nobody likes that."

Smiling, John dipped his spoon in the bowl again. "Not even Amanda. I don't know why she continually makes it."

"Anton told me that she reads magazines at the library and thinks she needs to eat more nuts and berries," Daed said as he pulled out the box and a bowl. After he joined John at the table, he quietly knelt his head and prayed. Then he spoke out loud. "You care to tell me why you are sitting here in the middle of the night talking to yourself?"

"You heard that, huh?"

"Only the tail end of it. The part about you fooling yourself."

"Ah." Glad his bowl was empty, John walked to the sink and washed it out with soap. And then he hid that cereal box again. His father never put back anything where it belonged. By the time he came back to the table, he'd made his decision.

"Daed, I've decided not to get baptized."

His father slowly put his spoon down. "Well, now. That's news."

"I'm sorry. I shouldn't have just blurted it like that. But I . . . well, I've been struggling with this for a while now."

"I see." He took another bite of cereal. Then another one.

John watched him, both appreciating the fact that his father was waiting a moment to comment on his bombshell and hating the fact that he was having to sit there and squirm and worry about what he was going to say.

After a couple more seconds passed, his father pushed the half-eaten bowl away. "You know, it's funny. I always used to love this stuff, but now I'm thinking it's too sweet."

"It is pretty late," John said as he stood up and poured the remainder in the garbage can. "Maybe that's the problem."

"Maybe . . . or maybe my tastes have changed." John looked over his shoulder at his father. He was in old navy sweatpants and a thick white undershirt . . . and wearing a sympathetic expression. "Leave the dish, son. I'll take care of it in a minute."

John sat back down. "What are you saying?"

"That it's okay to change your mind about things." He paused. "And to go your own path."

"You aren't mad at me?"

"*Nee*. I can't say it's much of a surprise, though. Your *mamm* and I knew you were happy working at the trailer factory."

"That wasn't it, Daed. Lots of Amish work there."

"*Jah*. But lots of Amish don't chat with the *Englischers* as much as you do. Or have a long-running friendship with Marie Hartman."

There it was. "Since I'm revealing all my secrets tonight, I guess I should tell you that things between me and Marie are changing. We're becoming closer."

His father smiled as he got up. "I'll look forward to seeing what happens next with you two, then."

John walked to his side. "Daed, wait. Is that it? Don't you want to talk to me about my faith or ask me if I've been praying about all of this?"

"*Nee*."

"No?"

"You might not be destined to be Amish but you'll always be my son, John. I know you've been doing those things." He squeezed his shoulder. "Now you best get some sleep. Morning comes early, ain't so?"

There were so many things John wanted to say to his father, to tell him. But he realized at last that words weren't necessary. "*Gut nacht*, Daed. *Danke*."

"Good night, John. Sleep well, and I'll see you in the morning."

As John walked up the stairs, he heard his father walk down the hall, his bowl in the sink obviously forgotten. Mamm was going to be questioning all of them in the morning about whose bowl it was.

He could hardly wait to see what his father would do about that.

ELEVEN

"Of course, I felt so sorry for the little kittens that I started crying, but Andy ignored me and started rubbing one, then another. Soon, E.A. and Harley were fussing over kittens, too."

"These are pretty good results, don't you think? Five out of seven of us were able to get together tonight," Katie Steury said from her seat in the back row of Marie's Escalade. "I think Andy would be proud."

Suddenly fighting a lump in her throat, Marie concentrated on maneuvering her vehicle around the parking area of Newman's Farm. There was a large number of attendants directing traffic. Their bright orange vests and flashlights were easy to see. All of the people and kids flowing out of their cars? Not so much.

"Boy, just when I thought I was going to be tear-free this evening," E.A. murmured.

"I'm sorry. I guess I shouldn't have said anything,"

Katie said. Looking around the vehicle, she asked, "Have I upset everyone by bringing up Andy's name?"

"No," Marie said as she at last set her parking brake for good measure. "You are right. Even though it hurts, we should talk about Andy from time to time. And it is good that we are all here."

"I'd say so," Will Kurtz said as he unbuckled, though his voice sounded a little flat. "I'm actually amazed that my schedule worked out the way it did. Lately I've been working odd hours at the trailer factory."

Marie noticed Will turn to John B., who was sitting in the back row next to Katie. "It's surprising that neither of us had to work tonight, ain't so?"

"*Jah.* Practically a miracle," John said. His voice sounded as strained as Marie's heart felt.

As she opened her door and grabbed her purse, Marie wondered if this was what their future get-togethers were going to be like. Full of stilted conversation and forced joviality—all hiding the pain that each was still feeling.

Did it even matter? She wasn't sure.

Instead she concentrated on smoothing out her jeans and blue-checked flannel shirt. Both were old and comfortable. She'd worn the old clothes on purpose, wanting to have something that was like it used to be.

As everyone continued to pile out of the SUV, the awkward conversation continued.

"Yes. It's a miracle and a blessing," E.A. said as she climbed out of the backseat, standing to one side as Will pulled the seat forward so everyone in the third row could get out. E.A., being Mennonite, had on a long skirt and a white T-shirt. Her red hair was bare except for a small lace covering. It was fastened in a low bun at the nape of her neck.

"Thanks for driving, Marie," Katie said.

She shrugged. "It's nothing. I'm glad I have a big car." Usually everyone would be teasing her. Well, Andy would be. Marie's parents had passed down their Escalade when they'd decided to buy a new, smaller vehicle. The Cadillac was far too big and expensive for her needs, but she hadn't had the heart to refuse the gift. It was comfortable, beautiful, and really good for occasions like this when a group of them wanted to go somewhere.

Remembering that several of their friends had already made arrangements to go home with other people, she said, "If any of you want me to give you a ride home, just let me know."

Elizabeth Anne pressed a hand on her arm. "Thanks, Marie."

The expression they shared spoke volumes, conveying how bittersweet the evening felt.

Holding up the key fob, she looked around. "Does everyone have all their stuff?"

"Yep. Lock it and let's get going," John said.

"Is Logan meeting us?" Will asked.

"I think so. He's with Tricia," John B. said as they all started walking toward the entrance of the festival.

As Marie watched him move ahead, a part of her felt disappointed. She'd hoped he would have chosen to walk by her side. But instead of showing any sort of preference for her companionship, he seemed to be going out of his way to not pay special attention to her.

It stung, especially when she recalled their kiss.

Scratch that. She'd had no trouble "recalling" anything. She'd actually relived their embrace so many times it was becoming embarrassing. She wasn't a sheltered girl. She'd kissed other boys.

So why was she fixating on John's kiss? Why could she not seem to think of anything else?

As they continued to walk through the crowded gravel parking lot, Katie kept pace with her. "Hey, you seem quieter than usual. Are you okay?"

"Yeah. It's just hard, you know? I miss Andy."

"I do, too. We all do." Staying by Marie's side, Katie's light green dress fluttering lightly in the evening breeze, she continued, "I keep thinking I'm going to hear his voice from behind me. I think part of me continually listens for it."

"I've found myself doing the same thing. I'll be working at the bank or out shopping at a store, or just cleaning my house. Hours will go by and I'll hardly think about him. Then I'll be doing the smallest thing and *bam*! His loss hits me so hard I can hardly catch my breath."

"You described how I'm feeling exactly. I started crying yesterday when I was eating Mexican food." She shook her head. "I can't believe that eating nachos brought me to tears."

"Andy did like nachos," Marie said. "But boy, would he be teasing you something awful if he saw you doing that."

Katie wiped her eyes. "He sure would."

E.A. came up to their side. "You two okay?"

"Yeah. We're . . . well, we're just missing Andy." Smiling at the other two girls, she shrugged. "I'll be fine."

"We'll get through it. Somehow," E.A. murmured.

Marie nodded, liking that. E.A. was right. It might not be pretty but they would all get through their grief somehow and in some way.

"Girls, you coming?" Will asked.

"We're here. Settle down," Marie said. She smiled at Will and felt her cheeks heat when she noticed that John was staring at her intently.

Boy, she was toast around him.

Five minutes later, they were all at the front of the donation booth. Because it was a community event, no one had to pay anything to get into the festival. But the organizers did ask for donations, both to help with the costs of the necessities and in order to give a donation for some of the area food banks.

As Marie watched everyone pull out a couple of dollars, and in some cases ten or twenty, a new feeling warmed her. This was something that she loved about their group. Giving to others wasn't something that they had to talk about. They simply did it. It was another example of how they might look very different but they really did have so much in common.

"Where to first?" she asked.

"I told my *mamm* I'd go see her at the booth in the back. She's in charge of the pie bake-off," Elizabeth Anne said. "Anyone want to come with me?"

"Sorry, E.A., but *nee*," Will said. "I wanted to look at the livestock."

"Marie and I are going to the corn maze," John B. announced. "We'll meet up with the rest of you later," he said as he walked to her side and pressed a hand to the center of her back.

Right away, her body shifted and relaxed. Almost as if she'd been needing his touch, his reassurance. It took her by surprise.

Just like the fact that their big outing seemed to

be disintegrating rapidly. "Wait a minute," she told them all. "We can't all wander off in different directions. We were going to all do something together, remember?"

Will raised his hands. "No offense, but I've no desire to watch John flirt with you under the cornstalks."

"We're not going to be flirting," Marie said.

John chuckled. "Speak for yourself, Marie."

Will grinned. "See what I mean?"

"I have an idea," E.A. said. "Let's all meet over where the food carts are in an hour."

"Perfect," John said.

Before Marie could reply, the rest of their group scattered. Even Katie.

"John, did you arrange something with everyone?"

"*Nee.*"

"Really? Because it seems like no one but me was surprised that we were separating from them."

"Well, maybe I did mention that I wanted to spend some time alone with you. But if I did, what's wrong with that?"

How come he kept turning everything she thought was obvious and flipping it on its side? "I don't know," she sputtered.

"That's because there isn't anything wrong with what I did."

"Maybe it was awfully high-handed of you."

He stopped and looked down at her. "Marie, don't make this harder than it has to be. I like spending time with you. I want to spend more time alone with you, but it's hard because we're both working and have other obligations."

"But what about everyone else?"

"What about them?"

"Don't you think they're wondering what's going on between us? Maybe they have questions."

John blinked. "Questions about what? The fact that you and I are enjoying spending time together?"

"You know that it's more than that."

His voice deepened as it lowered. "I absolutely know that. Do you not recall our kiss? Because I can't seem to forget it."

Talking with him was like jumping on board a roller coaster. He was taking her in circles and spins and she was simply trying to hold on and not fall. "I remember."

"Do you?" He stepped closer to her. Leaned closer to her ear. "Do you remember what it was like, Marie?"

Yes, she remembered. It had felt like she was coming home and stepping off the edge of a cliff at the same time. She'd alternated between wanting to wrap her arms around him and hold him close and stepping two feet away and reminding them both that it wasn't supposed to happen.

Still gazing into his eyes, Marie realized that her

heart was beating so fast. And . . . and her whole body felt like it wasn't aware of anything but him. Right there on the fairgrounds!

"*Gut*," he said, leading her to the corn maze. "Now, how should we do this?"

"What do you mean?"

"Should we race to see who gets out first?"

The sun was setting and the maze was huge. She'd been in it before, too. If they were lucky they might get through before the sun set completely, though that was doubtful. One year she and her girlfriends got so lost it took them almost an hour to get out.

The last thing she wanted was to be stuck in the middle of the stupid maze all alone. "Definitely not. We're going through the maze together."

"Should we time ourselves then? Guess how long it's going to take us?"

"John, you are such a boy. Why can't we just walk through the maze and enjoy the experience?"

"That's all you want to do?"

"I think that's enough." It was becoming rather hard to keep a straight face.

"All right," he said, though his voice was full of disappointment. "We'll go through your way."

"Thank you."

"Of course, Marie." He smiled at her before tensing up again.

"Now what's wrong?" Honestly, sometimes it felt as if he were her sibling, the way they could trade barbs back and forth.

"I'm not sure." Still looking just beyond her, his voice lowered. "*Mei shveshtah*'s here."

"Which one?" She had no idea why this was noteworthy!

"Molly. And look, she's talking with your gardener."

"Yes, she is talking with Danny Eberly." Feeling confused, Marie raised an eyebrow at John. He didn't notice, though. He was still staring at his sister like Molly was doing something wrong.

Marie had no idea what he could have been finding fault with. She didn't share it, but she didn't know if she'd ever seen Molly look so happy. Deciding she needed to get their tickets and move them on, she trotted forward. "My treat, John."

"Marie."

She kept walking. "Two tickets, Danny."

"Hiya, Miss Hartman. Having fun?"

"Very much. Hi, Molly. I'm Marie, your brother's friend."

"I remember ya. Hi, Marie." She lifted her chin. "Hey, John. You didn't tell me you were going to be here."

"Then we're even, aren't we? Because I sure didn't know you were going to be here either. How did you get here, anyway?"

"Anton and Amanda and Ezra. They hired a driver."

"Here you go, Marie," Danny said as he handed Marie two tickets . . . and directed a wary look at John.

"*Danke*," Marie said. Then, because John was embarrassing his sister something awful, she reached for John's hand and tugged. "Let's go."

He didn't budge. "Hold on a second. I want to ask Danny something."

"Not now John." With a wink in Molly's direction, Marie shook her head. "Let's get going. I've a mind to see how long it takes us to get through. That means we're going to have to time ourselves."

"Hold up, now. I need to—"

Marie cut him off. "No, you don't. What you need to do is get moving." Still holding his hand, a new, playful—and determined—light shone from her green eyes. "Therefore . . . one, two, three, go."

After giving his little sister a look that said he would talk to her later, he allowed Marie to tug him into the maze.

Within three feet, the scent of hay, cut grass, and cornstalks surrounded them. And even though it was still fairly light outside, the high walls made their world darken slightly.

Seeming to gather himself together, John turned his hand so their fingers linked.

Liking the feel of his calloused hand against her own, she looked up at him and smiled. John didn't return the smile, but his expression eased some more.

By the time they turned left and left again, they were walking slower . . . and then John grabbed ahold of her other hand. "Let's stop for a minute, Marie."

His voice was husky and full of promises.

And because she was a very smart girl, she stopped and turned to him. . . .

Looked up into his eyes . . . and waited to see what would happen next.

TWELVE

"God was so good. The kittens were all alive."

"Your *broodah* looked kind of mad," Danny said after John and Marie were out of sight. "Actually, he looks pretty mad at me. Why do you think that is?"

Oh, Molly knew. John hadn't liked seeing her doing anything with a boy, not even sitting at the front of a cornfield in plain view of their whole community. But even though she knew why John had been acting stupid, did that mean that she wanted to share that information with Danny?

Absolutely not.

"Don't worry about it. He likes to pretend I'm a child still. I don't have a problem reminding him that I'm sixteen and not six."

Danny laughed. "You really mean that, don'tcha?"

"*Jah*. Why are you surprised?"

"No reason . . . other than I didn't think you were so outspoken. You were always shy in school."

Danny wasn't wrong. She had been shy and self-conscious. As much as everyone pretended that her being in a wheelchair didn't make her any different, it felt like it was a dividing line between her and the rest of the kids. "Things were different in school for me."

"Even though I was only a year ahead of you, I don't remember much about you except that you were quiet."

"And that I was stuck in a wheelchair?"

"*Jah*. But you seemed timid, too. I remember thinking that you didn't seem like the kind of girl who could stand up for herself all that good." The moment the words were out of his mouth, he looked horrified. "I'm sorry. I didn't mean stand, like on two legs. I meant—"

She chuckled. "I knew what you meant," she said quickly. "Don't worry about it."

"Sure?"

"I know I'm in a wheelchair, Danny. I'm not sensitive about it. Well, not anymore. And not unless someone talks down to me because of it."

"I don't remember how you hurt your legs."

"It was my back. I injured my spine."

"Wait a minute. You had an accident, right? You fell off a horse or something?"

Thinking about that terrible moment, she nodded. "I was thrown. My horse got spooked by a snake or something and reared. It caught me off guard and I flew into a ravine and injured my spine."

"I bet it hurt bad."

"I don't really remember much of it, if you want to know the truth. I remember the horse rearing and making a terrible noise. I remember losing my grip on his reins and realizing I was gonna fall. And I remember landing and crying out. And then nothing until I was in the hospital and saw my whole family standing around my bed."

"I remember hearing about you being in the hospital for a long time."

It had been a horrible time. The hospital had been large and scary for her nine-year-old self. The tests they'd given her hadn't been pleasant or easy. Added that she'd realized she wasn't ever going to walk again?

It had been worse than hard.

Even now, all these years later, it was a struggle to keep her voice light. Though she truly didn't mind talking about her accident, or even about her hospital stay, the memories of the physical therapy and the times she'd been poked with needles still made her cringe. Even now, her palms got clammy every time she had to get a shot.

Danny lowered his voice. "What did you do when you found out about your legs? Did you cry?"

"I did. But I was mainly confused at first. I couldn't

accept that my paralysis was going to be permanent. I kept thinking if I prayed real hard that *Got* would listen and restore the feeling in my legs. But I soon learned that He doesn't answer every prayer."

Danny looked at her legs. "So you *canna* feel anything?"

"I was lucky. My T-12 vertebra was crushed but not completely ruined. I have some feeling in my lower thighs."

He looked skeptical.

Molly knew he probably had more questions about why that feeling was significant. She also had feeling above her thighs, which meant she didn't have to have a catheter and could even one day have a baby. But there was no way she was going to share such things with him.

Smiling at him, she said, "How has the fair been so far?"

He grinned back at her. "So far, so good. Everyone seems to really like the maze and I have fun sending everyone in."

Speaking of which, two more couples wandered over, and Danny was busy for the next couple of minutes selling them tickets and answering questions about the corn maze.

After they went in and disappeared, Molly chuckled. "That redheaded girl looked kind of scared."

He smiled at her. "I thought so, too."

"I don't know why she would go in if she was that afraid. It doesn't make sense to me."

"Who knows? I think a lot of people like to push themselves from time to time. Try something new."

"I guess so." Studying him, she realized that he'd been talking about himself. She wondered if he was talking about reaching out to her, though that seemed kind of silly. It wasn't like they were courting or anything. He was just being nice.

Sitting back down in the chair next to her, he looked at her closely. "Are you really not going to ask what I meant?"

"*Nee*. I mean, I know you'll share if you want to." Besides, what if he said something completely different from what she imagined? Then she'd feel kind of stupid.

Something new lit his eyes. Like he was seeing her in yet another way all over again. "You really mean that, don't you?"

She nodded, feeling suddenly confused. "I know what it's like to not want to talk about everything."

"You are sure different from other girls."

It was instinctive for her to flinch at the statement. But then, as she caught his tone, Molly realized that Danny meant it to mean *more* than it sounded. Like he wasn't talking about wheelchairs and legs that didn't work. Like he was talking in comparison to all the other girls he knew.

Like she had something good that they didn't.

She wasn't sure what that could be, but she held tight to the moment. Afraid to smile, she looked up at him, she searched his face, hoping he would say something else, if only to help her understand what he meant.

He stuffed his hands in his pockets. And for the first time since she'd known him, he looked a little self-conscious. "Hey, Molly? I was wondering . . ."

Inexplicably, he paused. She felt her heart start to pound. "*Jah*, Danny?"

"Well, what would you think . . ." His voice drifted off and he looked around. Then swallowed. "I mean. Do you think your parents would mind if I . . ." When he paused again, it was because he was looking at someone just behind her. "Uh-oh. Get ready."

Feeling like she'd just had a glass of cold water tossed on her face, she tried to keep up. "What's the matter?"

But then she saw them. Four kids from their school. Evan, Callie, Karl, and Mary Jane. They'd all been a year or two older than she was. But even though they were so close in age, she hadn't known them well. They'd been some of the most popular kids in their school. They'd also been some of Danny's best friends.

They weren't mean kids, not really. They were really nice to Amanda and Anton. But it was like none of them knew what to do with her, so they'd chosen to ignore her. It had been hard. Sometimes she'd felt invisible next to them.

She didn't really mind their differences, now that they were out of school and she hardly ever saw them. As she looked at what they were wearing she realized why. They seemed to be really enjoying their *rumspringa*. All four of them were dressed like *Englischers* and were conspicuously holding cell phones.

From the way they were acting, they might as well have been complete strangers.

If Molly were at the library she would have turned her wheelchair and sped out of sight. For a moment she wondered if Danny would invite them to hang out with them, making her feel awkward all over again.

That would be horrible, given the way she was stuck where she was.

On the heels of those doubts came a reminder that Danny wasn't like that. He'd invited her to hang out with him. She needed to stay. Plus, all of her siblings would get really mad at her if she took off, and then would probably refuse to take her anywhere ever again.

Therefore, she did the only thing she could. She sat there, watched them approach, and hoped and prayed that they would ignore her.

Which they did.

"Danny! Look at you. Working on a Saturday night."

After glancing at her quickly, Danny stood up and stepped forward. "Hey, guys. I didn't know you were coming out here tonight."

Evan shrugged. "It wasn't like there was a lot else to do."

"How's it going? Are you so bored?" Callie asked. "I would be."

"Nah. I've just been hanging out with Molly here." He placed a hand on the back of her chair.

Mary Jane glanced down at her. "Oh. Hey, Molly."

"Hi, Mary Jane," Molly said tightly. Because there wasn't really a choice, she smiled and raised a hand at all of them. "*Gut* to see you all," she lied.

Callie, who had always seemed to be the nicest of them all, smiled back. "It's *gut* to see you, too. It's been ages. What have you been doing since you graduated?"

Just as Molly was about to say she'd been working at the library, Karl nudged Callie. "Hey. Be nice."

"I was being nice. What's up with you?"

"Only that it's obvious that she can't do much."

Huh. It seemed Callie wasn't nice anymore, either.

Just as Danny looked like he was going to come to her defense, Molly spoke up. "Actually, I can do quite a bit. For instance, I work at the Walnut Creek Library."

"Oh. Well, I don't really read," Karl said. "I guess that's why I haven't seen ya."

"Probably."

Mary Jane laughed like she was embarrassed. "Sorry. We can't take Karl anywhere." When neither Danny nor Molly said anything, she giggled again. "Danny, when do you get off tonight?"

"Not for a couple of hours," he replied as he sat back down.

"Are you sure you can't just leave?" Evan asked, turning so it was obvious he was ignoring Molly. "My brother bought some beer. A whole case. We're going over to my barn to hang out. It's bound to be a lot better than walking around this place."

"Even Sam said he wanted to stop by," Karl said.

Danny's mouth tightened. "Sam is only fourteen. He shouldn't be drinking."

Karl continued. "Hey, he approached us. What could I say?"

"You should've said no." Looking like he was ready to punch Karl, Danny said, "I better not find out you've been hanging out with my little brother."

"Settle down, Danny," Evan said. "I have no desire to hang out with your little *broodah*. Karl just likes needling ya."

Mary Jane sighed. "I'm bored. Danny, are you sure you don't want to go with us? Or, you could meet us later?"

"*Jah.* I'm sure. I'm staying here until Mr. Newman closes for the night."

"Poor you," Mary Jane said.

To Molly's surprise, Danny moved his hand to her shoulder and squeezed gently. "Not poor me. It's been a *gut* night." His voice cooled. "Most of it, anyway."

Karl grunted. "If you change your mind, let us know." He held up his cell phone. "You want my number?"

"I won't need it," Danny replied, his voice still cold. "Look, there's some people coming, so sorry, you all need to either buy tickets and go in the maze or move on."

Evan's eyebrows rose as he turned to his friends. "Anyone want to spend money to go walk around the cornstalks?"

Karl shook his head. "*Mei daed* makes sure I do that plenty at home. Let's go."

"See you, Molly. Maybe I'll stop by the library soon," Callie said softly before Karl grabbed her hand and tugged her back toward the tents.

"*Jah.* See you," she said quietly, but she doubted anyone heard her. Mary Jane and Evan were whispering something to Danny and then laughed as they turned around and took off.

Molly watched them go, her insides a knot of emotions as she watched them blend in with the crowd. She was proud of standing up for herself but dismayed that they were all drinking and encouraging Danny to do the same, and irritated that those boys hadn't gotten any nicer.

"Four tickets." A customer speaking to Danny brought her out of her reverie.

She turned to see who it was, then was surprised to realize that she knew this group of people, too. "Oh! Hi."

"Hey, Molly," Will Kurtz said with a warm smile. "It's *gut* to see you here."

"*Danke*." She smiled at John's friend . . . and the three little girls in bright dresses and white *kapps* holding hands behind him. "Looks like you've got your hands full tonight."

"I do. I rode here with John and Marie but when I saw that my sister was interested in staying for the judging at the bake-off, I told my three favorite nieces that we could do something fun."

"I'm sure your sister is grateful. As are these girls." She smiled at the little ones. "Hiya."

"Hi," one little girl in a bright pink dress said.

"We're your *only* nieces, Uncle Will," one of them said.

"And thank heavens, too, seeing that there are three of ya."

"Have a good time," Danny said after he took Will's money.

"We will. Send in a search party if we don't come out in three hours."

"*Onkle* Will, we can't be in that long," one of the little girls in a dark pink dress whined. "I'll get hungry."

"Then you better lead the way, Violet," Will said as they disappeared from view.

Molly chuckled. "I've only seen Will's nieces from a distance. They're mighty cute, but I bet a handful, too."

Danny smiled. "Triplets! They would make me lose my mind."

"Maybe not." She chuckled again, feeling grateful that they'd shown up. If they hadn't, she didn't know what she would have done while Karl and Mary Jane and the others had been standing there.

He knelt down on one knee so they could see each other eye to eye. "Hey, are you okay? Karl and the others can be pretty rude."

"I'm fine. Are you? Are you wishing that you could have left with them?"

"What? No. I meant what I said. I'm here to work."

"Oh. Yes. Of course."

"But it's more than that, too, Molly. I like hanging out with you."

It took everything she had not to make a big deal

out of what he'd just said. "Do you think they'll really be drinking beer tonight?"

"Probably. They're into that right now."

She wanted to ask if he was, too, but she decided she didn't want to know. She wasn't naive, she had four older siblings, all of whom had experimented with different things during their running-around years. James had given their parents many a headache before abruptly changing his ways and wanting to be baptized.

Anton and Amanda did a few things but only because it was expected rather than because of some interest or need.

John was on the other side of the spectrum. He always said he never had any desire to drink, smoke, or even drive a vehicle because he was so close to his group of Eight. He said he'd always felt blessed that their parents allowed him to have such a broad range of close friends. Because of that, he had no worries or questions about what *Englischers* did.

Ironically, however, he didn't seem in any hurry to become baptized. Molly had even heard their grandparents tell their mother that they didn't think he would actually ever profess his faith.

Realizing she'd been quiet for too long, she smiled up at him. "I'm not much of a drinker myself."

Pure warmth lit those light blue eyes she liked so much. "Me neither, Molly."

When she giggled, he laughed, too, and stretched out his legs beside her. He now looked completely at ease. As relaxed as she felt, now that they were completely alone again. "Tell me about your brother and that woman."

"Marie? Well, she's one of his best friends. See, John developed a close association with a group of kids when he was about seven or eight. They all aren't Amish. Marie was one of them."

"They looked like they were more than just friends to me."

Remembering the proprietary way her brother had been standing next to Marie, she nodded. "I would never tell John this, but I think you're right."

He smiled as the sun continued to drift down over the horizon and the many lights that were strung from tent to tent came on, looking much like fireflies in the middle of July and mirroring the way she was feeling. Those lights had always been there, but now that they had been illuminated, they were twinkling happily.

Much like how she was feeling, too.

THIRTEEN

"Will, being Will, said we needed to go right to his parents and tell them what we found. That was the right thing to do. We probably would've done that very thing . . . if it hadn't started raining really hard."

Marie and John had been holding hands and staring into each other's eyes in the middle of the corn maze for at least fifteen minutes. Maybe even longer.

Long enough for a family of four to go running past them and disappear from sight.

Long enough for the sun to almost set and some twinkling lights to burst to life in the distance.

Long enough for two teenagers to glance their way, smirk, and then walk in the other direction.

No doubt, she and John were something of a sight to see.

For her part, Marie could not have cared less. She felt like she'd waited half her life for this moment. Maybe she had. She would be perfectly okay with standing with him for another hour, just drinking in the sight of him holding her hands. Of knowing that they might finally be done playing games with each other. But John worried more about appearances than she did.

She cleared her throat in a weak attempt to lighten the tension between them. "You know, I could be wrong, but I believe the point of stepping into these corn mazes is to try to find the way out. Unless we want to go back to the entrance, we should probably start moving."

"Is that what you want to do, Marie? Are you ready to start walking and get on out of here?"

No. It was definitely not what she was ready to do. But it wasn't like she could say that she would much rather be wrapped in his arms and kissing him.

As the seconds passed and he simply stood there, waiting for her answer, she became flustered. It was a new feeling. She rarely got flustered about much.

How honest should she be? How honest was she willing to be?

Right away the answer came to her. She was willing to be completely honest, because being patient and quiet had gotten her only years of pining for him.

It was time to make a move. And if it was the wrong move? Then so be it. With that in mind, she stepped a little closer to him. Close enough to notice the scruff on his cheeks. Close enough to notice the way the muscles bunched under the thin fabric of his shirt, reminding her of just how strong he was—and how different his body was from the handful of men she'd dated in Cleveland.

"I'm fine with whatever you want to do, John," she said at last. As she heard the words, she inwardly groaned. That sounded like something out of a bad TV movie.

His body seemed to tighten. "Is that right, Marie?"

He'd almost whispered that.

Okay, she was starting to feel a little tingly and it had nothing to do with the faint chill in the air. Hating and loving that he was making her lead the conversation, she swung their linked hands a bit. "You know I came here to spend time with you, John. Not to walk around cornstalks."

"Is that all you wanted?"

With any other man, she would be sure that was a suggestive comment. But with John? She just wasn't sure. Suddenly, all of her grand plans of finally making a move toward him crashed and burned. "I don't know how I'm supposed to answer that. Why don't you tell me what you want to do?"

He was looking at her intently now. Like if he turned his head he was worried she might disappear. "If I tell you the truth, I'm a little afraid of how you might take it."

"You won't know until you ask me."

His expression turned pained, but it wasn't serious. She didn't know how to describe it, except that she'd never seen it on his face outside of her dreams. "John B., just tell me."

"First, don't call me that anymore."

"What?"

"John B. The only reason Harley and Will started calling me that was because there were three other Johns in our school."

"I know that we talked about this months ago, but it's just a habit. Don't you think you're making too much of it?"

He shook his head. "I don't want you to think about another John but me."

In that moment, she wasn't sure if she could name any other man named John in her life. "I don't ever think about any other Johns. Just you."

"That's good. Because I never think of another Marie. Only you."

There it was. Further evidence of how he was brave enough to say all the words she was afraid to admit. "John."

"Should I be completely honest?" Before she could even nod, he murmured, "I haven't thought of another woman for months now."

Her breath didn't catch, but she felt like she was

slowly losing oxygen. Still too wary to share that she'd been feeling the same way, she stepped closer. Now her arms were pressed against his far larger ones and his fingers were brushing against the sides of her jeans. Tilting up her head, she licked her bottom lip. "So you're saying that I'm special to you?"

He exhaled. Then leaned down. Pressed his lips to her temple. Leaned a little closer. Then whispered, "What I'm trying to get up the nerve to tell ya is that I don't want to simply wander among the corn rows, Marie. I want to pull you close enough for me to wrap my arms around you."

"And then?"

He smiled. "And kiss you again."

The tingling she'd felt along every nerve ending dissolved into a great warm puddle of happiness and need in her middle. "Do you think that's wise?"

"I don't know. I don't even care."

Oh, John smelled so good. She knew being in his arms again would feel so good. Maybe she should stop worrying about what all of their friends were going to say or what kind of future they might have.

Maybe she should simply enjoy the moment, too.

"I might not be a naive Amish girl but I'm still used to the man making the first move, John. Are you going to kiss me or not?"

Maybe she shouldn't have phrased it quite like

that. Because less than two seconds passed before he did, indeed, pull her against him, wrap his arms around her back, and kiss her at last.

And then she couldn't really think of anything at all, because John B.—now only John to her forevermore—had parted his lips and was practically consuming her like she was his last meal.

She held on.

For the record, this kiss wasn't sweet and innocent. It wasn't tentative or even especially gentle.

Instead, it was a kiss of two people who had known each other for most of their lives and had each secretly dreamed of it happening for years. And now that they were in their midtwenties, they had experience and knew what they wanted.

It was lovely and passionate and everything she'd ever wanted. This kiss, this embrace made every other kiss she'd ever had seem forced and fake and wrong.

And while she had no idea what was going to happen next, she knew that it didn't really matter. Even if they didn't share another kiss for two months, everything between them had changed.

He wasn't just John to her now. He was simply everything.

FOURTEEN

"Next thing I knew, Andy was passing out baby kittens like it was Christmas Day, warning us all to tuck them under our clothes to keep them warm."

After John had kissed Marie until he was on the verge of losing control, he held her close and whispered to her about how perfect and special he thought she was, and she'd relaxed against him.

The feel of her in his arms had been so sweet. She'd been so trusting and responsive. She'd made him realize that every dream and every idea of how it would feel to finally have her in his arms had been completely inadequate.

When he realized he was tempted to kiss her again, John stepped away. He didn't want to embarrass her or do something that would make her regret having given him her trust.

Before he could change his mind, he took her hand

and started walking. "It's a pretty big maze. If we don't get going, we could be here all night."

Marie, in a very un-Marie-like way, didn't comment on his abrupt change or ask any questions. She just smiled up at him like he was something special and stayed by his side.

As they continued, cornstalks rustled in the wind on either side of them. Laughter and conversation floated around them, most of it muted, though every couple of minutes a loud exclamation or laugh would ring out. Overhead, the sun was slowly setting. A harvest moon was rising, just as the once bright blue sky faded into a steel gray.

Two teenagers appeared in their path, took one look at him and Marie, and turned right around.

Marie laughed. "Did you see the look on that boy's face? He looked like he was never going to find any privacy in this maze."

"All I noticed was that the girl was blushing."

Marie chuckled again. "Who knows? I might be still sporting a blush myself."

Looking down at her, all he saw was a pretty smile. "You look fine, Marie."

She smiled at him and squeezed his hand.

John had been in enough cornstalks to have a general idea about how most mazes were laid out. But still, at each juncture, he stopped and asked Marie which way she wanted to go.

Every time, Marie would smile slightly and simply say right or left. And then they would be on their way again. Meandering their way, both lost in thought.

He found the walk to be very much needed, since his whole body had felt like it was on fire when he'd kissed her. Within fifteen minutes, both he and Marie were joking with each other, just like old times.

As they neared the end, more people surrounded them. Marie began talking to a couple of ladies who were old enough to be their grandmothers. The tension between them lessened and became almost familiar.

John sighed in relief. Thank the good Lord that he hadn't forgotten everything that was right.

"Do you think we're close yet?" she asked.

Since he was pretty sure after they made two more right turns they would be at the exit, he nodded. "Pretty close."

"Oh."

He squeezed her hand. "What's wrong?"

"Nothing." After a pause, she looked up at him. "I just . . . well, I'm kind of sad it's over, you know?"

Feeling a lump form in his throat, he nodded. "*Jah*," he said at last. "I know." If he were another type of man, maybe he would have promised her more kisses, more stolen moments together . . . anything she wanted.

But he wasn't that man. More importantly, he wasn't in a position to offer her anything more. He was still Amish and she was still English. That difference didn't matter in the middle of a corn maze. But in the real world, where they were surrounded by their family and friends?

It made all the difference in the world.

After one last right turn, they came to a crowd of people standing near a wide opening. With reluctance, he let go of her hand.

"John?" Marie asked.

"You made it!" a twelve- or thirteen-year-old English girl chirped before he could say a word. "Would you like a ribbon?"

"A what?" he asked.

She held up the gaudy satin ribbon with NEWMAN'S FAMOUS CORN MAZE printed in white block letters. "Everyone who gets through the maze gets a prize." She thrust it toward his hand.

"*Nee, danke.*" The last thing he wanted was some silly ribbon memorializing what had just happened. He didn't want anything to taint or cheapen the way he was feeling.

"No, wait," Marie said. "I want mine."

"Truly?"

"It's a keepsake, John," she murmured, her green eyes looking sweet and languid under the twinkling white lights overhead.

"Let's get you one, then," he said, realizing once again that he might know how to navigate a corn maze but had much to learn about what women wanted.

"Thank you," Marie told the girl as she took both ribbons and carefully placed them in her purse.

"What would you like to do next?" he asked.

"Do you want to check on your sister?"

He couldn't believe it, but he actually had forgotten about her. After considering the pros and cons about getting into her business, he shook his head. "*Nee*. Molly looked to be just fine."

She lifted an eyebrow. "That's a bit of a turnaround from how you treated Danny earlier."

He shrugged. "You're right. Of course I want to keep her safe and protected. But . . ." His voice drifted off as he realized he'd been about to mention that he'd just done some things in the cornstalks that the rest of his family wouldn't be all that pleased about. "Um, what I mean, is that Molly has gotten pretty good at reminding me that she ain't a child anymore. Though we're all likely to still be looking out for her, I know she's right. I need to learn to give her some space and let her grow up. No good will come out of encouraging her to stay so sheltered."

Marie's expression softened. "I'm proud of you. I know it's in your nature to want to protect her."

Her approval made him feel good, like he'd done something worthwhile, though it wasn't anything more than accepting that his little sister wasn't a helpless girl—and that he, too, didn't want a family member commenting on every little thing that he did. "What would you like to do now? Are you hungry? Want some cider?"

"Not really." She pressed a hand to his forearm. "I . . . well, I think maybe we should talk about what just happened."

"*Jah.* We probably should. After we meet everyone at the food carts."

"I had forgotten all about them."

"Me, too."

She looked up at him. "I need to give everyone rides home who needs them. Could we talk after?"

"We can talk whenever you want, Marie," he said as he lifted a hand to greet Elizabeth Anne and Harley, who were both holding caramel apples.

However, fifteen minutes later, John was alone with Marie again. The rest of their friends had found other rides home. From the knowing smile Will had cast him, John wondered if they'd planned to leave on their own all along.

Marie had seemed surprised but hadn't argued with their decisions. Instead she simply bought a caramel apple for herself and ate it as they walked back to her vehicle. When they reached the Escalade and she was about to unlock it, he noticed that she still had a dab of caramel on her lip.

"Hold up, Marie," he murmured as he pressed his thumb across her mouth.

"John?"

"It was nothing. Just a bit of caramel." Then, because he couldn't help himself, he kissed her softly. "There," he murmured. "Now, you're perfect."

She pressed a hand to her lips, but her eyes lit up. "How about we go back to your place?"

"Um, all right?"

She sounded so hesitant, so un-Marie-like, he nudged her like he used to do back when they were teenagers. "I promise I won't attack you, Marie. I just . . . well, if we're going to be talking about what just happened, I'd rather do that in private."

Looking around them, at the crowds of people, she nodded. "I would, too. We know too many people here. Our luck, someone will overhear our conversation."

He had no doubt that if any one of their acquaintances got a hint that they had been kissing in the cornfield, it would be too tempting for them not to share . . . and maybe even add to the story a bit. "We'll just talk."

She chuckled. "Did you read my mind?"

"I didn't need to. You had a look on your face that said you were a little worried."

"I wasn't worried about how far you would want to go, John. I've been telling myself that I needed to practice some self-control around you."

"I've been thinking the same thing. It seems we're two of a kind, Marie."

He'd intentionally kept his tone light, but he knew that they really did have a lot to talk about. Losing control before they discussed what type of future they could possibly have would be wrong.

But though his head was telling him to keep his cool, John knew he was going to pull her into his arms before he told her good night. He was a patient man, but there were limits to how long he wanted to wait to hold her close again.

FIFTEEN

Remembering how awkward it had been, holding a tiny kitten and wondering how to get it close to her skin while still staying modest, Katie shook her head. "That was Andy for ya. He always had plans that made perfect sense to him . . . but not always to everybody else."

As she maneuvered her black Escalade through the crowded parking lot, Marie kept recalling a conversation the eight of them had had five or six years ago. It was about the time when Harley and John were graduating from the Amish school at fourteen. She had been secretly appalled that they weren't upset about not getting a better education. Andy had been plain jealous. But then Logan had reminded them all that the reason they all got along so well was because they'd respected each other's differences—and that had been all she'd needed to remember: they each had their own path to take in life. She was college bound, John was Amish and had a different type of education ahead of him.

That conversation had been one of the reasons she'd been okay with going to Cleveland and not staying in close contact with everyone. She'd assumed they wouldn't have much in common once they were adults and living on their own. She couldn't have been more wrong.

And though Andy's death had spurred the desire to reconnect with her friends, she'd quickly realized that they had been destined to remain close with the seven other people in their group.

But what was happening between her and John? This was something else entirely. She liked him. A lot. Found him attractive. Found him desirable. Wanted to be with him all the time.

Which meant that one of them was going to have to change. She couldn't pretend that their differences didn't matter in the real world. They did.

This realization was a surprise. She was a woman who liked things to be orderly. Liked for things to be how she expected them to be. This new development was throwing her for a loop, even though she knew it shouldn't have.

As if John sensed that she needed time to process it all—or maybe he, too, needed time to figure things out—John was quiet as she stopped to allow a very large family to cross in front of them.

Marie appreciated John's silence. Though she wasn't literally shaking, her insides felt a little unsteady. Tonight, everything between them had changed. It didn't matter what either of them had done with other people in the past. All that mattered was that the familiar platonic friendship she and John had enjoyed was now in the past. She didn't think she could ever look at John Byler again without recalling how it had felt to be in his arms.

Maybe she would be feeling different if she could dismiss their kisses as a mistake, a matter of the two of them getting carried away in the moment. Like neither of them could control themselves when they were standing in the middle of cornfields or something.

But even if nothing ever happened between them again, Marie knew that she would never consider those moments between them to have been a mistake.

Not when being in his arms felt so right.

"Marie, are you going to be all right?"

"Hmm?" She'd already driven out of the parking lot and was cruising down the highway.

"You've been quiet. I thought maybe you were having difficulty driving in the dark."

"No, I'm fine, John."

After a couple of seconds, John spoke again, his voice sounding a little rough. "I guess that was the wrong thing to say, huh? Sorry. It's just I sometimes hate that you are always the one having to be driving."

Surprised, she glanced at him. "John, I never even think about it. You've driven me around plenty of times in your buggy. This isn't that different."

"I think it might be."

"It isn't to me." She meant that, too. She never resented the fact that he didn't drive a vehicle and she did. There were many things he could do that she couldn't.

"I appreciate that. But still . . ." He took a breath then continued. "Lately I've been wondering what things would be like between us if I jumped the fence."

Jumped the fence. As in: left the Amish.

Marie tightened her grip on the steering wheel in a sorry attempt to not show any reaction. That was pretty difficult, considering what she really wanted to do was pull off on the side of the road and confide that she'd just been thinking the same thing. Then, maybe pepper him with about a thousand questions.

"Marie?"

As the tension emanated off of him, she realized he was waiting for her reaction.

"John B., I don't know what to say." She wanted to

share what she'd been thinking but needed to see his expression when they talked. Boy, she really wished he would have waited about thirty minutes until they were sitting in her living room, having their big discussion.

He reached out and pressed a hand to the top of her thigh. "Hey, did you already forget what we talked about? What you promised? Don't call me John B., Marie."

"That was a mistake. I didn't forget." She just happened to be a little rattled at the moment.

"*Gut.*"

He sounded so satisfied, so completely masculine and pleased, a tremor went through her. Both from his touch and his words . . . and the fact that she was driving fifty miles an hour down the highway in the dark.

"John, I can't believe you brought this up while I was driving."

"I know. I guess it just kind of came out. It's been on my mind for a while. So, what do you think?"

"I think we need to talk about this when we're at my place."

He pulled his hand away. "Are you upset?"

"No. Of course not."

"Sure?"

She was stunned. She was excited and scared, too.

Excited about the thought of having a real future with him. Scared about somehow disappointing him—and realizing that he'd made a huge sacrifice for her that he regretted. "It's . . . um, just a lot to take in." She glanced at him, intending to smile, when he jerked.

"Marie!"

She looked back at the road in time to see a car weaving toward them. It was going way too fast and veering into their lane.

There was no time to move her vehicle to the shoulder. No time to do anything but react. Crying out, she slammed on her brakes and laid hard on the horn, but they began to skid.

The sedan barreling toward them weaved again, going back to its lane, then crossing the yellow lines in the center once again.

Still skidding, Marie jerked the steering wheel hard to the right.

"Marie!" John called out.

She gasped as her heart pounded so fast she could hardly hear anything else. For two seconds, she thought they were in the clear, that she'd saved them.

But her actions hadn't been enough. The driver of the other vehicle had lost control and slammed into them on her side of the SUV, just behind her seat.

The crash created a scream of metal and screeching tires, blending in with her own screams.

John called out. Her Escalade slid farther off the shoulder and down the steep, gravel-covered ravine. Seconds later, they slammed into a line of fencing, the other car following on their heels.

Their air bags came out, hitting her hard in the chest and side. Her body was thrown forward. She held out her hands in an effort to shield her face.

And then she was aware of nothing but pain in her head and hands, the darkness that suddenly surrounded them, and the fact that John was not only silent, he wasn't moving at all.

Tears filled her eyes as she felt warm liquid touch her cheeks. Though she tried to fight it, she closed her eyes.

And then didn't feel anything else at all.

John had no idea how long he'd been lying in the dark, strapped to his seat, surrounded by air bags, peppered with small pebbles of glass.

Little by little, he slowly became aware of flashing lights, the piercing cry of sirens, and men's voices calling out to each other.

Then he was aware that Marie's SUV was tilted in a lopsided way. If he hadn't been strapped tight, he would no doubt be resting against his door.

"We're gonna get you out!" a man called out.

John blinked. Attempted to focus. After several tries, he was finally able to see two firefighters standing on Marie's side of the vehicle. They were leaning close, calling out to the crew of emergency workers who had just arrived.

What they were saying slowly registered. The whole side of Marie's vehicle was crumpled.

As the men continued to call out warnings and instructions to each other, more sirens rang through the air. At last, John came to his senses. He'd been riding with Marie, flirting and teasing with her . . . and then that car had been coming toward them.

Where was Marie?

Though his head was pounding, the vehicle was tilted, and the majority of her side was crumpled, he looked for her.

At last he found her, half buried in the collapsed air bag. But she wasn't moving.

Pure panic set in, holding hands with his worst fears.

"Marie?" he croaked out. "Marie?" His alarm increased as he attempted to shift and reach for her. "Marie, answer me, wouldja?"

No answer.

Suddenly fearing the worst, he started feeling for his seat belt, trying to unbuckle himself so he could get to her.

"No, buddy!" a voice called out.

He looked up. Realized the firefighter on his side was yelling at him. "I know you're hurting, and we know you want out, but don't touch that belt just yet, okay? Hold on. We're doing our best to get the two of you out."

Though the words made sense, John only had one goal in mind. "*Nee*, I'm trying to get to Marie."

"We know, buddy. I promise, we're working on that. Sit tight."

"But—"

"Trust us. Let us do our jobs." The voice was hard and firm but brooked no argument.

John would have nodded his understanding if his neck and head didn't feel like it had been wrenched from his shoulders. Now that his vision was working better, he tried his best to watch over Marie. She was sitting limply, strapped in as well. "Please, Lord," he whispered. "Please be with Marie. Please don't let her die."

Moments later, he heard the unmistakable sound of a saw cutting through metal. It was harsh and pierced through the rest of the noise and commotion circling them.

John gritted his teeth as the sound rose to a higher pitch. He stopped praying and stared at Marie, hoping for any sign of life.

As the noise at last abated, Marie jerked. All at once, she inhaled sharply and opened her eyes.

"John?"

Her voice sounded thin and weak. But she'd spoken. She was conscious. She was alive. Praise God. "I'm here, Marie," he whispered, wishing he could at least free an arm. He needed to touch her. "I'm okay."

She started shaking. Tried to turn her head his way. "John!" she said again, this time sounding scared and panicked.

"Hush, now, Marie. It's over. It's over and we're okay, and people are here, helping us. Don't you hear them?"

"I was so scared."

"I was, too. But it's all right now." When she started to struggle against her seat belt, he called out, "*Nee*, Marie. Don't move. Let the rescue workers help us."

Seconds later, a firefighter yelled out much the same thing from outside.

Before John could offer any more words of reassurance, the saw continued. More men and women arrived, surrounding them.

Beside him, Marie began to shake.

John had never felt more helpless in his life.

After what felt like hours but had probably only been a few minutes, a man came to his side and spoke to him through the broken glass. "What's your name, son?"

"John. I'm John Byler."

"Okay, John. Listen, I'm going to stay here with you, but it might be a little bit before we can get you out, okay? We've got to get the woman out first."

"I understand."

"What's her name?"

"She's Marie Hartman," John said.

The worker called out to the men on the other side.

Then, another worker leaned toward Marie. "Marie, hang in there, okay? We're gonna get you out."

John wasn't sure if Marie heard or not. Her eyes had closed again.

Tears filled his eyes as he closed his eyes to pray again. But it was hard. He was suddenly too tired to do much but listen to the saw and the emergency workers' raised voices.

His head pounded and a searing flash of pain made him wince. He didn't know what was wrong with him, but nothing mattered except Marie.

As red and blue lights illuminated the air, he

opened his eyes and gazed at Marie. And finally allowed himself a very selfish thought about how much it was going to hurt if he lost Marie the very night when he'd finally believed that she could one day be his.

SIXTEEN

"Somehow, I did get that kitten snuggled close. We all did. Then, with the rain still falling from the sky in heavy sheets, we all started walking. We might have gotten back to Will's house without another thought, too. If lightning hadn't hit a nearby tree."

The first sight of the hospital's waiting room brought Molly up short. It seemed as if half the population of Walnut Creek was in the hospital's waiting area. Everyone seemed to be sitting or standing on every available space—people were against the wall, on the tiled floor, or in one of the vinyl-covered chairs situated around the room. Two young women had even perched on the edges of one of the sturdy oak coffee tables.

As Molly scanned all the familiar faces, she had a difficult time not dissolving into tears. Each person in the room was wearing an expression that likely mirrored her own. One filled with worry and pain. Though she supposed some might find comfort in being surrounded by people who felt the same way she did, she didn't. The tension and tightly wound panic that filled the room only seemed to make things worse.

Wheeling her chair toward the side, she scanned the room some more, anxious to find a friendly face.

Sure enough, there were Katie, Harley, Will, Logan, and Elizabeth Anne. The remainder of her brother's original Eight. To see only five of them together was a difficult reminder of all that had happened. Now Andy Warner was up in Heaven while John and Marie were in one of the exam rooms of the emergency room.

Before her thoughts turned darker, she scanned the space some more. Scattered around were their parents, some of their friends and siblings, and even some of John's work friends, including his boss.

Of course, Mamm and Daed and her siblings were there as well. For once the twins weren't joking around. Instead they were sitting stoically side by side. Ezra was holding Amanda's hand.

In another section of the waiting area sat eight or ten kids that Molly had gone to school with. They were sitting close to each other but otherwise conspicuously silent. Molly's mother had told her that the driver of the vehicle who'd hit Marie's SUV was none other than Mary Jane. To make matters worse, there were even rumors that she'd been drinking.

Molly hoped that wasn't true. It was going to be hard enough for Mary Jane to deal with that fact that she was responsible for the accident—and for Evan's death.

Evan! Molly could hardly bear to even think about that. They weren't close, but he'd been nice to her. Even if he hadn't been, he'd surely been far too young to leave the world.

Swallowing back the lump in her throat, Molly attempted to focus on the latest report from the nurse on duty. She'd shared that Mary Jane was in serious condition and the other two—Karl and Callie—were being examined and would likely be admitted. Molly really hoped and prayed that all of them were going to be okay.

When she'd been in the waiting room earlier, a somber-looking doctor had come in and asked to speak to Evan's parents. Thirty minutes later, the news that Evan had died in the ambulance had spread and several kids had started crying.

When Evan's parents walked out, Molly hadn't been able to even look at them. Their expressions were a terrible combination of rage and shock—the same masks of grief that Mr. and Mrs. Warner had worn. As had John.

She still didn't understand why the Lord needed to take some people so early. She knew her parents would tell her that it wasn't for her to question His will. But still, it was hard to accept things that seemed so unfair.

After Evan's parents left, even more people entered the crowded room. Now, interspersed among everyone were police officers, firefighters, and their Amish preacher and a Catholic priest.

The only bright spot—if it could be called that—was that no one was trying to place blame on anyone's shoulders or yelling. Instead, the group of almost seventy people were all whispering to one another or talking quietly. People were sharing snacks, bringing in trays of drinks, and even helping to entertain some of the young children in the room.

"Hey, Molly?"

She looked over at her fourteen-year-old brother, Ezra. She hadn't noticed him walk to her side. "*Jah*?"

He swallowed. "Um, I thought I'd go get Mamm a fresh cup of *kaffi*. Want to come?"

She didn't. By the look of things, it didn't seem like their mother looked like she was eager for a cup either. But as she caught sight of the tension in her little brother's face, she knew he needed to get out of there. That, she could understand.

"Sure." She turned her chair and used the battery-operated mechanism to glide down the hall by his side.

Once they were out of sight of everyone, she slowed and looked up at him. "You okay?"

He shrugged. "I don't know."

"They said John was going to be okay. That's something."

"I know. Daed talked to one of the firefighters. He said that John was probably in the best shape of everyone who survived." He winced before looking away.

"That's a blessing."

He stopped and stared at her. "Is it?"

"It has to be."

"What about everyone else?" He took a deep breath and blurted, "What about Evan?"

Pain seared through her. "I don't know what you want me to say, Ezra. You know as well as I do that death isn't easy."

"I can't believe that we were just in school with Evan and now he's gone. I mean, he was in your grade."

"I know."

"Does his death feel real to you yet? It doesn't to me."

She shook her head. "*Nee*, but it probably won't for

a while. I feel so sorry for his family. They looked like they didn't know what to do. Almost like they weren't even sure if they could walk out of the hospital."

"Everyone's parents look upset. Did you notice Mr. and Mrs. Miller?"

"*Jah*," she said softly, remembering Mary Jane's parents. "They were both staring at the wall." They'd looked almost like statues.

He lowered his voice. "And what if it really was Mary Jane's fault? She was underage, drinking, and didn't have a driver's license."

"I imagine she'll have to pay the consequences."

After looking around to make sure he couldn't be heard, Ezra leaned closer to her. "Anton says she could go to prison. Do you think that could really happen? Would anyone send an Amish teenager to prison?"

She wasn't sure, but Molly had an idea that religion didn't matter too much when it came to causing another person's death.

But even though she wasn't too much older, she was old enough to want to protect her brother.

"Let's not think about what could happen. We don't know all the facts."

"Molly, come on. Tell me what you think."

"Ezra, I'm not trying to be difficult, I'm just saying that there's enough going on. We don't have to borrow trouble."

"It's still really bad."

"You're right about that. It is." She cleared her throat. "So, are we really going to get Mamm coffee?"

"I guess. I thought I'd get a Coke, too."

"Do you know where the cafeteria is?"

He pointed to a grouping of four elevators. "We have to go downstairs."

"Let's go do that, then."

He strode forward and pushed the button. It was dinging by the time she got there.

Then, just after they were in and the doors were about to close, Danny came running toward them.

"Hold it, will ya?"

Since she was situated near the front of the elevator, she leaned forward and pushed the button to hold it.

"*Danke*," Danny said as he smiled softly down at her.

She felt her cheeks pinken as she looked back up at him. "It was no problem."

"Danny, what floor do ya need?" Ezra asked from behind her.

"I don't know and I don't care. Where are you going?" Danny asked her.

"We're heading to the basement to the cafeteria. We decided to get our *mamm* a cup of *kaffi*."

"Sounds *gut*. I'll go there, too," Danny said as the doors closed.

"You're only going there because we are?" Ezra asked.

Danny crossed his arms over his chest. "*Jah.* Is that all right?"

"Of course it is," Molly said quickly.

When the doors opened again, she wheeled her chair out. Ezra mumbled something under his breath as he led the way.

Danny stepped behind her. "Is it okay if I push your chair?"

"There's no need," she said as she turned to look up at him. "I have a battery pack."

His light blue eyes didn't even blink. None of him moved, not even his hands, which were now settled on the handles of her chair. "You might as well save the batteries, right?"

Usually she didn't like anyone to treat her like she wasn't capable of getting herself around.

But when she looked up into Danny's face, she decided to make an exception. His expression was raw, like someone had brushed over his skin with a Brillo pad.

No doubt about it, Danny was feeling like he needed to do something. He needed to help her, to feel useful.

That, she could understand. Hadn't she just been feeling the same thing?

"*Danke*, Danny," she said softly as she looked up at him. "If you wouldn't mind pushing me around, I would really appreciate it." When Ezra grunted in front of them, she pretended she didn't hear him.

And Danny? Danny simply smiled.

SEVENTEEN

"And then Marie had to go and sprain her ankle."

Danny Eberly would have been the first person to say that he didn't usually like to tag along with people without being asked, but this time he couldn't help himself. Fact was, he needed to be near Molly Byler. Molly had a way about her that made everything seem better. The evening had been so terrible, he wasn't about to not be by her side if he could help it.

The hospital cafeteria wasn't crowded. It was actually fairly empty, and to his good fortune, there wasn't a person inside who he recognized. That was even better. He and Molly could sit and talk without anyone coming up to them and asking what they thought about the accident.

Even though her little brother Ezra was practically shooting daggers at him, Danny pretended not to notice. Ezra was just gonna have to deal.

"Where do you want to sit?" he asked before realizing how bad that sounded to a person in a wheelchair. "Sorry. I mean—"

"I knew what you meant," Molly said quickly. "How about we go sit over at that back table? It looks kind of private."

"That sounds *gut*. What do you want to eat or drink? I'll go get it and bring it to you."

She frowned. "I'm sorry. I only came down here to keep my brother company. I didn't bring any money with me."

"That's okay. I did."

Her eyes widened. "Oh, *nee*, Danny. You don't have to get me anything."

"I don't mind." Molly really was the sweetest girl.

"I'll have a Sprite then." She smiled. "*Danke*."

Ezra was still looking at him like he'd pushed his way into a private party. Which, of course, he had.

"We weren't going to stay here, Danny," he said. "We only came down here to get a cup of coffee."

"Is there a reason you want to rush back? The nurse said we wouldn't likely hear any news for at least another thirty minutes."

Ezra sighed. "*Nee*, but—"

"I'd like to stay for a little while," Molly interjected.

"Molly," Ezra muttered. "What about Mamm's *kaffi*? I'm sure she's expecting it."

And, there was his opportunity. Trying his best to look sincere and not foolishly pleased, Danny said, "I can help Molly get back to your family if you don't want to wait."

Before he could say anything to that, Molly spoke up quickly. "Ezra, let's all sit down for a couple of minutes. I need a break from that stuffy waiting room."

"Well. All right." Looking at Danny like he didn't have much of a choice, Ezra said, "Let's go get Molly that Sprite."

After making sure Molly was perfectly fine next to a table in the corner, Danny walked to Ezra's side. "Just to let you know, I'm not trying to do anything besides hang out with you two."

"You mean my *shveshtah*."

Danny had been going to treat the kid gently but changed tactics. "*Jah*. I mean your sister," he said.

"Why? Do you like her?"

With anyone else, even Molly's older brother John, Danny would have said he was trying to figure that out. Or he probably would've asked Ezra why it mattered to him, since it wasn't any of his business anyway.

But the kid had gotten himself worked up, and Danny could understand what it felt like to feel protective of a sister. He didn't have a sister but he had his cousin Rachel who he'd been practically raised with. He never gave into other men easily when they were flirting with her and wanted him to step aside.

"*Jah*. I do like her."

Ezra stopped and searched his face, almost as if he thought that Danny was joking. "Her chair doesn't bother you?"

"It might, if she acted like it stopped her. I don't think it does though."

"It doesn't." Sounding a little more relaxed, Ezra said, "Molly can just about do anything she wants."

Danny thought that was because she actually could. He figured Molly could do anything she wanted except stand on two feet and take off running. "To be honest, half the time I'm around her, I forget that she's in a wheelchair."

"Really?" Ezra's expression was incredulous.

"Really." He almost added the fact that she was sweet and really pretty with her hazel eyes and golden hair. But he wasn't ready to share that opinion with her little brother.

After waiting in line, Ezra bought himself a soda

and his mother a small coffee. Danny bought two Sprites and a package of pretzels. He wasn't sure how long Molly had been at the hospital, but he knew she hadn't eaten when they'd been together.

She smiled at both of them when they approached.

"I got you some pretzels, too," he added. "I didn't know if you were hungry."

"That's nice of you."

He shrugged off the compliment. "So, have you heard anything new? I just got here."

After glancing at her little brother, Molly said, "Only that Callie has a broken arm and Karl was just taken into surgery. I overheard his older brother say that the doctors fear he is bleeding internally."

"Karl's hurt that bad? Is he in danger? What if he—" Realizing what he had been about to say, Danny quickly shut up. No way did he want to worry Molly further—or give in to the tears that were now threatening.

He hadn't followed her to the cafeteria in order for her to have to comfort him.

Ezra turned to look at him directly. "Did you hear that Mary Jane's hands and face are all cut up? I heard she had to get over fifty stitches and even had to be given a pint of blood. " His voice was strained.

Danny shook his head. "When I walked in the downstairs lobby I saw a couple of people who we used to go to school with. They told me that she was cut up bad but I didn't know it was as dire as that. I wonder if we should donate blood."

Ezra blinked. "I hadn't thought about that. Can we?"

"I think so. I mean, I can. You can donate when you turn sixteen."

Molly's eyes were wide. "I feel sorry for them. Even though they did something terrible, I wouldn't wish them to be so hurt." Looking embarrassed, she said, "Do you think that's wrong?"

"*Nee.* You have a good heart, Molly. I'd be surprised if you didn't feel sorry for them."

"I don't feel that sorry for them," Ezra said. "All of them had been drinking, and that means one of them was driving drunk. I feel a little sorry for all of them and, of course, never wanted anything to happen to Evan. But both Marie and John were hurt bad."

Molly's eyes filled with tears.

Seeing them, Danny rushed to try to make her feel better.

"There's nothing wrong with not knowing how to feel right now," he said gently. "You can be mad or upset. There ain't a right way to act."

"Maybe so. I don't know."

She looked torn, and sounded so lost. "Molly, did you happen to notice all the people in the waiting room? No matter what we find out, we won't be alone. That's something, *jah*?"

When Molly gazed at him again, there was a new trust shining in her eyes. He'd done that. He'd helped her feel better. It made him feel ten feet tall. Almost invincible. Looking around the vast cafeteria, he wished they were someplace else. Someplace warmer, more private. Then he would maybe even be brave enough to share something else—that he wanted to be there for her.

Ezra got to his feet. "Mamm's *kaffi* is getting cold. We need to go back upstairs, Molly."

"Oh. All right."

Noticing that she didn't seem eager to go back upstairs either, Danny said, "If you want to wait another ten minutes I'll stay with you."

"I think I do." She turned to Ezra. "Tell Mamm and Daed that I'll be upstairs in ten minutes."

Ezra hesitated. "I don't know if you should do that."

Before Danny could interject and assure Ezra that he would look out for her, Molly spoke. "I'm not a child, Ezra. I don't need anyone to stay with me or escort me anywhere."

"So you want me to tell Mamm and Daed that you are choosing to stay here alone with Danny?"

She lifted her chin. "*Jah*. Even though I don't think

they'll be caring too much about where I'm sitting, you can tell them that if you really want to."

After casting a withering look in Danny's direction, Ezra stood up and walked to the elevator banks on the far side of the room.

After he was out of sight, Danny grinned. "I'm starting to get the idea he doesn't want me spending time with you."

Molly looked at him sharply before smiling. "Gee, I don't know where you ever got that idea."

"Is it because I'm hanging around you? Or is he just upset that John is in the hospital?" He wanted to also ask if he was being so protective because Molly was in a wheelchair, but he didn't dare. He was pretty sure no fourteen-year-old boy was going to be so protective toward an older sister unless he felt like he had a good reason.

She sighed. "It's because everyone is used to looking after me when we're out in public, and I've let them. What's embarrassing is that I thought I was looking out for myself pretty good already. I even thought I did a *gut* job of looking after Ezra. Now it seems like I've just been fooling myself. Even Ezra thinks I need constant help."

"Maybe they aren't being just overprotective. Maybe they simply care about you."

"I'm glad they do." Sounding exasperated, she

added, "However, I would still rather they try to care from more of a distance."

"How about this? Even though you don't actually need my help, we could pretend I like looking after you."

"Pretend?"

"I meant the looking-after part." Figuring it was time to be a little more direct, he murmured, "You know I like being with you, Molly."

Some of the cloudiness that had been in her eyes dissipated. And in its place?

Well, it was something that looked a lot like what had been lurking inside of him—a knowledge that whatever was between them was good. Too good to ignore.

"I like being with you, too," she said softly.

That was all he needed to know. Smiling, he talked with her for a few more minutes, changing the conversation to her job at the library and his job at Newman's Farm. When he told her a story about a few rambunctious goats scaring off a lady and her mastiff dog, she laughed.

Which made him feel like he'd done something pretty important.

After another five minutes passed, he stood up. "Are you done with your soda? We should probably go upstairs and see if there's any news."

"I'm done." After a second's pause, she handed him her empty cup. "Would you mind throwing this out for me?"

"Nope." Grabbing her cup with his own, he walked over to the trash can. Realizing all the while that she trusted him now.

All he had to do was continue to make sure that she didn't regret that trust.

EIGHTEEN

"Hey," Marie called out. "I didn't mean to slip. It was just really muddy."

"You have a concussion, multiple bruises and contusions on your face and arms, and a broken rib," the doctor told Marie.

Lying in the hospital bed with both of her parents perched on the edges of two chairs by the window, the emergency room doctor standing by her side, and a nurse holding a chart, Marie tried to make light of the situation. "That's all?"

He blinked as concern etched his features. "Why? Were you expecting something worse?"

"Since my body feels like it was hit by a freight train, I have to admit I thought it might be possible."

"Marie, this isn't the time to joke," her father called out.

"I wasn't making a joke, Dad," Marie protested as she looked back at the doctor and waved one bandaged hand. "Don't get me wrong, though. I'm glad that's the worst of it. That's enough."

"I'd say so," the doctor said with a smile. Looking over at her parents, he said, "And for the record, we encourage jokes around here. Every bit of levity always helps."

The doctor really was a nice man. So were all the nurses and physicians' assistants who'd helped her in the emergency room, as well as the many people who'd been taking care of her in this private room.

However, the whole place was noisy and too bright and smelled like disinfectant. More than anything, she wanted out of there. She wanted to go home.

Shifting on the uncomfortable mattress, she looked up at the doctor. "When can I get out of here?"

"Oh, Marie," her mother chided. "Your body has been through a terrible ordeal. Don't be so impatient."

"I'm trying not to be, Mom." Looking at the doctor again, she asked hopefully, "No offense, but can I go home soon?"

"Absolutely." The doctor smiled, though the amusement didn't really meet his eyes. "And, believe me, we're all thrilled that you feel well enough to want to get out of here. As long as you have a good night, you can leave first thing in the morning."

"In the morning?" She didn't even try to hide her dismay.

"We want to monitor you a little longer, Marie. Concussions aren't anything to mess with." His kindly voice lowered. "Plus, I have a feeling once your body relaxes a little bit more, you're going to be in a great deal of pain."

"I understand. Thank you."

"I wrote out some prescriptions for pain meds as well as some antibiotics, and the nursing staff will go over the guidelines for what to expect. Like I said, they'll go over all of this in the morning."

"Thank you, Doctor," her mother said as she stepped forward and shook his hand.

"Yes, thank you so much," Dad said. "We appreciate your time. I know you and the rest of the staff must be exhausted."

Sharing a look with the nurse, the doctor waved a hand. "It's our job, but I wouldn't mind a far quieter night than last night."

After the doctor and nurse left, Marie turned to her parents. It had been a few hours since she'd asked about the other survivors. She said, "How is everyone else? How is John?"

"John was in another room, but he's already been released," Dad said. "I think he's waiting to see you."

"So he really is okay?" she asked anxiously.

"He's okay. A little banged up and sore, of course," Dad replied as he walked to her side and gently smoothed back her hair from her forehead. "He's better than you, princess."

"Tell me what happened. All I remember is driving and noticing a car in front of us coming the wrong way."

Her parents exchanged looks before her father spoke. "I spoke with the police. The other vehicle was driven by a drunk driver."

That news felt like a crushing blow. "I hate that. They could have killed us!"

"Believe me, the same thought has crossed my mind," Dad said. "I'm hoping the police will arrest the driver as soon as she gets released."

"Released?" And hoping? Since when did drunk drivers get any leeway at all? "Dad, what is going on? Why would there be any question about what is going to happen?"

Her parents exchanged worried looks again just as John knocked on the door and peeked inside. He sported a few bandages on his face and neck, and he had a good-size bruise on his cheekbone. His shirt also was stained, with blood on the collar and on one of the cuffs.

"Marie," he murmured. "You're looking better, thank the Lord." As if remembering that he couldn't just barge in, he stood next to the door. "Is it okay if I step inside?"

To Marie's surprise, her mother walked over and gave him a quick hug. "Of course. We were just telling Marie that you have already been released."

Bemused, Marie watched John hug her mother back and shake her father's hand before walking to her side. "I've been so worried about you," he said quietly. "I can't tell you how *gut* it is to see you sitting up like this."

She could practically feel the tension and worry floating off of him. "Don't worry, John. I'm going to be all right. Come sit down."

Ignoring the chair, he perched on the edge of her mattress and ran a hand along her cheek. "You're a little worse for wear, but you still look like your usual pretty self."

Well aware that her parents were still in the room, though suspiciously not seeming all that surprised to see him touching her face, she said, "I know you were released, but it looks like you got banged up, too."

He looked over his shoulder and smiled at them before taking her hand. "I only have a few bumps and scrapes. Nothing to worry over. I'm practically as good as new."

She wouldn't go that far. "I'm glad you're okay. I'm so sorry, John."

He raised his eyebrows. "Sorry? For what?"

"I . . ." She looked over at her parents. "I'm sorry.

But . . . but could I speak to John on my own for a few minutes?"

"Of course," Mom said right away. "We'll, uh, go say hello to John's family. Are they still out in the waiting room, John?"

"Most of them are. My parents, definitely."

"We'll be back in a little while," Dad told Marie before he escorted her mother out of the room.

When the door closed behind them, Marie sat up and stared at the closed door. "What is going on with my parents? They are never this agreeable."

"Truly? They've always been kind to me."

"That's different. Did you notice that neither of them said a word when you sat down right next to me on this bed?"

Obviously stifling a laugh, John bent down and pressed his lips to her temple. "Calm down, Marie. You don't want to get yourself too worked up."

"But—"

"They are fine. All that matters is that you will be, too."

That reminded her of what she'd intended to tell him in the first place. "John, I am so sorry. I don't know what to say about that accident."

"That's because there ain't anything to say. None of this was your fault."

"Of course it was." She tried to remember the exact moment of impact, but it was all a hazy blob in her head. "I don't remember exactly what happened, but I know I tried to get out of the way."

"You did everything you could. Hush now."

Images flashed in her head. "I remember that car was swerving. It was, right?"

"It was, and you swerved so we wouldn't hit the other vehicle head-on. If you hadn't done that, things could have been much worse for you."

Remembering more details now, she recalled the way she'd turned the wheel sharply and sent the SUV into the deep ditch on the side of the road. "I still wish I could have handled everything better."

He shook his head as he gently ran a finger along her forearm. "Don't think like that. All you'll do is make yourself more upset. There was nothing you could do. Nothing at all. It's a miracle more people didn't die."

Everything inside her seized up. "More?"

John's jaw clenched as he looked away.

"John, what happened? Who died?" she whispered.

"What do you know?" His expression was guarded.

"My parents told me that a drunk driver hit us and that they hoped they would bring charges against her. But I guess she's hurt?" She didn't even try to withhold the disdain in her voice.

John released her hand and bent his head. She felt

a new tension between them, much like what had been drifting from her parents.

"What is wrong? What am I missing?"

He cleared his throat. "The driver was a young girl of sixteen."

"She was drunk?"

"It would seem so." Pure regret filled his voice.

She felt sorry for the girl, as well as for the poor girl's family. But even though Marie felt terrible for her, there was also a part of her that felt angry. The drunk driver could have killed John. Could have killed both of them. "Well, I'm sorry, but that's even worse. She shouldn't have been drinking in the first place. Especially not these days. Even out in Walnut Creek, it's possible to call for an Uber."

"They wouldn't have known about Uber," he said quietly. "You see, all the passengers in the car were Amish."

"What?" She heard the words, but it was hard to believe.

"They were Amish. In the middle of their *rumspringa.*"

Growing up in Walnut Creek, she was very familiar with the passage of time when some Amish teenagers experimented with the outside world. But she also had grown up as part of the Eight. None of the Amish kids she'd known—John included—had ever done anything like that. "Do you know them? Did you know the girl who was driving?"

John nodded. After taking a deep breath, he swallowed like every word was difficult for him to vocalize. "They all went to school with my sister Molly."

Her expression turned stricken. "Was she in the car with them?"

"Molly? Oh, *nee*," he replied, shaking his head. "She was still at the corn maze with that Danny Eberly and then she went home with Amanda and Anton."

"That's a blessing."

He nodded. "It is, but she wouldn't have been hanging out with those kids anyway."

"Are you sure?"

"*Jah*. They, well, of late, they've been earning a bit of a wild reputation. Molly has never been that way."

"It's too bad she knew the kids who were in the car, but I guess I shouldn't be surprised. Walnut Creek is a pretty tight-knit community."

"*Jah*. Especially the Amish one. But, I have to be honest with ya. Their involvement has shaken all of us up."

Her brain felt fuzzy but her heart seemed to know what to say. "Of course it has. All accidents catch people off guard."

John bent his head down. "The driver is going to

have a hard road to hoe. We're all going to have to pray for them."

Pray for the drunk driver who could have killed her and John? The idea was so painful, it was almost difficult to grasp. "Ah, John, no offense, but I don't understand why you sound so sorry for the driver."

His head snapped up. "Because the driver is Amish, of course."

"But she was driving a car without a license and driving recklessly. She was also drunk." Didn't he remember how terrifying it had been to see that car barreling toward them?

"I've heard it was Mary Jane."

For some reason, John naming the driver made it even more difficult for Marie to understand his sympathy.

Feeling her head pounding harder as her emotions got the best of her, she added, "This Mary Jane did something bad, John. She killed someone. She hurt you and me. I mean, you haven't forgotten that we're having this conversation in the hospital, have you?"

"Marie, don't be sarcastic."

"Then stop pretending that her actions and choices don't have serious consequences or that she isn't at fault."

His eyes widened in surprise. "I haven't said that at all."

"That's what it's sounding like."

"Don't twist my words," he said gruffly. "All I'm saying is that Mary Jane is going to have to live with the consequences of her actions for the rest of her life. Even after we forgive her, she's going to bear that burden."

After they *forgive her*? "John, surely you don't really think that she deserves much sympathy or forgiveness?"

"Everyone deserves forgiveness and sympathy. It's not our place to punish."

That "our" made it seem like the differences between them just grew a mile wide. Had he already forgotten that he'd told her he was thinking of jumping the fence? "Just because I'm willing to let the police and the courts decide her punishment doesn't mean that I should forgive her or feel sorry for her."

"I guess that's one of the differences between you and me. Isn't it?"

Marie jerked back, feeling like he'd just slapped her. "I don't know what to say. You've stunned me."

"If you were Amish, you would understand." His voice was still quiet, but it was threaded with steel, too. John Byler believed what he was saying completely.

"But I'm not Amish."

"Obviously."

Ouch. Maybe in time she would even admire the way he steadfastly clung to his beliefs.

But now? Well, all she could see was that she could be friends with him for most of her life, be attracted to him, and even kiss him passionately and cling to his arms just hours ago . . . but there were still huge differences in the way they viewed the world.

The very fact that he was insisting on pushing his point of view while she was still recovering in a hospital bed stunned her.

She realized then and there that maybe she'd been fooling herself. It wasn't the lack of electricity and technology that illustrated their differences. It was a whole way of thinking.

"Marie, you look pale," he said, his voice sounding on edge. Getting to his feet, he looked toward the door. "What's wrong? Has your pain medicine worn off? Or is it your rib? What do you need?"

What she needed was to figure things out. She needed the awful headache that was pounding against her eyes to ease. She needed John Byler to realize that she was feeling pretty confused.

"Time, I think."

"Ah. You'll feel better soon."

All she wanted to do was close her eyes and rest. But she didn't feel right just dropping the subject. "You know that's not what I'm talking about," she said wearily. "We have two completely different viewpoints about what happened."

"I know we do. But, we'll get through it."

"I don't know. These differences feel pretty substantial right now."

John winced. "Marie, I'm sorry. Let's not fight over who was at fault or what punishment they deserve. I came in here to tell ya that the rest of the Eight are here. They want to see you. Who should I send in first?"

Though she wanted to see them, too, Marie didn't know if she was ready to hear Harley or Will express the same sentiment about the drunk driver as John did. "I don't think I'm up for any more visitors right now."

"Truly? Oh, well, all right. Well, I also wanted you to know that I told my parents that I would stay at your place for a night or two after you got released tomorrow."

"Why would you do that?"

He looked even more uncomfortable. "You're going to still need a lot of help. I thought I could sleep on your couch and take care of you."

His offer felt like too much, too soon. They still hadn't really discussed their relationship, not in any great detail. Not what it might look like in the future. When she simply stared at him, he said slowly, "Or,

I'm sure Katie or E.A. would be happy to be there if you didn't want the two of us to be alone."

"John, I think I'm going to go home with my parents."

His expression shuttered. "Oh. Well, all right. I mean, if that's what you want."

"It is."

He got to his feet. "I, um, will tell everyone that you are resting right now."

"Thank you." She closed her eyes.

"Should I tell everyone to stop by to see you at your parents' *haus* tomorrow evening?"

"They won't have to do that."

"You know they'll want to. I'm going to want to see you. Like I said, everyone is worried."

"I think it might be best if everyone waited until I was more myself before they stopped by. You know how my parents are."

"I know your parents well. You know they won't mind, Marie. All of our families know how close we all are."

Opening her eyes again, she said, "John, what I'm trying to say is that I'm going to need a few days to get myself together. I don't want to see anyone until I've healed some and can wash my hair."

He smiled until it became obvious that he realized she wasn't making a joke. "I see." He stepped backward. "I'll wait, then, and tell everyone else to wait, too. Whatever you want."

"Thank you."

She wanted to understand what was happening between them. She wanted to understand how she was going to be able to meld her life with his.

But all she could seem to handle at the moment was the fact that all of those kisses they'd shared might not have changed everything between them as much as she thought they had.

It might not have changed anything at all.

NINETEEN

"We all thought it was broken. Marie's ankle looked like a softball had embedded itself under her skin. And even though she tried to act like it wasn't painful, we all knew it was."

"Molly, you don't have to do this," her mother said softly from her doorway on the following Monday.

Molly had just fastened her dress and apron and was sitting on the side of her bed when her mother had opened the door. Though it wasn't kind and there were far more important things to worry about, she couldn't seem to stop the burst of impatience that ran through her. Once again, her mother had opened her door without knocking.

The habit drove her crazy. She was sixteen, not six. And though she'd once needed a lot of help, she didn't anymore. However, no matter what Molly said, her mother ignored her wishes. She seemed to think that because Molly wasn't as mobile as her brothers and sister, she didn't need the same amount of privacy.

The opposite was true. Getting dressed took her a lot more time than it did for Amanda or her brothers. She didn't like having to be worried about her mother wandering in while she was changing clothes.

But, of course, that didn't matter right now. Evan would never have to worry about something so minor ever again. Today, during his funeral, the point would be driven home.

She swallowed the lump that had just formed in her throat and finally answered.

"I think I do, Mamm. I wasn't exactly friends with Evan, but I knew him. All of his former classmates are going to the funeral." Actually, most of Walnut Creek was going.

Though her mother's composure seemed to slip a bit, she still shook her head. "You can mourn for him without going to the viewing and funeral."

"Not properly. I want to do this." She needed to. Not only for herself, but for Danny, too. Even if they never became anything other than good friends, she knew he was hurting. And if he was hurting, then so was she.

Crossing the room, her mother sat down next to her—even though Molly's dress was still only half fastened. "Sometimes you have to think of yourself. You took Andy's death hard."

Andy. Molly looked down at her hands. The handsome, lively English boy's death had been rough on her. Though she wasn't sure anyone else knew it, he'd spent two hours by her side at the hospital a few weeks after her accident. On that day, she'd just been moved to the rehabilitation wing and had been feeling pretty sorry for herself. Half of her body was numb and the other half was in constant pain. Both had been difficult to bear.

She had also just begun to realize that her life was never going to be the way she'd imagined it. She couldn't stop thinking about all the things she was never going to do and how she was always going to be different. She'd even gotten mad at God and told Him that she didn't deserve to be in a wheelchair for the rest of her life.

Andy had come in the middle of one of her pity parties, had pulled out a deck of cards, and calmly asked if her hands still worked. She'd been so shocked, she'd nodded. That's when he'd told her that they were going to play hearts for pretzel sticks.

He'd then proceeded to win every hand . . . except for one. He told her to concentrate on that, that one success. She wasn't the same as before the accident, but she still stunk at cards, and that was familiar.

She'd been so shocked, she'd hardly blinked when he kissed her forehead and wandered out.

That had been a turning point for her. He'd been right. She was different now but she was also the same—and some of those same things could even be improved upon.

She'd always loved him for that.

But even though she'd loved him, she hadn't gone to his funeral. Andy was English, and though John and the rest of the Eight were going to be there, Molly hadn't wanted to be in the way. She'd ended up sitting in the back garden praying for hours, hoping that somehow her prayers would help heal Andy's family's grief and that the Lord's grace would shine upon Andy.

"I did take Andy's death hard," she finally said. "But so did a lot of people, especially John."

"*Jah.* John and he were *gut* friends. All of us loved that young man. But you never had that relationship with Evan, Molly."

"It doesn't matter. I'm still going to Evan's funeral. And for the record, John is, too."

A flash of impatience flared in her mother's eyes before she tamped it down. "There will be a lot of people there. And the graveyard will be crowded. You might have a difficult time getting around in your wheelchair."

"John and Anton said they'd help me with my chair."

"They really said that?"

"*Jah*, Mamm. They offered. I took them up on it."

After gazing at her for a long moment again, her mother stood up. "How about a hand getting into your chair? I'll tie your shoes, too."

"Mamm, I can do these things myself."

"Don't always push help away, dear. It's not always offered out of pity."

Her mother was right. "I'm sorry, Mamm," she said as she finished fastening her dress. Then, she held out her hands and allowed her mother to arrange her in the wheelchair. Then she knelt down, picked up a black boot, and slipped it on Molly's foot.

As she tied it, Molly felt like she was watching someone else's foot being shod. It was times like this when she thought about the conversations she'd had with the doctor about more physical therapy and getting fitted for braces to lend support to her legs.

After her mother tied her other shoe, she stood up. "I made an apple pie. It's already in a cardboard container. Would you take it to Evan's parents' *haus*?"

"Of course I will, Mamm."

Two hours later, Molly was situated on the sidewalk at the edge of the crowd, watching silently as Evan's casket was lowered into the ground. Anton was standing nearby. He'd waved off her offer to stand somewhere closer. Around them was a sea of black. Black dresses and *kapps* and bonnets. Black suits and shoes. They were a somber crowd. And for the most part a silent one.

She'd spoken to Danny before the funeral. He'd walked over to her as soon as he'd seen her. He looked tired and sad and confused—just like so many of them were.

Now, he was standing next to Kurt and some other friends from their class. His hands were in his pockets, and he looked like he was trying not to cry. On the other side of him was his brother, Samuel.

After speaking one last prayer, the crowd began to disperse. There was a meal being offered by the family's neighbors. Molly and Anton had already elected not to go, so they were heading home.

She'd just turned her chair and was moving it forward when Danny came back to her side.

"Are you two getting ready to leave?"

"*Jah.*" Looking up at Anton, who had just nodded, Molly said, "Being here for the service was enough for me. And since we already dropped off Mamm's pie, there isn't a reason to go back to their house. Are you going to go to the meal, Danny?"

"*Nee.*" He looked back at his brother, who was

standing off to the side, looking lost. "We've had enough, too."

"Why don't you both come to our *haus*?" Anton said.

Liking that idea, Molly nodded. "Please do."

Still Danny hesitated. "Do you mean Samuel also?"

"Sam is Ezra's age," Anton said. "They can talk if they want, or sit with us. Either way is fine." Smiling, he said, "And since you two are coming over, you should plan to have supper with us, too."

"Your mother won't mind?"

"Our mother will love to have you over," Molly said.

After glancing at his brother again, Danny nodded. "All right," he finally said. "*Danke*."

"No thanks needed." Anton pressed a hand on his shoulder. "We'll see you there."

As they continued on to their buggy, Molly looked up at her brother. "That was kind of you." Anton had never been as serious as James or as inherently kind as John. He'd always been more of a rough-and-tumble type of boy. That was why the offer meant so much.

"I know." He smiled slightly.

"I know I told Danny that Mamm would be happy about them coming over. But, do you think she might be upset after all?"

"About inviting them over for a meal? Of course

not, Mol. Besides, I think she has a soft spot for Danny and his brother."

"Oh? Why?" she asked as they stopped next to the buggy and Anton easily picked her up and deposited her on the seat. As he folded the wheelchair and put it in the back of the buggy, Molly thought about his words. She sure hoped Mamm wasn't liking Danny and Samuel so much on account of her.

After helping their horse back up and getting back in the buggy, Anton shook his head, like ten minutes hadn't passed in their conversation. "You know Mamm. She wants to take care of the world. If she *canna* do that, she at least wants to feed as many people as she can."

That was true. "What does that have to do with Danny and Samuel though?"

"She doesn't like that Danny and his brother aren't looked after good."

What? What did that even mean? Gaping at Anton, she asked, "Are you saying that they aren't being fed well?"

He gave her a look that said she should have known that.

She had not. "I can't believe you and Mamm knew that about them but I didn't."

Anton shrugged. "It hasn't been a big secret. All you have to do is look at those boys to see that they don't have anyone fussing over them like our mother."

She hadn't seen that. She'd never even thought about how his parents weren't around.

She realized then that she'd been just as guilty of only seeing certain things about Danny as other people had been about only noticing her chair. All she'd ever seen when she'd stared at Danny was what she'd wanted to see—that he was handsome, confident, and popular. The three things that she'd never felt about herself. "I'm embarrassed," she said after a moment. "I never thought either of them looked like they were being neglected."

"No?" He glanced at her again as North clip-clopped on the street. "Well, I suppose it's because you had your own problems to face."

She had, but that didn't make her feel any better. She'd always thought that she'd taken her accident and the paralysis she'd suffered after rather well. Oh, of course, that first year had been difficult, and she'd had many days along the way in pain. But even taking all of that into account, she'd considered herself to be rather aware and caring of others. For her to have missed something that even Anton had noticed made her feel ashamed.

"I wish I would have realized those things. I would have tried harder to help Danny."

Anton laughed softly. "Come now, Mol. You are only now sixteen. Most teenagers aren't thinking about much more than themselves." His voice turned tender. "And you've had more reason to be that way, I think. More reason than most, I reckon."

"But, still."

"No reason to worry about it. It's done. Ain't so?"

She nodded. Relaxing a bit, she said, "Do . . . do you think Danny and me are a bad fit?"

"How? Like as a couple?"

She liked that he acted like that could be a possibility. Even though it was embarrassing. "Well, *jah*."

He bent down slightly and looked at her. For once, he wasn't just skimming over her like he was checking to make sure she was okay, but rather he was seeing her. "Well . . ."

"Anton. Don't tease. Just tell me the truth and get on with it."

"All right. Well, first off, sitting here beside me, looking like you do . . . if I didn't know ya, I mean . . ." His voice trailed off.

"Yes?"

"I'd say you look to be a mighty pretty, sweet-tempered Amish girl." He raised his brows. "How did I do?"

"Not too well. You didn't answer my question."

"I kind of did, Mol. You are a pretty, sweet-tempered girl with a positive outlook on life. It don't matter what you and Danny—or any man—would think about how you look together. All that matters is that he would be blessed to have you by his side."

"Anton!" Tears pricked her eyes. It was truly one of the sweetest things she'd ever heard him say.

"Oh, no you don't. You may not start crying. I don't handle tears."

Hiccupping, she nodded. "I won't cry." Of course, two big, fat tears were trailing down her cheeks as she promised him.

"*Gut*. 'Cause we'll be there soon and Danny won't like ya if your face is all swollen and mottled."

She pretended to be offended. "Anton, what happened to me being pretty?"

Looking exactly like the older brother he was, he winked. "That was before your eyes turned all watery and red. Trust me, no man likes that."

She folded her arms over her chest and tried to look miffed. But she knew she wasn't doing a very good job of it.

She wasn't surprised, though. It was hard to look aggravated when one's heart was filled to bursting with love.

"*Danke*, Anton."

"Anything for you, Mol." Lowering his voice, he added, "You're my favorite sibling, you know."

"I know." She smiled. He always told her that. And whether it was true or not, it always, always made her feel loved.

TWENTY

"'We need to find a place to hunker down and wait for things to get better,' Andy had announced. 'Does anyone know where we can go?'"

Marie had been out of the hospital for twenty-four hours and was now settled back into her childhood room. That room, with its fairy princess four-poster bed, pink, cream, and light gray color schemes, and far too many pictures and awards from high school, sometimes felt way too confining. She wasn't that girl anymore. And though she didn't mind that she'd once been, she sometimes felt that her mother wished she still was.

Marie didn't always get along with her mother. She often found her mother to be too intrusive, too worried about everyone else's opinions, too loud, and too, well, everything.

But without a doubt, her mother would always be

the world's best "sick mom." All her life, whenever she was under the weather her mother transformed into a patient, quiet, and attentive nurse. Mom didn't have levels of care, either. No matter if she had two skinned knees when she was five, strep throat at fifteen, or had just survived a car accident at twenty-four, her mother was an equal-opportunity caregiver.

Case in point—from the time she and Dad had driven Marie back home, her mother had gotten her set up in her old room like she was visiting royalty. They'd brought in a flat-screen TV from her father's study, put fresh, cool sheets on the bed, and had bought her a new fluffy robe.

Her mother had even put a pitcher of water, a jar of her favorite kind of crackers, and a plate of chocolate chip cookies on her nightstand. It was all heavenly.

She'd also left Marie alone quite a bit. Yesterday, she'd slept most of the day away. Today, however, she was finally feeling more like herself.

All that was why when her mother poked her head in the room, Marie waved her inside.

"Hi, Mom. Come on in."

Her mother was dressed in one of her casual outfits, which meant she was wearing pressed khakis, designer loafers, and a light sweater. Her hair was pulled back from her face in a red leather headband, and she smelled like she always did, like jasmine and roses and Ivory soap. "How are you feeling?"

Marie could practically feel her mother's gaze drift over her face and bare arms. Not wanting to lie, she shrugged. "Not great. Pretty sore."

"I bet." Walking over to the medicine bottles neatly lined up on the dresser, her mother eyed the directions, and her note of when Marie had last taken the painkillers. "Looks like you can have another dose in one hour. Can you wait that long?"

"Yeah. It's not that bad."

She turned around, hesitated, then perched on the edge of the light blue velvet chair near the window. "My cell phone's been ringing off the hook. My Facebook page, too. Everyone is worried about you, Marie."

Her mother's love of social media was a mystery. Marie found it kind of cute and alarming at the same time.

Picking up her cell phone, Marie scanned her notifications. She'd placed it on silent and saw that she'd received quite a few text messages and three missed calls. "News travels fast around here, doesn't it?"

"It does." Mom sighed. "I haven't called Kurt's

mother yet, but I heard that the kids from the other vehicle are all home now." She paled. "Except for Evan, of course."

"Poor Evan."

She nodded. "I hate that our community has lost another child. He was even younger than Andy, too. I know the Lord never gives us more than we can handle, but this sure feels awfully hard."

Marie felt the same way. "I haven't allowed myself to think about it too much." She shook her head, trying to form her thoughts more coherently. "I mean, not about Evan's death, or even the accident."

"I'm glad. You'll have plenty of time to think about those things when you're back on your feet. You need to rest as much as possible right now."

"I'll do my best."

"Do . . . do you think John will be stopping by today?"

"I'm not sure. I kind of doubt it. When we talked at the hospital, I told him that I was going to need some time to sleep and rest." Thinking about how stunned he'd looked at the hospital, she added, "I know he's going to have a difficult time with Evan's death, too. I didn't know the boy, but he did."

"If he does stop by, do you want me to send him right in, or do you want me to check with you first?"

Ah, so that was where the conversation was going. "You can send him in if you'd like. Or check with me first. This is your house."

"It might be just me and Dad who live here now, but it will always be your house, too. We'll do whatever you want. Marie, are you and him close now?" She closed her eyes. "Sorry. I guess you can tell I'm flustered and don't want to say the wrong thing. But, um, what I'm trying to ask is, are you two serious?"

And if she was serious about John, what were they going to do? "I think we're getting that way, Mom. But we don't have all the answers yet."

"You know I like John. I like all of your friends here." Her voice was tentative.

"But . . ."

"But, what do you think his family thinks? I'm not trying to be mean, but I can't imagine that they would be too happy about the two of you becoming a couple."

"I don't know what they think."

"John didn't tell you?"

"I haven't asked. I do know that they have six children, and they're all pretty different. I have a feeling they are used to each child going their own way."

Her mother nodded slowly. "I can see that happening. As much as Dad and I have wanted to worry about every little thing you do, we've learned to give you some space."

Marie thought they were still learning that.

Realizing that they'd left out an important part of the conversation, Marie looked at her mother. "What do you think about me and John?"

"You already know I like him."

Boy, her mother was trying so hard to be considerate and open! "Mom, what would you think if he and I became a couple?"

She stood up and folded a towel that Marie had left hanging on the back of a chair. "I think I came to terms with you having a mind of your own your senior year in high school, dear."

"Oh, Mom. We aren't going to rehash homecoming again, are we?" She'd gone to the dance with Parker Hawley, who'd been both very cool and very unsuitable—at least to Marie's parents.

"Of course not," she replied primly. "All I'm trying to say is that I learned a lesson back then about paying attention to your dreams and wishes instead of my own."

Her mother had been over the moon about Marie being crowned homecoming queen. She? Not so much.

"After Andy's death, dear, I learned something else. All that really matters is happiness. I want you to be happy. If you think that John Byler is the man you want to spend the rest of your life with, then I do, too." She smiled. "Daddy feels the same way."

"Thanks, Mom."

She sat down beside her again. "Now, how about some soup or some ice cream?"

Those were her two favorite things. Again, she had the best sick mom ever. "What kind?"

"Homemade chicken and rice soup and strawberry ice cream from Graeters."

Both were her favorites. "Can I have them both at the same time?"

"I think that's a wonderful deal, Marie. I'll bring them and some warm rolls in here, too. I'll be right back."

After she left, Marie leaned back on the pillows and thought about how far they'd come. Back when she was fifteen, she would have never believed that life could be sweeter. But in a lot of ways it really was.

When her door opened again, Marie sat up. "Thanks, Mom."

"You're welcome," Mom replied as she put the tray on Marie's bedside table. "And look who I've brought with me."

There was Katie Steury, dressed in a dark blue dress

and black apron. As usual, her straight blond hair was neatly confined under her *kapp*. "Katie, hi!"

"Hiya back."

"I'll leave you two alone," Mom said before walking back out the door.

Eyes wide, Katie walked in. "Boy, this room looks the same . . . and for some reason, better."

She grinned. "I know, right? My mother still spoils me rotten."

"Not rotten. Not yet." Katie winked as she sat down.

"Thanks for coming, but you didn't have to visit. You visited me at the hospital."

Instead of shrugging off Marie's thanks, Katie frowned. "Don't say things like that."

That took her off guard. "I'm sorry . . ." Her voice drifted off. She wasn't exactly sure what she was apologizing about.

Katie exhaled. Loudly. "Marie, you are one of my best friends. Of course I'm going to visit you. I'm sorry I snapped at you. But sometimes, you just act like anything any of us does for you is surprising."

She swallowed, hurt by the accusation. Even though it might have had a kernel of truth to it. "I don't know what to say again."

She waved a hand. "Never mind. This is my fault." Looking troubled, she said, "I've had some things going on at home that have made me short-tempered. I shouldn't have taken it out on you."

"What happened?"

Katie pursed her lips, then murmured, "My mother decided to move to Kentucky. She left me the *haus*."

Marie knew Katie had grown up in a pretty worn-down house. It was the opposite of what everyone thought of a well-run, neat-as-a-pin typical Amish home. She also knew that the house wasn't the only thing that hadn't run well in Katie's life. Though Katie hated to talk about it, they'd all known that she wished things were different between her and her mother.

And, maybe sometimes that her parents were a lot different, too. "Do you want to talk about it?" She smiled. "I might be stuck in bed, but my ears work fine."

Katie's blue eyes cleared for a moment before being replaced by shadows. "*Danke*, but I ain't ready to talk about it."

"Okay."

Gesturing at the tray she'd just brought in, Katie said, "How about we sit and eat instead?"

Marie grinned. There were two bowls of soup, a big plate of the warm rolls her mother had promised, and two dishes of ice cream, too. "You don't mind soup and ice cream?"

"Your mother said she's making grilled cheese squares, too. I might never leave."

"You make grilled cheese sound like filet mignon."

"You might yearn for fancy steak with French names, but I could eat your mother's cooking every night, Marie."

"Even grilled cheese squares."

"She grills sourdough bread and Amish white cheddar and Swiss cheese on a cast iron pan and somehow makes little grill marks on them. They're incredible."

They really were. Of course, she usually asked her mother to not make her any because she always ate too many and they were fattening. But today, sitting beside Katie? Nothing sounded better. "You better take off your shoes then and climb up next to me. We can eat and talk and then even watch a movie."

Katie slipped off her tennis shoes and scrambled up on the bed. After fluffing up a pillow and sprawling out next to her, Katie sighed.

"You look happy."

"I am." Looking around the room, Katie got a look of complete bliss on her face. "Oh, Marie. Soup, grilled cheese, ice cream, all to be consumed while sitting on this comfy bed? I am *frayt*, indeed.

Why, I'm so happy right this minute, I may never leave."

Marie chuckled as she took a spoonful of ice cream. And, for the first time in two days, finally allowed herself to relax.

TWENTY-ONE

"But of course we didn't, I mean, we were all only fourteen, you know. We just stood there and stared at one another." Looking at Marie, Katie said, "Since Andy never had been one for standing around, he decided to take things into his own hands. Erm. Or, rather, Marie."

"Didn't expect to see you here today," Will told John on Tuesday while he set his lunch cooler on the linoleum floor near his locker at work. "Are you feeling all right?"

"Well enough. Why?"

Will pressed two fingers against his cheek. "You got a good-size bruise there. It looks pretty sore."

John shrugged. "I'm good and banged up, that's for sure. But other than feeling stiff and tired, I'm good enough. Good enough to work."

"I'm sure Mr. Kerrigan wouldn't have minded if you stayed home for a few days."

"There was no need." His injuries weren't as bad as

Marie's. Still thinking about her concussion and hurt ribs, he frowned. He really wished they had parted in a better way.

As if Will read his mind, he said, "How's Marie? Did she let you go by and see her yesterday?"

"*Nee.* I even talked to her father on the phone. He said he didn't know what was going on with her, but she wasn't wanting to have people over. So far she's only let Katie see her." He didn't even try to conceal his disappointment. Of course, he'd known exactly what she was upset about. Him, and his need to talk to her about forgiveness and compassion while she was still in a hospital bed.

Now, thinking back on it, he wished he hadn't sounded so sanctimonious. He'd meant everything he'd said, but there was a time and a place for everything, and arguing with her while she was just recovering from the accident hadn't been it.

Pulling out the work order waiting for him, Will skimmed it. "I talked to Elizabeth Anne and Harley. We're going to go by and see her tonight. Maybe she'll be up for visitors. We can only try, ain't so?"

John nodded. "I hope the visit goes well."

"Do you want to come with us? Maybe if Marie sees you in person, she'll want to talk to ya."

He shook his head slowly. "I said some things that upset her. I don't think she wants to see me right now."

"Uh-oh. What did you do?"

"Nothing I care to talk about right now."

Will didn't move. "Are you sure?"

Pulling out the plans for the art design he'd been working on, John said, "Very sure. I need to go show Mr. Kerrigan what I've come up with."

Will grinned. "You already came up with the design? Come on, let me see it."

Eager to get some feedback, John carefully unrolled the drawing paper and smoothed it out on their lunch table. "What do you think?" He was right proud of the design. It was a combination of desert silhouettes and sunset. He thought it would be perfect for the new owners and would look nice rolling down the highway.

Will whistled low. "John, this is a work of art."

"Well, *jah*." He winked. It was his work of art, after all.

"*Nee*, I mean it." Smoothing a hand over the top of the paper, he continued, "I think it could be in an art gallery or something. It is that good."

"You really mean it?" It wasn't until right that minute that he realized he wanted this design to help him to achieve his goals of being a real designer for the company.

"I wouldn't lie about this."

"*Danke*. I'm pleased with it. I thought it would

convey what the customer wanted without making everyone who saw it need sunglasses."

"How do you plan to paint it?"

"In stages. I'm going to stencil in the design and then work on it in layers." Already picturing the finished product, he added, "I think it's going to give some dimension to it, too."

Will blew out a breath of air. "It's gonna be something to be proud of, John."

"I hope Mr. Kerrigan and our customer feel the same way." He already did feel mighty proud of it.

Will slapped him on the back. "I'll see you in the garage. While you are imagining sunsets and coyotes, I'm going to be contorting myself while I install hardware."

John was tempted to roll his eyes. If he knew anything, it was that only by all of the employees working together could they produce something of worth. Each of their jobs—from the designers, to the assembly line workers, to the men and women who prepped the parts to be installed, to the people who kept the space spotless—had a vital job to do. Mr. Kerrigan told all of them this all the time.

After Will walked out, John rolled up his paper and knocked on his boss's door.

Mr. Kerrigan was bent over his desk and staring at several work orders. "Hey, John. Good morning."

"Good morning. I brought my design to show you."

"I'm looking forward to seeing it. Have a seat."

John sat down, eager to share his work but when he placed the rolled paper on his boss's desk, the other man placed a hand on the top, preventing John from opening it. "Before we talk business, I want to know how you are doing. How are you feeling? Do you need anything? I've been concerned."

"Concerned about me?"

Mr. Kerrigan's gray eyebrows snapped together. "Come, now. I know we don't often see each other outside of work, but I heard about your car accident." He pointed to a list of notes on an index card. "I was going to leave a message on your phone to see how you were doing."

"I'm a little stiff and sore, but well enough."

Instead of smiling, his boss looked even more concerned. "I see the bruise on your face. Should you even be thinking about working today?"

"I wanted to give it a try. If it gets to be too much, I'll let you know."

Instead of looking satisfied with his answers, his boss still hesitated. "I heard you were with your girlfriend when you got in the accident. Is that true?"

"You mean Marie?"

His expression relaxed. "Yes. Marie. Marie Hartman, right?" When John nodded, Mr. Kerrigan said,

"I read in the newspaper that she was hospitalized overnight."

"She was," he said awkwardly. "But Marie is home now. Well, home with her parents." Why he was sharing so much but not making clear that Marie wasn't exactly his girlfriend, he didn't know.

Mr. Kerrigan leaned back in his chair. "I hope she'll make a full recovery as well."

"Thank you." Gesturing to the paper, he said, "Can we talk about the drawings now?"

"Of course." He smiled, looking tired. "I was just trying to get these work orders organized. A couple of parts are on back order, so everything is going to have to be juggled and completed out of order."

"It's going to get crowded." Such things happened from time to time, and the consequences of any change in schedules created a ripple effect that rivaled any rock tossed into a pond.

"Yep. And I'm going to have to schedule everyone for odd hours again." He sighed. "Oh well, it can't be helped."

"Do you want me to try to make heads and tails of the work schedule? I've a knack for that."

"You truly are gifted at arranging everyone, but let me make some phone calls first." After he straightened the sheets and cleared a space on his desktop, he motioned with his hands. "I can't wait to see what you came up with for our Arizona couple."

John rolled out the paper. "This is what I've been thinking. What do you think?"

Mr. Kerrigan stared at the drawings, examining the three of them, as well as John's careful notes, before speaking. One minute passed, then two. Then three.

It felt like an eternity.

Anxious, John got to his feet. He found it easier to see the whole drawing looking straight down on it. After allowing himself to imagine how nice it would be to have a real artist's drawing table to work from, he pushed the whim from his head.

There was no telling what would happen next. Maybe the Lord would lead him toward something different. Maybe not.

As the seconds passed, John watched his boss's expression, feeling vaguely like the man held his life in his hands. Of course he didn't, but he now realized that he didn't just want to be a designer; he was hoping such a thing would come true with all his heart. He felt as if God had given him these talents and he was finally putting them to good use.

At last Mr. Kerrigan straightened and looked him in the eye. "I think if everything comes out the way you have indicated that it will, it's going to be one of our finest works yet." He grinned. "You should be real proud of yourself, John. It's fantastic."

"*Danke*," he blurted. "Um, I mean, I'm glad you feel that way." And that was certainly an understatement! He knew it wasn't right to feel so prideful, but the man's words meant a lot to him. He felt a satisfaction deep in his chest.

"I really do. I'm going to scan these drawings and e-mail them to our client." He grinned. "As soon as he replies, I'll come find you, but I'm telling you now, I know he's going to be thrilled."

"I hope so. I'd hate to redo it." Realizing how that sounded, he cleared his throat. "I meant, I like how it is, but I'll be happy to make changes if the clients want me to."

"I feel the same way," his boss replied with a grin. "Now, how would you feel about tackling a couple of more project designs?"

"I'd enjoy working on them."

"Would you be comfortable corresponding with the clients and getting specific information? It would help me a lot, and I think it would save time, too. If you hear what they all want from their lips, you won't have to wonder what I'm trying to describe." Looking a little sheepish, his boss said, "We both know describing colors isn't my strong point."

"I'd be happy to chat with them," John said. "More than happy."

His boss pointed to the worktable at the side of his office. "Why don't you get started there? I'll get you a laptop and a company cell phone to use."

Though he was used to talking on a cell phone—the bishop had given him permission to use one for work long ago—the fancy laptop was another story. "I'm not sure how to use that computer."

"That's why I thought you could work in here with me today. I'll help you. You'll get the hang of it in no time."

As John sat down, he realized that he'd just started something that was going to change everything he did at work. It was exciting and nerve-wracking, too. And truly amazing! The Lord was so good.

John just hoped he didn't let himself, his boss, or their clients down. With that in mind, he cleared off his space and got ready. He could hardly wait.

It was just too bad that he couldn't make plans to rush over to tell Marie. That would have made the moment even sweeter.

TWENTY-TWO

"What Katie isn't saying is that 'taking things into his own hands' meant Andy threw me over his shoulder and started hiking up the hill," Marie explained to the crowd. "I was so surprised, all I could do was try to hold on."

Marie lasted only two nights at her parents' house. Though her mother was a terrific "sick mom" and her parents were trying their best to give her space, it wasn't enough. She needed more time to process her thoughts about the accident, John, and even her original reasons for wanting to return to Walnut Creek. She was actually starting to wonder if she'd returned to be closer to all of her close friends . . . or just to John in particular.

Ironically, her parents didn't seem all that concerned anymore about the fact that she'd gotten in a car accident while on a date with John Byler. Oh, of course they were worried about her head and the cuts and bruises. They spent a good amount of time talking about the kids in the other vehicle, both expressing their disappointment about the drinking and confiding that they were praying just as much for the teenagers' parents as for the boy who'd passed away.

But as far as concern went about Marie being with John?

Not a peep.

It was strange, really.

If anything, her parents were acting like she and John had been in a serious relationship for years. It was both kind of cute and extremely awkward—almost as if they'd forgotten that John was Amish.

When Marie had found herself wanting to ask why they were taking her relationship with John in stride, she knew it was time to go home. Her mother might be trying hard to not dwell on this on-again, off-again relationship, but if Marie gave her enough reasons to bring it up, she would change her mind real quick.

After she'd had breakfast, Marie asked her father to drive her home, saying she was going to rest better in her own bed. Dad had agreed to drive her home after a few halfhearted attempts to change her mind.

Now she was home and on sick leave for the rest of the week, doctor's orders. She was also without a vehicle. Currently, the auto repair shop and insurance company were talking about whether her car should be considered totaled. She was privately hoping everyone would decide her SUV wasn't salvageable. She was still having awful flashbacks of the accident. She didn't know how she was going to be able to handle getting behind the wheel again.

When she'd been resting in her old bedroom, she hadn't been too worried about being without a car. Her mother had been catering to her every whim, and Marie hadn't felt like going anywhere.

But now that she was home?

She realized she was now stuck in her house with only meager supplies in her refrigerator and freezer. One day, she vowed, as she stood and stared at the two eggs, three TV dinners, and a frozen package of hamburger meat, she would do a better job of keeping her pantry stocked.

When her doorbell rang, she opened the door as quickly as she was able, thinking that it was going to be her mother with a shopping bag full of food.

Instead, Elizabeth Anne and Katie were on her doorstep. E.A. held two Pyrex containers in her hands. Katie was holding a heavy-looking brown grocery bag.

"Oh, *gut*! You're home," Katie said as she walked

in, looking bright and pretty in a cranberry-colored dress. "I was hoping you would be here."

Well aware she was wearing flannel pajamas that had dancing dogs in sweaters all over them, Marie tried to pretend that she didn't care about how she looked.

Well, almost. She peeked over her girlfriends' shoulders. "There aren't any boys on the way, are there?"

Katie chuckled as she closed the door behind her. "Nope. It's strictly girls."

"*Jah*, at first Will and I were gonna visit you tonight at your parents' house, but after we learned you had come home, I decided he needed to wait to pay you a visit."

"Really? Wow." This was a new level to E.A.'s bossiness.

"It was no trouble," E.A. said with a smile. "Your penchant for doggy pajamas is safe with us."

After Katie put the groceries in the kitchen, she looked Marie over. "Interesting choice in sleepwear though, Marie."

She lifted a foot and kind of kicked it out. "They're comfortable."

"They certainly look it," Elizabeth Anne said with a smile. "They are big enough for two Maries to fit inside."

Realizing that was probably true, Marie tugged on a roomy pant leg. "No one wants snug pajamas."

"Especially not you," E.A. teased.

"Oh, leave her alone, E.A.," Katie said. "You're just jealous that you don't have a pair like them in your own bedroom drawer."

"*Nee*, I'm jealous that I'm wearing this dress instead of cozy pajamas." She ran a hand down the light gray dress. It had tiny white flowers printed on the fabric.

Marie hid a smile as she let the girls' teasing banter float over her. All of them had known each other for so long, they sometimes commented on too much, kind of like sisters.

"What are you two doing here?" she asked when she could get a word in edgewise.

"Feeding you," E.A. answered, just like that explained everything. "Now, go sit back down on the couch and rest. We'll dish up some food and join you."

"You brought me supper?"

"We did," Katie said with a smile. "Supper and milk, juice, and strawberry ice cream."

"And a coffee cake," E.A. added. "Because I know you like your sweets in the morning."

"You girls are lifesavers," Marie said as she took E.A.'s advice and went back to the couch. "I was just standing in front of my refrigerator wondering what to do with two eggs."

E.A. looked at the other girls and smiled. "We figured it would look something like that. You're hopeless when it comes to keeping a good kitchen."

"Hey, that isn't exactly true." Though, since E.A. was Mennonite and Katie was Amish, they sometimes considered her lack of cooking skills rather curious.

"How about this, then?" Katie asked with a wink. "You never learned how to properly grocery shop."

"I know, I just chose to concentrate on other things." Like banking, for example.

"It's time you learned, then. It's a *gut* skill to have," Katie said as she began bustling around Marie's kitchen.

"Ha-ha. You're sounding pretty bossy this evening."

"It's only because you caught us off guard. We thought you were staying at your parents' house," Katie explained. Eyeing her carefully, she said, "That's where you were last night. What happened?"

"I think I was simply ready to get home."

"Your father said that you wanted to sleep in your own bed."

"I do." But even to her own ears her voice sounded kind of thin and doubtful. She bit her lip and tried once again to figure out what was wrong with her. Was she still simply reeling from the effects of the accident?

Or did it have more to do with her conversation with John?

Luckily, she didn't have too much time to dwell on those questions because Elizabeth Anne approached with a wooden tray piled high with chicken and dumplings, fresh rolls, green beans, and a slice of chocolate pie. "This looks amazing."

Katie smiled. "*Danke.*"

Marie was happy to see that each of them had given themselves small portions of the meal as well.

That was just another reason why they were her best girlfriends in the world. They knew the last thing she wanted was to eat while they stared at her.

"You girls are the best. Thank you for making all of this and coming over." Marie smiled at all of them. "I'm so glad you're eating with me, too."

"Well, you know what they say, friends don't let friends eat pie alone," Katie teased.

"I can't disagree."

Holding out her hand, E.A. said, "Let's pray, shall we?"

Used to the Amish way of praying silently before meals, Marie bent her head and fervently gave thanks. She was so very thankful for the food, the hands that made it, and her friends' company.

Once everyone was finished, Marie ate a spoonful of the chicken and dumplings. "This is so good. Thank you."

"No thanks are needed. It was the least we could do," Katie said. "We've been worried about you."

"I'm all right. I'm just sorry that John got hurt, too. And, of course, about Evan and the other kids."

Elizabeth Anne winced. "Evan's funeral was as difficult as I expected. That poor boy."

Katie nodded. "And Mary Jane, too. I've been praying for her, too."

There was that forgiveness that was such a part of the Amish way of life. Surprisingly, though, she didn't find herself getting as upset as she had when John had confided that he had already forgiven Mary Jane for driving underage and intoxicated. She wondered why. Was it because she was slowly coming to terms with the Amish way of forgiving others? Or, was it because she was simply feeling better and had some time to think about how Mary Jane must have been feeling?

E.A. broke the silence. "John went to work today. Did you know that?"

"No." She picked up her roll and took a bite. "I haven't talked to John today." Or yesterday.

Katie sighed. "You still haven't talked to him since you were in the hospital?"

"We had some words." Way too many words. How she wished she could take back half of what she had said or at least a good part of her anger! "I told you that, Katie."

E.A. looked confused. "I stopped by John's house yesterday. I could have sworn he told us all that he was going to stop by your parents' house soon."

"Our argument in the hospital didn't end well. I kind of asked him not to come over."

Elizabeth Anne leaned forward. "It was that bad? Why were you arguing?"

Marie groaned. "E.A., don't you think that's kind of personal?"

"Well, yes. And I would never expect you to answer me if other girls who weren't us were here," Elizabeth Anne said. "But it is us, Marie. We're your best friends and we love you."

That simple declaration brought tears to her eyes.

Katie noticed immediately. "Oh, Marie. What is really wrong?"

"I don't know. You're all probably going to think I'm being selfish but I was pretty harsh on the kids who crashed into us. John said that he was already trying hard to forgive them." Each word came out grudgingly. She didn't exactly want to rehash her feelings with the girls.

Especially not while she was eating their delicious

food—and after Katie said she was praying for Mary Jane.

As she feared, the two girls exchanged worried looks. Before one of them could launch into a lecture, she raised her hand. "I know. This is something I need to work on. I understand."

"*Nee*, what I was going to say is that you have every right to feel that way," Katie said softly.

Marie studied her expression. "Do you mean that?"

"Of course. The accident was scary."

Setting her dish down, she felt one of the tears that had threatened to fall begin a slow march down her face. "It was awful. I didn't know how to get out of the way of that oncoming car."

"Of course not," E.A. murmured.

Marie kept talking. "And then there was John. I was driving, of course, so I didn't want him to get hurt. But really, it all happened so fast, I could hardly think."

"Even though we've all been praying for Mary Jane, I can't deny that I was shocked about what she did," Katie said quietly.

"And Evan! He was so young. It was such a waste," E.A. murmured. "They all knew better. I know they did."

Marie was almost afraid to say anything more, but she felt like she owed their friendship too much to not be honest. "I was pretty harsh when I shared my opinion. John wasn't happy." Looking from one girl to the other, she continued, "It felt like everything I loved about him didn't matter. Only our differences."

She paused, ready for the other girls to nod in agreement. Maybe even share some of their experiences about how everyone's chosen way of life did matter in the real world.

But instead of agreeing, the other two seemed to be gaping at her.

"What?" Marie asked at last. "What did I say?"

"Do you really not know?" Katie asked gently.

She shook her head. Feeling hurt, she said, "I already told you I feel bad about making John upset."

Elizabeth Anne stood up. "I think all of us need pie for this conversation. Not just Marie. Does everyone want a slice?"

"We all need a piece, you know that," Katie said.

Marie was getting a little irritated. "Just to remind you all, I was in a car accident two nights ago. I'm not at my best right now. Maybe you could give me a bit of a break and tell me what I said that has gotten you two in a dither?"

"You said 'everything I loved about him.' You love John," Katie said.

Marie blinked. "Well, of course I love him. I love all of the Eight."

"It's different with you and John," Katie murmured.

Just as Marie was going to protest, she closed her mouth. Katie was right. It was time to stop pretending to herself and to her friends and family. She really did love John. Maybe she always had.

"Um, let's say that I agreed with you. Do you really think it's okay that John and I have completely opposite opinions about those kids in the other car?"

"I think it is, especially since when you talked you were both under a lot of stress and both in pain," Katie said. "Maybe you should consider that neither of you were thinking clearly when you talked."

"And that even people who love each other don't always agree," E.A. murmured.

"Thank you. I . . . well, you both have really helped me tonight."

E.A. smiled at her. "That makes me happy."

Marie took her slice of pie from the tray and set it in her lap. "Now, which one of you made the pie?"

"Neither of us. Tricia Warner did," E.A. said.

"Really?" Until recently, they'd only known her as Andy's little sister. But now that she had started dating Logan, she was slowly becoming integrated into their close-knit group, much like Kendra had a few years ago.

"I know," Katie said with a smile. "It turns out Tricia has a lot of skills none of us ever knew about, one of which is that she's a mighty fine baker."

Marie was glad the talk had turned from her but was starting to think maybe Trish's name coming up in conversation wasn't an accident. "She and Logan have gotten close."

"At first I thought they had gotten closer because they both were hurting from Andy's death. But now I think they really have fallen in love."

"Do you think the rumors are true about Tricia wanting to become Amish?" E.A. asked.

"I know she is serious. Logan took her to church last week, and they stayed late and met with Preacher Able and the bishop," Katie said. Smiling at Marie, she said, "Maybe one day you and John will finally become a real couple."

"Um, actually, I think we might already be. Last Saturday night we kissed."

Elizabeth Anne chuckled. "Marie, you always do make mountains out of molehills. What did he do, kiss you on the cheek when you picked him up at his house?"

"No." After debating how to describe what happened, Marie plunged forward. "We um, well, we kind of made out in the middle of the corn maze." There. She said it.

Katie laughed. "*Ack*, Marie . . . You mean you two made out in the corn maze just like all the teenagers do?"

"We did." It was a struggle to not blush profusely, though she had a feeling she was already doing that.

"What happened?"

"I don't know. One minute we were walking, and then the next? John was holding me close and we were kissing like it was our last day on Earth."

And it felt just as embarrassing to say out loud as she'd feared it would.

After a brief moment of silence, both of her girlfriends grinned even wider.

"I'm so glad I came over," Elizabeth Anne said as she playfully fanned her face. "Tell us all about it."

"I just did."

"Details, girl." Katie smiled. "I'm never going to be kissing John Byler. I never even thought about it, but now I'm kind of thinking that I should have been!"

"I'm not going to share anything more," Marie said primly. "I'm not that kind of girl."

"Spoilsport," Katie teased as she leaned back on the couch and tucked her feet under her dress. "Well, at least we know that the two of you are serious."

"And that argument of yours now makes a whole lot more sense," Elizabeth Anne added.

"How do you figure that?"

"Everything matters more when you're in love, Marie. Surely even you English girls have learned that?"

TWENTY-THREE

"Andy carried you for a good long while, Marie," Katie said. Glancing at John, she said, "Though I'm pretty sure that John B. carried you even longer."

Maybe it was the accident that had triggered everything, but the dreams that had plagued Marie for most of her life were now happening almost nightly. Each night, just after one or two, they came to visit, each one a carbon copy of the previous evening, alike in every sense, just starring different characters.

But it didn't matter, the outcome was always the same. She would be walking through some kind of store, holding one of those handheld plastic baskets that she always regretted taking because they inevitably got too heavy too fast, when she'd hear a loud bang and then someone unexpected would appear in front of her.

Because she had never liked surprises, she would

stop abruptly, raise her hands in protest, and then ultimately veer off in a different direction.

When she was a child, she used to run into all sorts of scary things at night: cliffs, dark caves, dangerous-looking alleyways. On a really bad night, she would run into her absolute worst fear—a clown. When that happened, she would wake up screaming, and either her mother or father would rush to her side and sit with her until she fell asleep again.

Her latest dreams had nothing to do with dark alleyways or scary-looking clowns. Instead, she always ended standing next to Andy's grave.

The first time Marie had come upon his grave, she'd burst into tears. Over the last few nights, though, she'd begun to realize that his grave wasn't something to be feared. No, it was something that she needed to see in person.

Which was why that Sunday, after barely making it through church, she'd begged off from sharing lunch with her parents and did what she'd needed to do—what she had felt like she couldn't wait another day to do—she went to sit by his grave.

As it had the day of the funeral, the sight of Andy's place of rest made her feel disoriented. She couldn't see the neat rows of headstones without thinking about how much Andy would have hated the orderliness of it. He'd been brilliant, kind, often funny, and always full of himself. Yeah, he'd been a great many things, but he'd never, ever been one for following the rules.

Even seeing his headstone, on which his parents had placed his name, dates of birth and death, and BELOVED SON, BROTHER, AND FRIEND didn't do him justice.

But really, how could five simple words ever describe the boy who used to light up a room just by entering it?

Because she didn't believe in making a visit without bringing a gift along with her, she brought him a package of his favorite red Twizzlers.

As she weaved her way down the walkways toward Andy's grave, Marie scanned the area. When she realized no one was around, she breathed a sigh of relief.

Hardly caring about what the grass was going to do to her cream-colored pants, she sat down and placed the package of Twizzlers next to his headstone.

Immediately, she felt his surprise.

"I know. It's kind of a waste, isn't it? I probably should've split the package up before I gave you some. But what would I do with it? You know I never did like them." She pointed to her mouth. "I've always been afraid that they'd hurt my teeth."

She felt his eye-roll.

"Come on, Andy, don't be too harsh. We can't all be like you and eat junk food all your life and never gain a pound."

This time, she didn't imagine he said anything to her back. Instead, only silence. It left her feeling empty. Okay, maybe more empty.

Tears formed in her eyes. "You know, I'm just going to say it. I could have really used your advice over these last couple of days, Andy. I don't know what I'm doing with John. Worse, I don't have any idea about what I should be doing. Everyone seems to be so intent to keep us all in our own areas in life. We're supposed to be Amish or English, and only fall in love with people like us. But what happens when it feels like we never had a choice, when everything we do becomes so hard?"

Stewing and suddenly needing something to do, she reached over, opened the package of Twizzlers, and pulled out one long strand and bit down. The sweet cherry taste exploded in her mouth . . . and seemed to fasten like super glue to the three fillings in her back molars.

"Andy, I swear, if this thing pulls out a filling I'm going to be so mad." Then, perversely, she bit off another bite and chewed, and wondered if that Twizzler was like her current situation in life. She kept doing things she knew she shouldn't.

Like making out with John in the middle of a corn maze.

She sighed. "Is life supposed to be this hard?"

"I don't know."

Stunned to hear another voice, Marie turned. "Tricia! You scared me."

Andy's little sister raised her eyebrows. "I have to say that you kind of scared me, too. This is the first time I've turned the corner and saw someone practically sitting on top of Andy's grave." She narrowed her eyes. "Did you bring him Twizzlers?"

"Yeah." She lifted the open package. "Want one?"

Tricia eyed the package suspiciously. "How long has it been sitting there?"

"I just opened it. A couple of minutes."

"Oh. Well, then sure. Thanks." Tricia got on her knees, kind of scooted onto the grass, pulled out a strand, and took a bite. "Boy, I haven't had one of these in years."

"You don't love them like Andy did?"

She rolled her eyes. "Uh, no. I don't think anyone does." She kicked out her legs. "You know, what's funny is that none of us could ever figure out when he became such a big fan of them." She lowered her voice. "Mom was always sure that he was going to get a mouthful of cavities, but he never did. Always had the best teeth in the family."

The comment sparked a memory from high school. "He used to have a smile that made girls go weak in the knees."

Tricia laughed. "He did have a great smile. He knew it, too. Every once in a while, he'd try it on me or Mom to try to get his way."

"Did it work?"

She laughed. "Uh, no. We loved him, but we knew better than to always let him get his way." She flashed another smile, showing Marie that Andy wasn't the only one with a blinding smile. "My dad used to say he should write a children's book about boys like Andy."

"Why?"

"Because Andy was manipulative. I adored him, but if you gave my brother an inch, he'd try to steal a mile."

"Maybe that's why we always let him be our leader," Marie mused.

"I don't think he actually cared who made all the decisions, Marie." Tricia's voice softened. "Logan and I have talked about my brother a lot. And you know what? I don't think Andy ever intended to boss around the Eight, it just kind of happened from time to time. I know Andy never considered himself to be the Eight's leader."

"You might be right," Marie said softly. "What's funny is that whether he was our leader or not didn't really matter. He was just Andy. Andy with the good ideas and the really good smile." Thinking about that, she bit down on another chunk of licorice, letting the sweetness melt on her tongue before swallowing. When Tricia smiled at her, Marie grinned. "I never noticed it before, but you have Andy's same smile."

"You think so?" Trish looked genuinely surprised.

"What, you haven't noticed that before?"

She shook her head. "Andy was so bright, I don't think it ever occurred to me to compare myself to him."

"You might not agree, but I think he would have said that was a mistake."

"Yeah. Maybe." Her voice was faint. Not doubtful, but more like Marie had told her something that she had never considered before.

After a few moments passed, Marie looked at Tricia again. "Do you come here very often?"

"About once a week." Looking at Andy's stone, she said, "I like to come here and tell him how everyone is doing. Tell him about me." Her voice cracked. "He was always sure I was going to do something stupid. He used to say I was the smartest silly girl he knew."

"Does it help, talking to him?"

"Some weeks talking to this darn stone is the

only thing that gets me through it." Her brown eyes widened, doubts filling her head. "Do you think, you know, that hanging out in a graveyard is bad?"

"I'm the last person to judge you." She swallowed. "Actually, I think what you've been doing might have been the smartest thing I've heard of any of us doing."

"Really?"

Marie nodded as she stood up. "I'm going to leave you alone so y'all can talk."

"I feel bad. I didn't mean to make you leave."

"No, I think I was ready."

Tricia nodded as she stood up and gave her a hug. "Hey, Marie?"

"Yeah?"

"Thanks."

"For what? I didn't do anything."

"You've done more than you realize. Really, you've helped a lot." She shrugged. "I guess I needed to be reminded that it was okay to miss Andy."

"You helped me remember that, too." Marie leaned close, hugged Andy's little sister again, then picked up her purse. "Tell Logan I said hey."

"I will. And, um, tell John B. that we're all glad you and him are okay after the accident."

Marie studied her, realizing that she and John had become an official couple. Even though she still hadn't talked to him. "Thanks. I'll do that."

Trish smiled at her again before turning back to her brother.

Marie could hear the other woman's voice, low and faint, as she began to talk. Reassuring Andy that she was okay.

Right before Marie got in her rental car, she looked up at the sky. "Thanks," she whispered. "Thanks for reminding me that it's okay to still need you."

She knew then what she needed to do. It was time to stop thinking only about herself, her doubts, and her pain. With that in mind, she drove the short distance to the Byler farm—it was time to pay a call of her own.

TWENTY-FOUR

"We ended up finding an old hunting cabin in the woods. It didn't have much, but it did have an old fireplace."

Marie had always loved the long drive that led to the Bylers' large, imposing house. John had told her once that it was an old thing and full of nooks, crannies, and a dozen aches and pains. She'd laughed at his description until he'd described the number of things that were a part of life in their home—leaky pipes, drafty windows, and creaking floors.

Though she'd been sympathetic, there were times like now when she thought no house could be prettier. The Byler house sported a black roof, white paint, and dozens of trees currently dressed up for fall. Their red, golden, and bright orange leaves rustled a greeting when she got out of the car.

Just as she reached into the backseat to grab her purse, John's little brother Ezra called out to her.

"Hiya, Marie."

"Hey there, Ezra. How are you?" She smiled at him, loving how with his dark brown hair and hazel eyes, he looked like a mini John.

Walking toward her, all arms and legs, she realized that he wasn't all that small anymore. Nope, he was now even two or three inches taller than she was! "Boy, you got tall all of a sudden."

He smirked. "*Mei daed* says that I might even be taller than Anton one day."

"That would be impressive," she teased. Anton was the burliest of the brothers. She'd always thought he looked like he could have been one of those MMA fighters if he was a different type of person. "Is John here?"

"Uh-huh." Looking her over, his private smirk turned into a full-blown grin. "You've got grass stains on your white pants."

"Do I?" She looked down at her knees. Sure enough, there were twin marks spotting the wool slacks. "Ugh." The green smudges were dark enough she didn't know if even the dry cleaners was going to be able to get them clean.

"Why are ya here? You going courtin'?"

"Ezra, leave her alone," Molly called out from the front door.

"Mol, don't act like Mamm."

She lifted her chin. "I'm not, though Mamm did say to come on in."

"See ya, Marie," Ezra said before turning back to the house.

When Marie started walking toward the front door, too, Molly smiled much more warmly. "Hi, Marie. John's on his way downstairs."

"Thanks for letting me know." The Bylers' front porch was so long and wide, there were two sets of chairs and tables on it. "I'll just wait out here."

"Sounds *gut*." She smiled before rolling back through the open front door and into the dim foyer.

As she sat down on one of the comfy white wicker chairs that had a candy-red cushion, she sighed in relief. Coming here had been the right decision. She had always loved John's family, and seeing his sister and brother reminded her of their long friendship. She remembered the day Mrs. Byler gave birth to Ezra, and John had been so excited. Just two days later, all of the Eight had gotten to come over and see the baby. Marie had talked about that tiny baby for days.

She heard John saying something to one of his siblings before walking out to the porch. He had on his usual dark blue pants and a short-sleeved light blue shirt. To her surprise, his feet were bare and his hair was damp.

"Did you just get out of the shower?" The moment the words were out, she realized that those were the first words she had said to him after their argument. Boy, when was she ever going to actually say the words she actually wanted to when they were together?

Luckily, John just grinned. "*Gut* afternoon to you, too, Marie. And *jah*, I did. I helped with the horses and the barn after church today."

She stood up. "Let me try this again. Hi. Is now an okay time for me to stop by?"

He walked to her side. "Hi back. And anytime you want to visit is fine. You never have to wonder."

Those were swoon-worthy words. "So . . . do you forgive me?"

His expression was sweet and patient. "There ain't nothing to forgive, Marie. I think we both said some things we wished we hadn't." Linking his fingers with hers, he added, "Plus, I've done some thinking, and I kind of think it's just fine that we have different opinions."

"I don't think I was myself when we argued."

"I wasn't myself, either." He smiled suddenly.

"Now come sit down before I do something crazy like pull you into my arms on my parents' front porch."

She sat down but was pretty sure her mouth was hanging open. "John Byler, I can't believe you said that."

He shrugged, not looking the least bit embarrassed. "Why not? It's true."

She swallowed. He kind of did have a point.

"Now, why are you all dressed up? And how come you have green knees?"

"You've noticed that, huh?"

"Hard not to . . . though Ezra made sure to tell me, too."

"I'm dressed up because I went straight from church to Andy's grave." She hesitated, then decided to give him the full story. "And . . . my knees are green because I knelt next to his headstone and ate half a pack of Twizzlers while I talked to him."

John blinked, like she caught him by surprise.

"I know. Kind of weird, huh?"

He nodded. "I didn't think you liked Twizzlers at all."

That comment startled a laugh out of her. "That's all you have to say?"

"That's all for now. I want to hear what you have to say. Why did you decide to visit Andy today?"

"Because I missed him." Opening her heart, she decided to share a little more. Slowly, she told him about staying in her old bedroom and E.A. and Katie's visit. She told him about how she'd started having her dreams again and how she was struggling with Evan's death.

John stayed silent the whole time, letting her talk and explain and backtrack. She knew she was explaining things like a pinball machine, jumping from one topic to the next.

When she finally stopped to take a breath, he spoke.

"I'm sorry I stayed away. I thought we needed some time apart, to think about things." He looked away. "I was wrong."

"I missed you," she blurted. "That's why I came over here today. I realized that it was wrong of me to always make you do the visiting. I can come see you."

His gaze warmed again. "When Anton told me that you were here, I felt happier than I've been in two days. I'm glad you came over."

"Wait, Anton told you I was here? He knows, too?"

He chuckled. "Marie, you know my family. Nothing is private around here. No doubt half of them are standing at the windows watching us." He leaned closer and linked his hands with hers. "Why, I betcha half of them are even brazenly trying to listen to our conversation."

"Oh, no. Ezra teased me, asking if I was going courting. Do . . . do you think that's what they think is going on?"

He studied her for a moment, then nodded. "*Jah.*"

She closed her eyes in embarrassment. "I'm so sorry. I bet they're all going to tease you when I leave."

"No doubt they will." His voice sounded put-upon.

Eyeing him again, she noticed that he didn't look upset by that at all. "John?"

With a groan, he got to his feet, pulling her up with him, since their hands were still linked. "Oh, Marie. Come here."

And before she could do more than give a little squeak, he'd pulled her into his arms and held her close. "What about your family?" she whispered.

"*Ack.* I figured if they're gonna talk and give me grief, I might as well give them something to talk about," he murmured.

She leaned back to see his smile. "I'm glad I came by."

He lightly kissed her cheek before pulling her close again. "Me, too, Marie. Now just relax and let me hold you. 'Kay?"

Wrapping her arms around his middle and resting her head against his chest, she did as he asked.

He smelled like soap and sunshine, and she'd never felt more secure and treasured and warm in his embrace.

It felt like after several days of trying to find a place to feel comfortable again, she had finally found the place where she belonged.

TWENTY-FIVE

"John placed Marie on the floor while Will tested the fireplace. The rest of us either tried to open windows or watched Will. While I was fairly sure the old fireplace was gonna push a ton of smoke into the room, it worked just fine. Within ten minutes, a cozy fire was going."

Molly's parents had wanted her to stay home from work for the whole week after John's accident. They'd said she'd been through a traumatic experience and that the Lord sometimes gave out pain and sadness in small doses, meaning that He was sure to make her feel even more upset about the accident and Evan's death than she already did.

Molly had nodded obediently but had privately thought that her parents were completely wrong. She'd been hurting plenty already. When she'd heard about the accident, John being possibly injured, and then Evan's death and Mary Jane's drinking, she'd felt so overwhelmed, she'd had a difficult time breathing. She'd only calmed down after visiting with Ezra and Danny in the hospital cafeteria.

Then, she'd had to get through the funeral, which had been difficult as well. She'd started helping more with laundry and other jobs around the house. As long as her hands were busy, her private worries eased, and a hazy kind of numbness had fallen over her. She thought that was the Lord's doing. He knew this whole experience was difficult for her to deal with, so He'd elected to give her a way to deal with it the best she could.

After another day passed and all the hoopla of Marie's visit to John had died down, Molly knew she had to get out of the house. She told her mother that James had volunteered to take her for a walk to clear her head. But what she really had done was ask her big brother to help her get to the library so she could ask to be put on the schedule.

James, to her relief, hadn't batted an eye at his little sister's duplicity. Instead, he walked beside her on the sidewalk as she moved her chair forward.

Mrs. Laramie had taken one look at Molly's eager and, well, needy expression and given her a four-hour slot for Thursday and a full day on Friday.

"*Danke*, Mrs. Laramie," she said, finally feeling lighter than she had in days.

"No reason to thank me, Molly. We'll be glad to have you back. Some of the patrons have even been asking about you."

That made her happy. "I've missed them, too. I'll see you on Thursday."

After they exited the building, James bought them ice-cream cones from a nearby stand and sat beside her to eat. She'd gotten something called "moose tracks"—peanut butter ice cream filled with peanut butter cups, dollops of fudge, and parts of waffle cones. James got plain vanilla.

"You always get the craziest ice cream choices, Mol," he teased.

"And you always get plain vanilla."

"I like simple things."

She smiled at him. "I guess I like them more complicated." As soon as she said that, she realized their ice cream choices weren't far off the mark. James was as perfect and straightforward as a man could be. All of their siblings and their parents depended on him.

And she? Well, even before she'd gotten in her accident she'd never taken the easy way. She wondered why that was.

She was still thinking about that when halfway home James said, "Molly, tell me the truth. How are you doing with Evan's loss?"

With Anton, she might have fibbed. Never with her eldest brother, though. "I feel sorry for him and his family."

"And?"

She forced herself to voice the thoughts that had been plaguing her. "And I also feel guilty that I'm not sadder than I am."

"Ah."

"Don't tell Mamm," she said in a rush.

"Why? You don't think she'd understand?"

"Not even a little bit."

He raised an eyebrow. "You seem certain."

"James, you know as well as I do that Mamm wants us all to love everyone."

"She wants us to be kind to everyone and give people the benefit of the doubt." He paused, looking like he was giving the matter some more thought. "And she wants us to love each other."

A little piece of her heart hurt. She'd been secretly hoping he would understand. "You think I'm wrong."

"I think you are being hard on yourself. No one expects you to be perfect or to always think perfect thoughts. I sure don't."

In spite of the serious conversation, Molly found herself smiling.

James looked shocked. "What is that smile for?"

"Because you're James."

"I'm not following you."

"Oh, James. You are the oldest and almost perfect. You never gave Mamm and Daed any trouble, are now working by Daed's side, and you're courting Patsy Kauffman, who's your equal in almost every way."

He groaned. "I feel like I should bow or something, you make me sound so commendable."

"You're welcome to, if you'd like."

"I am the oldest, but I'm not near perfect, sister. And for the record, I think you're mighty special, too."

As always, his praise filled her with warmth. "*Danke*, James."

He looked down at her. "Molly, I think when we get home you should tell our parents how you are feeling and that you're going back to work at the library."

"I will." Well, she wanted to. . . .

"*Nee*, I know you as well as you know me. You'll put it off until you can't any longer. Just tell them everything."

"I'll try."

"*Gut*." Their house was in sight now. "So, do you want to tell me what is going on with you and Danny Eberly?"

"Oh, James. Do we have to talk about this?"

He smiled, looking even more handsome than he usually did. "Anything you tell me will stay between us."

"I've already gotten a talking-to from John."

He waved a hand. "We both know John is a great many things, but he's not a person to give relationship advice."

This was news to her. "Do you mean because of how he acts around Marie?"

"Of course. We all know he's liked her forever, but she was the one who stopped over here yesterday."

"They did hug, James. I saw them."

"*Nee*, you spied on them."

"If you're gonna chide me, you better chide Daed, too. I was right next to him at the living room window."

"I was watching with Ezra from upstairs," he said with a sheepish grin. "And since we're revealing secrets, I'll admit I was disappointed he didn't kiss her."

"Me, too." She smiled up at him.

He winked back. "See? John don't know much."

"But you do?" She was starting to think they'd all been spying on the wrong brother!

"Come on, Molly. Talk to me."

After debating a couple of seconds, she blurted, "If I tell you something, will you promise not to go to John—or anyone else?"

"I already told you I'd keep our conversation private."

"*Nee*, you said you wouldn't share what I told you with anyone. This is about John."

"I promise. Tell me."

"Well, when I was at the ticket booth with Danny, John and Marie went into the corn maze and not long after, one of the *kinner* that had bought a ticket after came running back out giggling, saying that he saw a blond *Englischer* girl and an Amish boy kissing."

"Huh. So maybe he hasn't been waiting on Marie to make the first move after all." James's eyes brightened as he looked down at her. "Have you told John about what you heard?"

"No way."

"Why not? I would have."

"First, right after that was the accident, and second, I don't know. There's a part of me that kind of likes knowing that John has a secret."

"Ha. He only thinks he does."

Molly noticed that James didn't sound particularly upset about John and Marie. "Are you upset that Marie is English?"

"*Nee*. I mean, that's who Marie is, ain't so?" After Molly nodded, James added, "Besides, John is too old for me to be judging his relationships."

"Amanda told me once that you can't help who you love. It just happens."

James's expression softened. "That sounds like our Amanda, don't it? She's always been both a romantic and matter-of-fact about most things."

"I suppose." Though it was probably because of their birth order, Molly always considered her older sister to be far more interested in getting her way and being heard than interested in anything of a romantic nature.

"So, about Danny?"

James wasn't going to let this go. "We are friends, James. That's all."

"That's it?"

Though it was painful, she waved a hand in front of herself. "Come now. When you look at me, what do you see?"

"A pretty sixteen-year-old who is kind and generous?"

"*Nee*, I mean, what would you see if you looked at me as a man?"

He made a choking sound. "Molly."

"I'm serious."

"I don't know. A pretty girl with a nice smile?"

She mentally rolled her eyes. "You are still being a *broodah*. If you were simply a regular *boo* interested in courting a girl my age, the first thing you would see would be a wheelchair, James." She shook her head. "No, actually, *all* you would see would be a wheelchair."

"I hate it when you talk like that, Molly. There's a lot more to you than that."

"I know," she said impatiently. "I mean, I feel like I've spent most of my life trying to get people to see something besides my wheelchair when they look at me."

He nodded. "That means the right man will see something more, too. Who knows? Maybe it will be Danny."

"I doubt that will ever happen. He could have any girl he wanted."

"I doubt that."

"It's true." She swallowed. "He's well liked, James."

"You are, too."

"He's going to want someone better."

"Molly—"

Forcing herself to say the words, she continued. "He's gonna want someone who can walk, James. A woman who won't have to ask for help when she has toddlers at home."

Pausing next to the ramp they'd installed after her accident, James continued. "You are selling yourself short, Molly. And before you say a word about that, let me tell you this—as long as you continue to do that, everyone else is going to do that, too."

She opened her mouth, then shut it just as quickly. Hadn't she learned that lesson at the library? When she acted capable and professional, the patrons treated her that way, too.

James grinned. "Did I finally render you speechless?"

"Maybe. You've given me a lot to think about."

Just as he looked about to answer, his smile broadened. "I'd say that's perfect timing, then."

"Oh?"

"You have company, Molly."

Turning her chair to the side, she spied Danny himself walking up their drive. When he saw her look at him, he waved. "Hey, Molly."

Feeling a little weak, she raised her hand, too. "Hi." Lowering her voice, she said, "James, what should I do?"

"Smile and get ready for Mamm to bring out lemonade and a plate of cookies."

Just imagining her busy, inquisitive mother chatting with Danny made her wince. "Do you think she really will?"

"You have a suitor come courting, Mol," he said, amusement in his voice. "She'll be out here real soon. For sure and for certain."

She stayed where she was while James walked over and said something quietly to Danny.

Then her heart started to pound when, three minutes later, James walked by, winked at her, and then trotted inside.

TWENTY-SIX

"After Will got the fire going, he helped get Marie settled on an old cushion he found in the corner, proving to us all that he was the man to have around in any emergency."

Molly was staring at him like she was shocked that he'd come over to her house. Her expression kind of caught Danny off guard. She'd seemed really happy to be around him at the Fall Festival. At the hospital, too.

Had her feelings for him changed already? Or maybe she was embarrassed to have a caller. Belatedly, he realized he should have asked her if it was okay for him to visit.

Feeling a little less sure of himself, he walked up the front steps. She'd gone up the side ramp that led to the front porch. "How are you, Molly?"

She shrugged. "I don't know, exactly. What about you?"

"About the same. Is it okay that I showed up unannounced like this?"

"Of course. Since I'm not allowed to work for a couple of days, I just went out for a walk with James."

"That's nice." Liking the thought that another one of her brothers looked out for her, he added, "Boy, I haven't talked to James in months."

"He's ten years older than us, so I wouldn't expect you to see him much." She smiled. "I mean, besides church and everything."

"Is he married yet?"

"*Nee*. But we're all thinking it'll happen soon. He and Patsy Kauffman have been courting for a while."

"Ah."

Looking pensive, she said, "Have you talked to Mary Jane, Callie, or Karl?"

"I don't really know Callie that well, but I talked to Karl. I went to his *haus* with my parents."

"He looked awfully pale at the funeral. Is he still badly injured?"

Danny couldn't help but wince. "He had to get his spleen removed at the hospital and says he's real bruised from the seat belt he was wearing."

"That's awful."

"*Jah*." What Danny wasn't sure how to describe was the way Karl had looked—haunted and exhausted. Those were two things that a doctor couldn't heal.

Molly looked down at her hands, which were folded in her lap, before meeting his gaze again. "I haven't known what to say to anyone. Even at the funeral, I tried to stay in the background."

"Is that because your *broodah* was in the other vehicle?"

She shrugged. "Maybe. But more because it feels like everyone has an opinion about the accident. I never know what to say."

"Do you have an opinion?" He felt like he was opening a can of worms, but he also knew it had to be done. They needed to clear the air between them.

"I'm not really sure." Looking embarrassed, she said, "Isn't that stupid? I mean, I thought I had opinions about everything. But now? Now, I wonder if my opinions even matter."

He scooted to the edge of his chair, wanting to reach out to her but not sure how she would react. "It's not stupid at all. I think it's smart. It's easy to pass judgment. It's harder to want to really think about another person's perspective."

"I fear you're giving more credit than is due, Danny."

"Why is that?"

Looking even more pained, she said, "I feel guilty."

His first impulse was to shrug off her words. After all, they hadn't had a single thing to do with their friends deciding to drink and drive. "I don't understand."

"It's because I kind of feel like we should have done something."

"When?"

"When they said that they were going to the barn to drink."

Now he did shrug. "Molly, come on. What do you think would have happened? You and me tell them about the dangers of drinking and they would be so impressed with our logic that they would change their plans?"

"I know they wouldn't have listened to me. But they might have listened to you."

"They wouldn't have listened to me. Besides, I wouldn't have told them that."

"Why?"

"Because it wasn't any of our business. No one wants to be around people who tell them how they should run their lives."

She frowned. "I know. But I can't help but think if more people stepped in and said things then maybe some of the bad things that happened could have been prevented."

Her words didn't sit well with him. He didn't like how she was trying to give them, and him especially, any responsibility for Evan's death. "What happened was not our fault," he blurted. "We didn't even know they were going to drive."

"I know."

"You might not have been friends with Evan, but I knew him and liked him. I would have never done anything to cause him harm."

"I didn't say that you did."

"But you insinuated it." Angry now, and yes, also a little hurt, he added, "It's not fair of you to say that I should have told them not to go to that barn and drink because they might have listened to me."

"I'm sorry." Tears were in her eyes now. "Danny, I told you I was having a difficult time explaining my feelings."

"It seemed to me like you were explaining them just fine. What's too bad is that you are wrong."

"I'm sorry," she said again. "Please don't be mad."

Just then her front door opened and her mother came out, holding two glasses of lemonade. "Hi, Danny. It's a long walk over here. Would you like something to drink?"

He glanced at Molly, but she had her face averted.

Suddenly he wasn't even sure why he'd come over in the first place. "*Danke*, Mrs. Byler, but I've gotta go."

Eyes wide, she looked from him to Molly. "But you just got here. Is everything all right?"

"It's fine, Mamm," Molly said before he could say a word. "Danny only came over to tell me something. We're finished now."

He felt her words straight to his gut. Without another word, he turned and started down the steps, Molly's last statement ringing in his ears.

She wasn't right about everything, but she was surely right that they were finished.

As far as he was concerned, he had no need to ever attempt to call on her again. They were too different.

As he continued the long walk home, he had thought their differences would always revolve around her disability, or maybe even the fact that she came from a well-off large family and he and his little brother lived in a far different situation.

But it seemed that there were now other things that were just as powerful that could keep them apart.

TWENTY-SEVEN

"Will always was a show-off," Elizabeth Anne said.

After coming clean to his father about not getting baptized, John had thought he would have felt more relaxed about his future. After all, it had been a big decision and a life-changing one. Unfortunately, he still found himself debating what to do next—and perhaps, when to take the first step in this new direction. What he needed were not only friends who he trusted, but who knew Marie well, too.

And who could, perhaps, understand why he was thinking about the things he was.

There were only two people he felt comfortable being completely honest with—Logan and Will. Will was his best friend. They'd gone to Amish school together, had sat together during church. They'd even goofed off together when they were little boys and everything in the world seemed like a better idea than being obedient and hardworking.

Even though Logan was New Order Amish, he was currently having to deal with many of the same issues John was, since he was now courting Tricia Warner seriously.

With all that in mind, John made arrangements for the three of them to go fishing in Will's creek that evening after work. The three of them had spent many an hour there. When they were little boys, they'd built tree forts along the banks. Later, they'd walked along the banks for miles with their siblings. One crazy day, the Eight of them had had quite an adventure in the rain.

But the three of them had always most enjoyed fishing together in a section just off the edge of the Kurtzes' property. There, the fishing hole was deeper, the area was fairly secluded by a grouping of trees, and time seemed to stand still.

He needed that space, and those two men, now.

When John arrived at their usual spot, walking barefoot and holding his old fishing pole, he discovered Logan had already arrived. He was perched on the edge of a log and sipping what was no doubt coffee from a large red travel mug. "Hey, I thought I left too early," John told him. "I'm surprised you beat me."

Logan shrugged. "I got off early. I was looking forward to seeing you guys, too. As soon as I brewed a fresh pot of *kaffi* I started walking over."

"I worked with Will, but I know he likes to check in with his mother when he gets home," John said. "I reckon he'll be along in a few."

"I imagine so. You got bait?"

"I do." Opening up a container he'd tossed in the top of his tackle box, he said, "I asked Ezra to get us a mess of night crawlers."

Logan raised an eyebrow. "And he did it?"

"He's still young enough to not mind digging for worms from time to time." Grinning, John added, "He left them for me in the refrigerator. Mamm was none too happy about that."

"We used to do the same thing," Logan said.

"What did we used to do?" Will asked as he approached.

"We stored our *voahms* in our *muddah*'s Tupperware."

Will winced. "You might have. I did not. *Mei mamm* would have blistered my rear end if I did that. You know she liked keeping a clean refrigerator."

"Oh, we know," John said. Remembering all the summers he'd spent at the Kurtz house, either being babysat or simply playing, he shuddered dramatically. "Your *mamm* had to keep a tight rein on it, though. Otherwise we would have eaten everything in your kitchen."

"I'm thinking my father said the same things from time to time." Will pulled out his rod and reel from its case and started adjusting the fishing line and hook. After he walked over to a particularly wide boulder—the source of many discussions over the years—he reached out a hand. "Send one of those worms this way."

John sat down and handed him the open container. After Will pulled a worm out and attached it to his hook, John baited his own line. He poked the hook through the worm, wincing slightly as the worm wiggled in his fingers. "This used to bother me none. Now? Well, it feels a bit mean."

"You're getting soft there, John," Will said as he approached. "Next thing you know, you'll be wanting to become an *Englischer*."

Here it was. His opportunity. John felt his cheeks flush. "*Jah*. Well, that's something I wanted to talk to you about."

Will smiled at Logan. "Told you."

"Told you?" he sputtered.

"Logan and I have been guessing why you wanted to get together to fish. Looks like I was right."

It wasn't a shock that his friends read his mind so easily. But it still was a bit disconcerting to realize that it hadn't taken them more than a minute or two to figure out what had been on his mind. "No need to be quite so full of yourself there."

Will didn't even attempt to hide his amusement. "Come on, John. Surely you didn't think your relationship with Marie was a secret."

"I didn't think it was that obvious."

Logan, who had always been more diplomatic than Will had ever tried to be, easily baited his hook and cast the line. "It might not have been real obvious to everyone. But for those of us who've known you both all our lives?" He waved a hand. "It was hard to miss."

"What was hard to miss?"

"The fact that you've always been smitten with our Marie," Logan said. "Not that anyone would blame ya."

Will winked. "Don't you remember Andy telling us how half the boys in the high school had set their caps for her?"

"I remember."

Logan grinned. "I think we met at least four or five of them. Remember the black-haired guy with all the freckles?"

Oh, John remembered. "He was a know-it-all."

"*Nee*, he was annoying, that's what he was," Logan said. "I'm pretty sure I told Marie never to bring him by again."

"I don't think he was all that fond of us either," Will said. "We didn't have much in common."

Knowing he was one of Marie's many admirers didn't make John feel any better. Nor, he realized, did grouping him with the other boys she used to date convey the depth of his feelings for Marie. "You know it's not like that."

"It's not like what?" Will asked.

"I'm not just taken in by a pretty smile and a bunch of golden hair." Thinking about Marie, he stared out into the creek. "You know what? Marie Hartman is more than just a pretty face. She's a hard worker, and is genuinely kind. She's been a *gut* friend to us all, too."

Will looked taken aback. "I know that, John. I didn't say she wasn't special."

"Sorry." John took a deep breath. "Obviously I am having some trouble talking about my feelings, and what I want to do."

"You're doing fine. All we're trying to say is that our Marie has been a *gut* friend, indeed," Logan murmured.

Feeling encouraged, John continued. "What's more, returning to Walnut Creek after being gone so long hasn't been easy, you know."

"I'm sure it has been an adjustment. She was in the city for years," said Will.

The words tumbled onward, practically falling from his mouth. "She came to a smaller bank and is having to prove herself all over again. And then there are her parents. You know how her mother is. Mrs. Hartman has her own goals for her. Poor Marie has been having to remind them that she's not a little girl anymore, that she's her own person."

Logan cleared his throat. "*Jah*. She's *wunderbaar*."

Still looking out at the creek, John ignored the faintly snarky tone of his buddy, still concentrating on trying to find the right words. "I'm being serious. Marie's been trying hard to find her place. That ain't easy."

"It might not be easy, but I'd wager that her struggles might be over," Will said.

Taken aback by the statement, John glanced at him in confusion. "What do you mean by that?"

"You know what I mean. She has you on her side now. If she has you, she won't ever have to face things on her own again."

"Me and Marie being together isn't going to be that easy," John said quickly.

"It might not be easy, but you don't have to make it seem so hard," Logan said. "Things will work out."

John sighed. "You both know as well as I do that just because someone might want something, it don't mean that getting it is the right choice."

"I would agree with you if we were talking about a new fishing pole or a horse. But you are talking about your feelings for her. You can't stop those," Logan said.

"Do you really think so?"

"I'm falling in love with Andy's little sister," Logan said. "If you don't think that took me off guard, then you would be mistaken. Even though I've never regretted my feelings for Trish, I can't deny that I did have some doubts about whether it was realistic to be together."

"But you two are still together."

Logan nodded. "Having Tricia has been worth all our struggles. I bet you already feel the same way about Marie."

"That brings up the next thing. She's not Amish."

Will laughed. "I noticed that, too."

"Come on. You know what I'm getting at. Logan, what did your parents say? How did you feel when you started thinking about courting Tricia?"

After taking a generous sip of his coffee, Logan turned to him. "I felt confused, I'll tell you that. I couldn't even fool myself into pretending that my feelings for her took me by surprise. I've spent the last couple of years hoping that I wouldn't see Tricia because I thought she was too young, she was English, and she was Andy's sister, which was a whole other can of worms." Glancing at the Tupperware container, he rolled his eyes. "No pun intended."

"Did you ask her to change or did she volunteer to become Amish?"

"We didn't have much choice. I had already been

baptized. I told her that I wasn't going to break my vows. They were too important to me."

"I can't see Marie being Amish."

Both Logan and Will started laughing. "That's putting it mildly there, John," Will said. "You're gonna have to be the one who jumps the fence."

"I know."

"And?"

"And . . . I think I'm ready." Even saying that much out loud felt scary. "I value our beliefs and love Jesus, but I love Marie, too."

"I reckon it's going to be hard," Will said, "but other men and women we know have gone the same direction. What do your parents say, John?"

"I spoke with my *daed*. He wasn't surprised."

Logan, who had been reeling in a catch, glanced over at him. "I wouldn't think he would be. Everyone knew there was a reason you didn't want to get baptized when I did."

He was starting to think the only person he'd been fooling was himself. "I was relieved that my father wasn't upset with me, but to be honest, I felt too old to be asking my parents for permission about my choice. I'm going to want their blessing, of course, but this is my life, not theirs."

"No offense, John, but I think you came here to ask our blessing, too," Will murmured.

"What?"

"Your mind is made up. We all know it. You need to simply come to peace with it," Logan added.

"I guess that's what I'll do, then." Steeling his spine, he added, "I'm going to do this then. I'm going to soon begin to be an *Englischer*."

"You'll be fine. We've all spent the night at each other's houses enough to not be too scared about the changes," Logan said.

"Plus, you already work at the trailer company with *Englischers*. You and me both do," Will said. "It ain't a different world."

"We're thinking what you're really going to have to do is think about buying a pair of jeans and a T-shirt and visit Marie and tell her you want to move forward."

John swallowed. "And hope and pray that she hasn't changed her mind."

To his surprise, Will and Logan started laughing again. "What's so funny?"

"Well, she is a woman, John," Will said. "They change their minds all the time."

Casting his line again, John grinned because he knew they were teasing him.

But Will had just brought up his biggest fear.

TWENTY-EIGHT

"When it started thundering and lightning, we closed the cabin door, let the kittens free, and huddled in front of the fireplace. We decided to wait out the storm. But it was really hard, because by that time, it felt like we were having our own little squall right there in the cabin. From time to time, even the best of friends can get annoyed with each other."

By five o'clock Wednesday evening, Marie was certain it had been one of the longest days of her life. From spilling hot coffee on herself to running late to meetings, to getting yelled at by a customer, everything had gone wrong.

She'd skipped breakfast, missed lunch, and couldn't seem to do anything right. Things had gotten so bad, she'd ended up leaving at four thirty. She hadn't cared one bit that she was the first employee to walk toward the parking lot.

As soon as she got home she put on a pair of old

shorts and a sweatshirt and made a huge BLT, her favorite stressed-out snack. Then, eager to spend at least part of the day outside, she walked out to the front porch of her little house, popped in her earbuds, and turned on her favorite playlist.

She'd just taken a massive bite of the sandwich when John walked up the driveway.

Or, it was someone who looked a lot like John. But couldn't be, because this man was definitely not dressed Amish.

Thinking that her headache, lack of food, and generally bad day had gotten the best of her, she continued to stare. The man was wearing a navy baseball cap, soft-looking denim jeans, and an untucked oxford shirt.

Looking at the way that shirt hugged the man's muscles, she almost choked. She knew those lines of that body.

Putting down the half of sandwich she'd almost forgotten she was holding, Marie took off her earbuds and got to her feet. "John, what is going on?"

"Can't a man visit you without an invitation?"

She felt herself flush. "Of course, you don't need an invitation to come over. I'm always happy to see you."

"Is that right?"

When his smile widened, she shook her head at

him. Sometimes it felt like he could take anything she said and give it a new meaning. "You know what I meant. What's with the clothes?"

He paused on the first step, suddenly looking a lot less sure of himself. "Do I really look that different to ya, Marie?"

"Well, yes . . . and no."

He grinned. "That ain't much of an answer."

She honestly wasn't sure what to say. She settled for honesty. "I've never seen you wear a hat like that before."

John pulled the ball cap off his head and examined the bill, which was emblazoned by a red C. "This stands for Cleveland, you know. For the Cleveland Indians baseball team."

His gaze was so intent, she had a hard time looking away. She knew what the C stood for. What she didn't know was why he had decided to wear that instead of his usual straw hat. "Um, are you a fan now?"

"*Jah.*" Some of his confidence seemed to crack. "Well, I mean, I like baseball and I've seen the Indians play before."

This day—and their conversation—just kept getting stranger and stranger. "I didn't know you liked going to the Indians games," she murmured. Looking down at the table next to her chair, she noticed her sandwich sitting there, calling to her like a tasty beacon. "I was just having a sandwich. Would you like one? It's no trouble."

His gaze softened. "*Nee*. But you sit down and eat."

"Are you sure?" She was having a hard time deciding whether to give more importance to good manners or to her growling stomach. "I would usually put the food away, but I didn't eat lunch. Or breakfast."

"Oh, Marie." He waved a hand at her, gesturing for her to sit back down. "Finish your sandwich."

His voice was soft. Different. That tone, combined with his completely different look, turned her mind to mush.

Was she even hungry anymore? She wasn't sure.

"Actually, um, I think the sandwich can wait. It looks like we've got something pretty important to talk about instead."

"It's important, but not urgent. I'm thinking I should be more worried about you eating for the first time all day after five." His voice softened. "What's going on, Marie? I thought you usually packed your lunch."

"I did. I mean, I do." To her surprise, tears pricked her eyes. "It's nothing to worry about. I just had a busy day."

"Too busy to eat?"

"It was really busy." And awful.

He sighed. "Marie, it's obvious that it's more than that, *jah?*"

"It was. It was filled with all kinds of things that went wrong."

"Going hungry now won't help. Eat a little bit more, 'kay?" He eyed her seriously, reminding her that he might be very sweet but he was also the kind of man who was used to being listened to.

Feeling frustrated all over again, she took another big bite of her sandwich and chewed. Then took another bite.

Sitting across from her, his elbows resting on his knees, John smiled as she self-consciously finished her meal.

After she was done, she smiled weakly at him. "I'm finished." And yes, that was completely obvious.

His expression softened. "What happened, Marie?"

"Oh, everything." When he remained quiet another minute, she blurted, "The truth is . . . I'm not liking my boss much right now."

"What did he do?" he asked as he shifted, crossing his denim-covered legs.

"My morning started with me spilling coffee on my leg." Though it was silly, she kicked out a foot and lifted the hem of her shorts up an inch. She now sported three red marks on her thigh.

His eyes widened. “Marie, you burned yourself.”

“I know. It hurt pretty bad.” Attempting to laugh it off, she said, “Next time I say I like my coffee really hot remind me about this.”

He was still frowning. “You’re lucky you didn’t blister.”

“I’m glad about that, for sure. The last thing I need is a couple of scars on my leg from hot coffee.”

“What does the spill have to do with your boss?”

“Well, I had to try to clean up the stain and put cold water on my leg, so I was five minutes late to a meeting. Mr. Black was pretty angry.”

“I’m getting kind of angry, thinking about him being so uncaring.”

She smiled at him. “Thanks.” Taking a deep breath, she told him about the other parts of her day, none of which—except for the mean woman—was all that bad. But when put together it had felt overwhelming.

“I’m real glad I came over then.”

“Me, too.” Taking a chance, she added, “Talking about it all with you has helped a lot. But I think I would have been glad to see you no matter what.”

“I feel the same way about you. I probably haven’t told you this enough, but I’m really glad you moved back to Walnut Creek.” He looked down at his feet before meeting her eyes again. “I missed you.”

“I missed you, too.” She smiled at him, then took a

deep breath. "John, are you ever going to tell me about your clothes? And don't even start talking about baseball again. This outfit is not normal for you."

After a pause, he spoke. "Marie, after what happened in that cornfield, after those kisses we shared, you know things between us changed."

"So you didn't think of it as just a simple kiss either?" Of course, the moment she asked her question, she knew she was being silly. First, no one in their right mind would call what they'd done in that cornfield just a simple kiss. And second? She knew he would never have kissed her like that if his feelings weren't involved.

"*Nee*. It was anything but a simple kiss, Marie. I've kissed other women. This was something different." He waved a hand. "I don't know what happened, but there's something about the two of us. Ain't so?"

He might be dressed as an *Englischer*, but he still spoke like an Amish man. It was oddly comforting to know he hadn't completely changed overnight.

She swiped a crumb off her lap and nodded. "It's different with you."

He clasped his hands together. "Different, *jah*. But maybe it's better to say it was also intense. Passionate, maybe?"

Her cheeks heated again. "It was certainly passionate."

"Things could have gotten out of control if we hadn't been careful." He sighed. "By the time we walked back to your car, I knew everything had changed between us. At first, I wasn't sure what I wanted to do about it. I guess I needed time to think about it, and to figure out what I wanted to do."

She was trying to keep up. "But . . ."

"But then we had the accident."

She swallowed, still feeling responsible. "That accident changed everything, didn't it?"

He nodded. "I know we both felt that it was a reminder that anything can happen." He stood up. "After Andy's death—I'm not going to lie—it shook me up. But now, going to Evan's funeral? Realizing that the Lord took him so quickly? Well, it made me realize that maybe I've been thinking too much."

It almost seemed like she was hearing a buzzing in her ears. Everything John was saying was so sweet. But it felt intense, too, like every word he was saying could change her life. Could change both of their lives.

Though, maybe that was his point. Their lives already had changed. She'd tried to be everything her parents had wanted. She'd tried to make corporate life and the big city her focus. Maybe had even tried to slip the Eight into her past, tried to pretend their long friendships didn't mean what they used to. Of course, she'd learned fairly quickly that she'd been wrong. She didn't want to worry about work or start new relationships with people who had never lived outside the city. She needed people who shared her roots.

With Andy's death, she had realized that she'd needed to make the change sooner rather than later.

So maybe she, just like John, had been ready to make a change.

Still looking at her directly, he said, "I don't want to think anymore. It's time for action, don't you think?"

Realizing that he'd just voiced her thoughts, she nodded.

"Since I know you could never fit completely into my world, I decided to bend a little and move farther into yours."

Was he really saying what she thought? A whole mixture of emotions ran through her. Excitement. Worry about him making the right decision. Gratitude that he would do something so life altering for her. "You are going to leave the Amish?"

"I don't know if I've ever really been there. I've come to the conclusion that I've been straddling two worlds for some time. I've finally just decided to pick a side and stand tall." His voice lowered. "I realized that if I'm going to stand tall, I want to be standing next to you."

While she gaped at him, he continued. "All you have to do, Marie, is decide whether you want me standing there or not."

Staring at John, her heart was so full. Realizing what he had done, knowing that she was the first person he'd come to outside of his family after he'd made that decision? It was humbling.

While she had secretly dreamed of such a thing, she hadn't really thought John would choose her over his faith and his family's traditions. So it was a surprise, too. Actually, she felt a little like a child on Christmas morning who had been given a new pony but wasn't quite sure what to do with it.

She wanted to honor the moment by saying the right thing, to make John glad that he'd made such a big sacrifice. However, right at that moment, she wasn't sure if she could think of anything to say that would even come close to what his choice meant to her.

Then, she suddenly remembered something that Andy had said to her long ago, back when she'd been so scared to give Katie Steury one of her dolls for Christmas, thinking Katie or her parents would get mad at her. Andy had said that actions always meant more than words.

So, she stood, looped her hands around John's shoulders, and gave him a hug.

When he immediately hugged her back, she relaxed against him. She'd done the right thing.

TWENTY-NINE

Katie paused, looking at everyone gathered in the room. Andy's relatives, friends, and neighbors. All the people who had loved him so much. Each one was dressed in black. But maybe they all no longer looked quite so ravaged by grief? Bracing herself, she continued, hoping her words would help them as much as they helped her.

Marie was in his arms. Though he was holding her against him and loved how she was relaxed and seemed pleased, John was a little dismayed.

To be honest, he'd expected a far different reaction. On his way over to her house, he'd imagined all kinds of things. Marie dissolving into a torrent of happy tears. Her gaping at him, obviously overwhelmed and overcome by what he was saying.

His favorite scenario had involved her talking a mile a minute, asking him a million questions, all interspersed with words of excitement and a whole lot of heartfelt words about how pleased she was about the changes he was willing to make in order to be by her side.

He'd even thought about her peppering his face with kisses, being so joyous that she couldn't contain herself.

Never had he thought that she'd simply stand in front of him for a few minutes, gaping at him. Or calmly walk into his arms and give him a hug.

Obviously, he should have given a little more thought about the way he told Marie about his decision.

He'd shocked her. Maybe made her upset. Nothing in his life had been more humbling. For all of his talk about being patient, it seemed he should have been a little more patient, waited a little bit longer.

Maybe even given her some warning.

All of a sudden he felt silly in his ball cap and jeans, like he was an imposter, or a little boy playing dress up. Maybe he looked silly. Turning embarrassed, John just wanted to walk back down her driveway. Go for a walk, but not go home yet.

Maybe he could go back to Will's creek and do a little bit more praying before he returned back home? He was going to need as much support as he could get for when he faced his family again. Both Amanda and Molly had sent him off with big smiles and dreamy expressions, loving the idea that true love conquered all.

Now he was going to have to tell them that Marie . . . well Marie was rather quiet about the whole thing. A knot formed in his stomach as he imagined what James and Anton would say to that.

Boy, his grandfather would probably act disappointed in him and call him back into his kitchen for another pep talk.

Striving to keep his voice a whole lot lighter than he felt inside, he pulled away and then stepped backward, giving them both some space.

"John?" Marie asked. "What's wrong?"

What was wrong was that nothing was feeling very right. He cleared his throat, hoping to sound less devastated and more . . . casual. "You know what? I think I'm gonna just head out."

Her green eyes widened. "Now?"

"Ah, *jah*. I mean, yes." Fumbling over each word, he glanced at her face again, then concentrated on a point just above her head. "It's obvious that you are stunned." Maybe disappointed. "I realize now that I well, um, rushed things a bit."

"Rushed what?" She looked completely confused.

Which was exactly how he was feeling.

"Marie, I think I was too hasty about telling you

about my decision." Boy, he was sounding stranger and stranger. So stiff and formal. He tried to smile. "You know, maybe I've put the cart before the horse or something."

Her eyes brightened. "You think you've put the cart before the horse when it comes to telling me about your news?"

Now he felt even more stupid. Because yep, only he would show up like an eager *Englischer* all while spouting Amish-themed analogies. He took another step back. "Never mind. Look. I'm sorry, Marie. I don't know what I was thinking."

All traces of amusement vanished. "You don't?"

"Obviously. So, how about this? I'll get on my way and give you some space. Then, um, tomorrow or the next day I'll come back and we can talk about our future." There he went again! "I mean, my future." And if she wanted to be in it. "You know what? How about we just forget the last fifteen minutes?"

"Oh, John. I don't think I am going to be able to do that."

His heart sank. He'd ruined everything between them before they'd even had a chance. "All right, then. I understand."

She shook her head as she stepped forward, reaching out and taking hold of his hand. "I can see we have a problem here."

Ah, yes. Yes, they did. "*Jah.* That is why—"

"No, I don't think you understand what I'm getting at, John," she said, her eyes brightening again. "You see, what you just said to me, and what . . . well . . ." She waved a hand at his clothes. "What you have done . . . What you intend to do . . ." Her voice drifted off.

Feeling a small kernel of hope, he ran a finger along one of her knuckles. "Finish your thought, Marie. I'm afraid I need to hear the words."

"All right." She inhaled and smiled at him brightly. "What I'm trying to say, even though I'm terribly tongue-tied, is that what you have done is one of the most meaningful things anyone has ever done for me."

Meaningful sounded good. But it wasn't really saying that she liked what he'd done, now was it? Or that she wanted to spend the rest of her life living with him. "I'm glad you aren't mad."

"John, I'm the opposite of that! I'm floored. I'm amazed. I'm so, so happy that I can hardly form any words." She grinned at him. "Obviously."

"You really mean that?"

"Of course."

Now he felt tongue-tied. "Ah. Well, then. *Danke.*"

She stepped closer to him. "I don't think you're supposed to do that anymore."

Her perfume floated around her again, teasing him, making it difficult to concentrate. "What shouldn't I do?"

"Speak Pennsylvania Dutch," she said softly as she reached out a hand.

He curved his fingers around her own. Tugged her closer. It seemed his body was no more able to pull away from her than his heart was. "Marie?"

"You're going to have to practice speaking English a lot more, since, you know, I don't know much Amish."

Finally her words were sinking in. "Because?"

She stepped even closer, so close that her blouse was brushing against his shirt. So close that their arms were sliding against each other. So close that he could smell the mint shampoo in her hair and the flowery lotion she rubbed into her skin. "Because I'm not going to let you leave just yet, John Byler." Her voice turned husky. "Just like I'm not gonna let you take back a single word that you just said."

"Is that right?"

"Yep. You might as well face it, John. You're my boyfriend now."

No, he was more than that. He was simply just hers.

Maybe he should have pulled out more words from

his head. Attempted to tell her how much her acceptance of what he was doing meant to him.

But they'd talked enough.

Instead, he bent down and claimed her lips again. Kissed her softly. When she wrapped her arms around his neck and pressed closer, he curved his own arms around her waist and kissed her some more in an attempt to show her how precious she was to him. How much she meant to him.

Marie responded in much the same way, seeming just as eager as he was to seal what had happened.

When he at last lifted his head, he looked down into her eyes. Her eyelids were a little lower, and she had a soft expression in her face that he'd only seen once before—when he'd kissed her in the cornfield.

Suddenly, he hoped another person would never see that expression. He wanted it to be his own.

Even though it looked like she would step into his arms again with only the slightest bit of encouragement, he dropped her hands. "Sit down, Marie, and we'll talk."

"You only want to talk now?"

He smiled. "*Nee*. But I think we need to put some space between us before things get out of control. No, I mean before I get out of control."

Looking bemused, she nodded. "All right, John."

Sitting across from her, he made a mental note to remember that if he really needed Marie to do something, all he had to do was kiss her and then admit that he wanted to do more than that.

Since it now seemed that they might have many more moments like this in their future, he planned to put that plan to good use.

No matter what John said, she knew he wasn't the only person who was struggling for control. It felt like they'd been waiting for this moment for most of their lives.

When they'd been little, she'd always wanted to be near him because he was nice and had never made fun of the frilly sundresses her mother used to make her wear. Later, when they were young teenagers, she used to admire how steady and quiet he was. So many boys in her classes at school bragged too much or made too many jokes at the expense of others.

Then, when they were sixteen, everything between them had changed again. He'd gotten so handsome, and sometimes she'd even catch him watching her. They'd begun lightly flirting and would always seek to sit next to each other when the Eight got together.

She'd spent many a lazy afternoon dreaming of doing more than flirting. To imagine that there could one day be more to them than something clandestine or fleeting.

Leaning toward him, she said, "Tell me everything, John. What did your family say? Are they upset with you?" Suddenly worried, she blurted, "Are they upset with me?"

His eyebrows rose. "Why would they be upset with you?"

Because he'd done this to be with her. Because he'd known that she would never have made such a sacrifice for him. "You know," she hedged. "Because you're changing."

"Well, they ain't thrilled, I'll tell you that. But they don't seem to think it's the end of the world either."

"Really?"

He nodded. "I wouldn't lie about this."

"What happens now?"

"I'm afraid whatever happens in our future is up to you."

"I meant for you. For your life at your home. Do you have to move out?"

He hesitated. "My parents haven't said anything, but I think that would be best. I'm going to need to make some changes. That's going to be hard, and I don't want to disrespect them by adopting new things in front of them."

She nodded. Everything he was saying made sense. "Do you know where you're going to look for a place? I would invite you here, but I don't think that would be a good idea."

He laughed. "I don't think so either." He shrugged. "I'll look around tomorrow and make a choice. It's not really that important to me right now."

John was making it all sound so easy, but she knew it was anything but. No matter how close he was to his parents and siblings, there was no denying that he was going to be different now. They'd never be able to go back, either.

"Let me know how I can help you." Realizing something, she said, "If you need help with a loan or something, I could help you at the bank."

"I'll be okay. I have a bank account, Marie."

"Of course you do. You know I'm just flustered."

"Because you weren't ready?" he asked softly. "Or maybe you didn't want me to go English?"

Wanting to do justice to his question, she spent a moment thinking about it, then said, "John, I kind of feel like I had a dream for all my life that I wanted to happen but was sure that it never would. And now, suddenly, it has all become true. Part of me is afraid to open my eyes wide. If I do, maybe I'll realize that it's all just a dream."

"I might have been the man you've been dreaming about, Marie, but I ain't no figment of your imagination."

"Ah. There you are. Still the same, full-of-yourself man that I've always known." Getting to her feet, she said, "Maybe things haven't changed all that much between us after all."

Getting to his feet as well, he said, "I hope not."

"What do you want to do now? I guess we could go look at apartments."

"How about you go put on some clothes that you can relax in, and then we sit down on your couch and watch TV?"

"That's it?"

"It sounds like a good idea to me. You need to relax, I need to become more English."

"And you think hanging out on the couch and watching television is an English activity?"

"It for sure ain't Amish, Marie." He picked up her now-empty plate. "Go change now."

"I can handle my plate."

"I need to practice putting it in the dishwasher, right?"

Shaking her head at his teasing, Marie walked back

to her bedroom and got ready to put on old leggings and an oversized T-shirt.

Spending a couple of hours curled next to John while they watched mindless shows sounded like heaven.

After all, they had far more important things on their minds.

THIRTY

"He said that one day all of us were going to look back on that afternoon and be glad for it. He said that what made life memorable wasn't when everything went so right that it was easy . . . it was when everything felt so wrong that the only thing to do was accept it for what it was—a memory in the making."

"Miss, can you help me, please?"

Molly turned to the English man who'd just called out, hoping that he hadn't noticed that she'd been staring into space for at least five minutes. "Of course. What do you need?"

Looking completely confused, he held up a pair of cookbooks. One was a Martha Stewart book, the other from Betty Crocker. "Do you know anything about these?"

He seemed nice. He looked to be about the age of James or John and had kind-looking brown eyes. "Beyond that they're both cookbooks?" she teased.

He smiled. "Yeah. Beyond that."

"Well, I know a little bit about them." Her mother didn't really use cookbooks but had never minded if Molly tried out new recipes from time to time. Enjoying the various authors' stories and all the pictures, Molly had sat down and skimmed through all of the cookbooks at one time or another. "What is your question? I'll help if I can."

"I'm trying to make a meal for my girlfriend. I don't know which one to use, though. I've heard of Martha Stewart, but some of the ingredients in her recipes are unfamiliar. Some of them look complicated, too."

"Well, now. I'm no cooking expert, but I think Martha Stewart might have more difficult recipes. Are you a good cook?"

"Not exactly." He looked at her, almost as if he thought she was going to laugh about that. When she didn't, he continued. "I can make simple things. You know, grill. And I can make eggs and bacon." He brightened. "And a lasagna."

"Lasagna is *gut*."

He nodded. "I thought so. But my Melissa is a great cook. I don't think she's going to be too impressed by my lasagna." Looking at the two books that were now spread out on the table in front of him, he murmured, "I know she likes Martha Stewart. Do you think she makes an easy lasagna?"

Molly thought Martha Stewart would probably make a very delicious lasagna with fresh-from-the-garden sauce and homemade noodles. "It sounds like you are planning a pretty nice supper. Are you, um, sure that it needs to be fancy?"

"Doesn't *fancy* mean 'special'?"

She couldn't help it, she laughed. "I'm Amish. We aren't real comfortable with fancy."

He smiled sheepishly. "I guess not. Anyway, I still want to do something special, something that she knows I went to a lot of trouble to do. We've been going out for a while now. Four months. I thought it was probably time to do something that meant something, you know?"

She nodded. "I'm thinking you could either check out both books and look at them at home on your own, or we could flip through a couple of the recipes together now. What do you think?"

"Do you really have time for that?"

"Of course I do. Helping patrons is my job."

He pointed to one of the higher tables. "Let's go over them and figure this out."

She laughed. "*Jah.* Let's figure out something for this Melissa."

Over the next fifteen minutes, they talked about the merits of chicken casseroles and Mexican enchiladas, and even something called beef Wellington, which needed goose liver pâté. After deciding that neither he nor his Melissa liked that, they decided on a whole meal from the Betty Crocker cookbook.

They even got out some scraps of paper and marked the pages for a chicken casserole with spinach and wild rice, a green salad with homemade dressing, and a pan of brownies because Melissa was a real fan of chocolate.

When they finished, Craig—they were now on a first-name basis—held up his hand. "Give me a high-five."

She chuckled as she playfully slapped her palm against his. "*Gut* job, Craig. It's a mighty fine meal."

He grinned at her. "Thanks for your help, Molly. I couldn't have done the planning without you."

Molly didn't know if she'd ever gotten as nice a compliment as that at work. "You are welcome. Take your time and don't worry too much. Cooking is easy if you can follow directions."

He handed her the Martha Stewart cookbook. "Would you mind putting this one away? I don't think I'm ready for Martha yet."

"I'll be happy to. Good luck with your supper. I hope Melissa enjoys it."

"I hope so, too." Just as he turned away, he said,

"Hey, thanks for helping me. I . . . well, you really helped a lot. At first, I was sure you were going to think it was kind of weird that a guy like me was trying to learn to cook."

"A guy like you?"

He waved a hand over his jeans and dark red T-shirt that Molly now realized had CAMERON AND SONS emblazoned across the front. "You know. I probably look like just a dumb construction worker."

She shook her head. "I think you look like a man who cares enough about his girlfriend to step out of his comfort zone." Taking a chance, she admitted, "I was just glad my wheelchair didn't make you think that I wouldn't be of use."

Two lines formed on his forehead. "What? Like that you can't cook because you're in a chair?"

"Well, *jah*."

He smiled softly. "I'd never think that." When she must have still looked skeptical, he leaned down a little closer. "See, my Melissa? She's in a wheelchair, too."

Before Molly could respond, he winked and walked toward the checkout desk. Seconds later, he was out the door, a spring in his step that might just be from his plans to make that Betty Crocker supper.

Realizing she was still holding the cookbook he'd

decided against, she turned her chair to the right and headed over to the cookbook aisle.

She put it neatly away, thinking all the while that the conversation she'd had with that man had been rather eye-opening. He had been waiting for her to question his goals, and she had been expecting him to think that she couldn't help him plan his menu because either he hadn't thought she was knowledgeable enough in the library or probably didn't cook.

But none of those things had happened. Instead, they'd proved each other wrong.

"What was going on with that man?"

She turned her head and was surprised to see Danny standing at the end of the aisle. "I didn't hear you approach. Hiya, Danny."

"Hi back." Still looking at her intently, he said, "Do you know that man well?"

"Um, *nee*. I don't know Craig well at all."

"But you know his name?"

"We were planning supper for his girlfriend. It took a while, so we introduced ourselves." What was going on? He was sure acting odd.

"Oh."

Searching his face, she tried to guess what he was thinking then gave up. She shrugged. "What are you doing here?"

"Obviously, I came here to talk to you."

"That don't seem all that obvious to me, Danny. You made your point about how you felt about me pretty clear the other afternoon."

He stuffed his hands in his pockets. "Yeah. Well, about that. I have started to think that maybe I was a bit harsh with you."

"You were more than that. You made me feel pretty bad, Danny."

"You're so sweet. I didn't expect you to argue with me."

"Discovering that I have a mind of my own is what upset you?"

He nodded. "*Jah*." He stopped. "*Nee*! I mean, no." Looking pained, he finished. "I mean, I don't know." Danny sighed. "I don't know what's gotten into me, Molly. I thought I knew everything I believed in. But after getting to know you better? I'm starting to realize that I didn't actually know anything at all."

Hearing him flustered did more to repair the damage that their argument had done than a sweetly worded apology would have. To her, his unease meant this relationship was just as new and foreign to him as it was to her. And that, of course, made her feel like in this area, at least, they were on the same footing.

"I know you're close with your brother. Surely with your parents, too?" She searched his face. "Aren't you used to not agreeing with people you care about all the time?"

Instead of answering, he smiled. "Are you saying that you care about me, Molly?"

Oh, boy. She sure walked into that one! She figured she could either fib and say she didn't mean anything or tell him the truth. "Of course I do."

He smiled at her. "I care about you, too."

Even though she was sure she was bright red, she didn't dare look away. She wanted to remember everything about this moment.

"Molly, I stopped by your house earlier and talked to your mother."

"You talked to my *mamm?*" Dread and embarrassment started circling in her head. "What about?"

"You. I mean about courting you."

"You did?" She was pretty sure her voice was squeaking.

"*Jah.* I told her that though I like coming to your house, I want to take you out to do other things, too."

"What did she say?"

He smiled at her. "Your *mamm* told me that it wasn't up to her, it was up to you."

Molly didn't know whether to laugh or cover her face in embarrassment. "Wow," she murmured. Because, well, what else could she say?

Looking pleased, Danny stuffed his hands in his

pockets. "So, um I was thinking . . . could you ever ride in a courting buggy?"

He wanted to take her for a ride in a courting buggy! "Sure," she said quickly, just as she realized what he was asking. He was asking if she *could* ride in one. Not if she wanted to.

Luckily, though Molly didn't have much romantic experience, she had quite a bit of practice discussing her physical needs. "Danny, are you asking how to go about moving me?"

He nodded. "I don't know how much of you is paralyzed. I don't want to hurt you." He lowered his voice. "Should I not be mentioning anything like that? Is it too personal?"

"Not at all." She shrugged, hoping to make their awkward conversation a little easier. "I've had to deal with my disability since I was nine, Danny. You wouldn't believe the conversations I've had to have about my body." Realizing that he was looking even more embarrassed, she laughed softly. "I'm sorry. I guess I should also say that the majority of these conversations have been with my siblings."

"No. No, I want to be able to talk to you about this. If, you know, you don't mind."

She realized then that Mrs. Laramie was looking over at them. No doubt she was wondering when Molly was going to get back to work! "Would you mind if we talked about this later? It's kind of personal and I am supposed to be working."

Now he was the one with bright red cheeks. "Oh. *Jah*, sure."

"*Danke*."

Leaning down so they were eye to eye, he said, "How about I come to your house tonight and we talk?"

"If you come at five, you could join us for supper."

Danny's dark eyes looked panicked. "I'm not ready to share a meal with your whole family yet. I'll be there at six."

She chuckled. "I don't blame you for wanting to dodge a meal with them. Come over at six and I'll save you some dessert."

He smiled at her before turning away. She watched him leave before turning her chair toward the main circulation desk.

When she stopped at the front of it, she saw that Mrs. Laramie was watching her with a smile. "Looks like you've got an admirer, Molly."

Everything about him felt too new to share, especially with her boss. "Danny is nice. We're friends."

"Friends? Well, that's nice."

It was actually more than nice. In a way, it was kind of remarkable. It was remarkable that someone she'd always had feelings for suddenly liked her back.

Almost like the Lord was gifting her for being so patient.

Mrs. Laramie was still smiling at her. "I also noticed that you helped one very appreciative patron. He couldn't sing your praises high enough when he checked out his cookbook."

That, Molly could talk about. "He was funny. He wanted to make a fancy dinner for his girlfriend but couldn't really cook. We planned out a menu from the Betty Crocker cookbook."

"I'm glad you were there to help him. Not every employee here likes doing things like that."

"I do. It was fun. He was mighty eager. Like a puppy."

Mrs. Laramie chuckled. "He told everyone around the desk about his menu. Good job."

Molly smiled. It was tempting to share his compliment, or maybe even that his girlfriend was also wheelchair bound, but that all sounded too prideful. "What would you like me to work on now?"

Her boss pointed to the clock. "Go pick out a children's book. It's almost story time."

She loved reading with the preschoolers. "*Danke*, Mrs. Laramie," she said as she started guiding her wheelchair to the children's section.

"Enjoy yourself. And brace yourself for all those hugs."

Molly smiled to herself as she wheeled over to choose two books for the story time. The last time she'd read, she'd answered almost as many questions about her wheelchair as she had about the book. One little boy had even wanted to hop in her lap.

This library really was proving that almost anything could happen, if one had the right attitude.

THIRTY-ONE

"So even though it doesn't make a lot of sense, and maybe isn't even all that happy, that's the story about Andy that I wanted to share with you—a couple of hours when we were hurt, lost, soaking wet, and surrounded by kittens and felt like we only had each other to depend on.

"It was everything and it was nothing. Special and inconsequential. Easily forgotten yet completely memorable."

Later that night, when Danny realized who was answering the door at the Byler house, he bit back a groan. It wasn't that he didn't like Molly's brother John, it was that he seemed determined to go out of his way to make him uncomfortable.

But maybe this time would be different? All John did after he answered Danny's knock was stand back and let him inside.

Ironically, that made him feel more ill at ease. "Hi," he said. "I'm here to see Molly. Is she home?"

"*Jah*. Come on in."

"*Danke*." He noticed then that John wasn't dressed Amish. He had on a soft oxford and faded jeans. Unable to help himself, he stared.

Before Danny could ask John about his unusual outfit, John kind of half-smiled. "Well, if you're back, I guess we haven't scared you off yet."

Danny shook his head and looked him in the eye. "I've had to deal with a far sight more than protective older brothers at my *haus*. I'm glad you all care so much about Molly."

A glimmer of respect entered John's eyes. "What did you want to talk to Molly about?"

"Nothing special." Nothing that he wanted to talk to her brother about, that was.

"If it's nothing special, how come you came over, then?"

"John, you apologize right now," Mrs. Byler called out as she strode forward. "Now, if you please."

"Sorry, Danny," John said obediently, though it was obvious he wasn't sorry at all.

Danny shrugged. "Nothing to be sorry about." Turning to Molly's mom, he smiled. "Hiya, Mrs. Byler."

She smiled right back, making him realize that she really was one of the nicest ladies he'd ever met. "How are you today? Did you work at Newman's?"

"*Nee*. I was finishing up a job over at Marie's *haus*."

"John's Marie?"

John groaned. "Mamm."

"If you're moving heaven and earth to be with her, she'd better be your girl, son."

"Yes, Mamm."

Danny bit back a smile. He personally was hoping that John was feeling just as awkward as he was. "*Jah*, it was at Marie Hartman's *haus*, Mrs. Byler." It took just about everything he had not to say "John's Marie."

"You've done a great job with her yard. It looks a whole lot better," John said.

Hoping he didn't look as shocked as he felt, Danny said, "*Danke*. It wasn't hard."

"I would disagree. You've got a knack for it," John said, continuing to surprise him. "And it ain't easy, either, carving out flower beds in land that's been ignored for so long."

"I like working with the land."

"When do you go back again? Maybe I'll see you there."

"I don't know if I'll be over there anytime soon. Marie already paid me."

John smiled at him. "Hey, that's great."

Danny would have gaped at the man's reaction if his mother wasn't standing right there.

"Oh my stars," she said as she clasped her hands together. "I'm sorry again, Danny. He's a bit besotted with Marie."

"All I'm doing is making sure she is taken care of, Mamm."

"She's fine. And so is Molly."

He inhaled. "Now, Molly—"

Making a shooing motion, she said, "Go make yourself useful, John. Ezra needs a hand in the barn."

He hesitated before turning away.

She sighed. "You'll have to excuse him. He's a bit protective over our Molly. I guess we all are."

"I see." Was she trying to warn him off?

She smiled sweetly. "However, when I was speaking to your mother today, I realized that Molly couldn't be in better hands. You are a mighty grown-up seventeen-year-old."

Wait a minute. "You spoke to my mother?"

"*Jah.* She had a couple of questions. I guess she didn't tell you?"

"*Nee*, but I didn't see her when I got home." All he did was take a quick shower, change clothes, and grab an apple to eat on the way over to the Bylers' house. But, of course, even if he had seen his mother, they wouldn't have had much to say to each other.

"No matter. Molly will tell you everything I told your mother. Oh! And here she is now."

"Mamm, please tell me that everyone didn't wait to tell me Danny was here so you could talk to him first," Molly called out, diverting his attention.

Today she had on a bright royal blue dress and flip-flops on her feet. She looked pretty. Almost like she had also gotten cleaned up for his visit.

"Hey, Molly."

"Hiya, Danny. I'm sorry. I was going to try to wait at the door for you, but my sister took forever in the bathroom."

He laughed. "I was fine."

Mrs. Byler folded her hands in front of her chest. "Now that Molly is here, I'll leave you both alone. Go take him into the parlor, dear. I told Ezra to do his homework someplace else."

"He didn't care?"

"Of course not, seeing as how I didn't give him a choice," she said before walking away.

Molly sighed. "This is my life. I'm surrounded by way too many people all of the time. I bet you're never going to want to come back."

"I might."

Cheeks turning pink, she reached down to move her wheels. "Come on. Let's go where there's at least a little privacy."

After watching her move the wheels, he said, "Hey Mol?"

"Yes?"

"How about you let me push you?"

"There's no need," she said quickly, sounding flustered. "I'm pretty *gut* at getting myself around."

"Maybe I want to push you for a change."

"Um, all right."

Grasping the handles of her wheelchair, he started pushing, kind of liking the idea that he was helping her get somewhere. When they got to the room her mother mentioned, he sat down on a chair near where she'd motioned him to stop in front of.

"So, I heard John and my mother talking to you. What were they talking about?" she asked.

"I don't know. Marie Hartman and your brother."

"Isn't it something how they are together now?"

He nodded. "Does it bother you that he fell in love with an *Englischer*?"

"*Nee*. I think there's been a lot of things between them for a while now. Even my parents are glad that everything is out in the open."

Danny nodded. He could see that. He was slowly learning that things were a lot easier if people were honest instead of hiding secrets. Now that he was alone with Molly, he supposed that he should finally ask her to tell him about her life in a wheelchair. But how did he even start that conversation?

"Hey, Danny?"

"*Jah?*"

"Were . . . were you still wanting to understand more about my paralysis?"

"*Jah*. Can you talk about it? I mean, do you mind?"

She shook her head. "It's who I am. Talking about my legs and my paralysis doesn't upset me. I live with this all the time, you know."

Although she was acting like she wasn't self-conscious, he could tell that she was. Figuring it was better to simply get everything out in the open, he said, "So, you told me once that you have some feeling in your upper legs."

"I do. I didn't for about a year after my accident, but then I slowly regained some feeling there."

Her statement made him realize just how much he didn't know about her condition. "What does that mean?"

"Well, it's a good sign, especially since once it returned it didn't vanish again. For me, it means that they aren't steadily getting worse."

If they weren't getting worse, did that mean they could get better? "Does that mean you might one day walk again?"

"Well, um, not exactly."

"I don't understand."

"My doctor told me that some soldiers can get electrodes and all kinds of things to help their nerves and muscles work better. Some men and women are even able to walk a bit."

He was stunned. "Really?" Her news sounded like a miracle! But he was also confused as to why she didn't seem happier about it.

She smiled sadly. "I'm afraid that's never going to be me, though. We relied on lots of doctors and technology after the accident in order for me to survive. That was enough. Most likely, I'll spend the rest of my life in a wheelchair."

"Not to be mean, but do you ever want to change your mind?"

"To be able to walk around and look like everyone else? I'm not sure. Sometimes I think I would. Other times, I tell myself that I should be happy living the rest of my life in a chair."

"What does your family think?"

"They're supportive. By now, I think they realize that no matter what I decide to do, it's going to affect me a lot more than them." She looked just beyond him. "They're the best. I'm blessed to have such caring parents and siblings."

She was more blessed than she probably ever imagined. "If, say, we ever wanted to go for a buggy ride . . . could you do that?"

She nodded. "You would just have to lift me onto it."

Just thinking how he would do that made him wary. "Would your parents be okay with that?"

She laughed. "I understand that you are worried that it might be um . . . too personal, but I promise, it ain't like that. And I would help you."

"But . . ."

She laughed again. "Danny, how about we try this out? Come help me sit on that chair." She pointed to the dark blue lounger next to him.

He stood up and looked down at her. "What do I do first?"

"First, let me move my chair closer so you don't have to carry me too far."

He felt like telling her that he was strong and that lifting her wouldn't be too much for him at all. But he knew that wasn't what she wanted. So he stood to one side while she moved her chair to the side of the lounger and then popped the brake. Then, with her hands on the sides of the chair, she twisted her body.

"Danny, you can help me now. You can either put one arm under my thighs and the other around my waist and pull me off, or I can kind of wrap my arms around your neck, you hold me close, and then shift me from the wheelchair to the other chair."

He was scared of hurting her. "Which is easier for you?"

"Both are fine. I'll help you, I just need to be prepared for how you want to move me."

After eyeing Molly again and seeing her determined expression, he said, "How about we try the second way?"

"Sounds good. Bend down so I can loop my hands around your neck."

He leaned and she pressed her hands on his shoulders. He found himself closing his eyes, enjoying being so close to her.

"Danny, wrap your arms around my ribs and pull me up."

Forcing himself to get back on track, he placed his hands on either side of her, inhaled, and pulled her toward him.

But instead of feeling like he was lifting a dead weight, Molly was helping him.

"Now turn and put me down on the lounger."

Anxious to not hurt her, he did just that. Automatically, she used her arms to situate herself. When he leaned back, she smiled. "You did it."

"No, we did it."

"It wasn't so hard, was it?" Her voice was chipper, like he was a child and she was spurring him on.

He smiled. "I think it only took a minute or two."

"My brothers are so used to moving me around, it

hardly takes any time. Half the time I get into chairs by myself."

"You can do that?"

She nodded. "It's not always graceful in a dress, but it gets done."

She was being so upbeat, but still, thinking about how much she'd had to learn to deal with made him sad. "I guess it does."

"Oh, no." Looking stricken, she said, "Was this all too much? Did . . . did I gross you out or something?"

He was shocked. "Why would you think that?"

"What we just did is a big reminder about my handicap. Some people don't want to be around people who aren't whole."

"Well, you certainly are whole. Don't talk about yourself like that."

Her eyes widened. "All right."

He pulled over a ladder-back chair and sat down next to her. "Molly, you know I like you. It's . . . just that, well, sometimes I feel like I must seem like a little kid around you. You are able to discuss all of this so easily."

"I have to be able to do that. It's my life."

"I wish I had your confidence sometimes. I'm still trying to figure out my life and my future."

"Danny, I might know how to deal with my handicap, but that doesn't mean I have everything about my future figured out. I'm fumbling around, too."

He shook his head. "*Nee*, I feel more selfish."

"Danny, just because I've had a lot of surgeries and doctor visits doesn't mean that I'm any more mature when it comes to the rest of my life. Not like you are."

"Why would you say that?"

"Well, I know you have always looked after your brother." She swallowed. "Because, um, of your parents." When he gaped at her, she blushed. "Sorry, I guess I shouldn't have mentioned them."

He looked down at his hands. "It's no secret that my family ain't like yours, Molly." His parents didn't fight and they weren't mean to him and his brother. But it was clear—especially when he was someplace like the Byler house—that it wasn't a very happy house.

"It must have been hard, wishing your parents were happier."

It was hard, coming to terms with the realization that his parents weren't ever going to be happier. Or more giving. Or less selfish. "Like you, I've come to terms with it. You have gotten used to your limitations, and I've gotten used to the fact that being in my *haus* is going to be anything but a place to sleep until I'm old enough to get my own place."

"What about your little brother?"

"Samuel has always seemed kind of lost. I've tried to help him, but even a pretty good brother can't fill in all the gaps, you know? He's been acting up since he was old enough to act up. Right now I just hope he stays around until next May, when he finishes the eighth grade."

"Then?"

"Then I bet he'll find someone to help him move on."

"Maybe the bishop could do something?" Her voice was full of hope, thick with the belief that good things could still happen if a person really wanted them to.

As much as he hated to dispel her hopes, Danny shook his head. "Sam doesn't want to stay around here, Molly. Too much has happened, and he's too unhappy."

"But maybe if you talk to him, you could convince him to try some more." Hesitantly, she said, "I mean, it ain't the same, but I wasn't always all right with me being like this." Her voice thick with emotion, she said, "I had to give up a lot of dreams after I woke up in the hospital. I had to reimagine my future. It was hard."

Looking at the pained expression in Molly's eyes, Danny once again realized that he'd mistaken Molly's quiet ways and generally even temper as one of complacency. Or maybe he'd imagined her to be perpetually optimistic.

He'd never fully imagined how hard it must have been for her. How difficult and painful her surgeries had been.

"I'm sorry I never thought about what you'd gone through."

She shook her head impatiently. "*Nee*, this isn't about me, Danny. I'm trying to tell you that the Lord has given all of us times when things are hard and painful. But just because He has, it doesn't mean that it's not a *gut* idea to stick it out."

"I believe you. I think I agree, too. But that ain't the same with Sam." When she continued to look at him with her wide eyes, he murmured, "See, Molly, you could get through your accident because you have faith and the knowledge that there are lots of people who love you and will help you. Sam doesn't have that."

"But doesn't he have you?"

"I'm seventeen, not twenty-seven."

"But, still you could do something."

"I've been trying." Gathering himself together, he forced himself to continue. Made himself reveal his weaknesses. "But don't you hear what I'm saying? Everything that Sam has been going through? I went through it, too."

"Oh, Danny." Her eyes had filled with tears.

He knew he couldn't handle sharing his secrets and her tears at the same time. "Don't cry for me."

She sniffed. "I'm trying not to. But I feel so badly for you."

"Molly, like you said, we each have our own hardships and pain. That's why I made peace with the fact that I'm not going to try to force Sam to stay if he doesn't want to."

"But anything can happen. Doesn't what happened to Evan not scare him?"

After glancing at the door, he lowered his voice. "I think what happened with your brother's friend Andy Warner scares him more, Molly."

"Why?"

She looked so sweet. So completely confused, he almost didn't want to be completely honest. He would have liked to let her keep her innocence. "Because for people like me and Samuel, the only thing worse than being in the situation that we're in is knowing that there's no hope for the future. As bad as things have been at our house, it would be worse if Sam thought he couldn't hope for anything better."

Molly sighed. "I understand now."

"*Gut*. So, can we just hang out? Maybe play a game or cards or something?"

"*Jah.* Over in that cabinet are some board games. Pick one out and we'll play."

As Danny got to his feet to retrieve a game, he realized he felt ten pounds lighter. He'd never intended to reveal so much.

But maybe it was time he did.

THIRTY-TWO

"It was exactly like Andy said." Katie opened her mouth to say more, to try to explain why that memory was so dear to her, but she couldn't seem to form the words.

As quietly as he'd approached, John turned and walked down the hall, Danny's words echoing in his ears.

He'd intended to simply ask Molly and Danny if they wanted anything. He, James, Mamm, and Daed had all gotten to talking in the kitchen and lost track of time. After thirty minutes or so, Daed had remembered that no one had checked on Molly since she and Danny had entered the back parlor.

John had volunteered to go check on them, mainly because he'd been feeling restless, waiting for Marie to get home.

But hearing the tail end of their conversation had left him stunned.

Never had he imagined that Danny had been fighting his own demons or carried his own burdens that might be too hard for him to bear. Though he was older and supposedly grown up, John had behaved like a spoiled child around him, only caring about himself and his feelings. He was going to need to apologize to Danny one day very soon.

The conversation also gave him something to think about in terms of Andy's death. He and the rest of the Eight had been having such a hard time, he hadn't thought about everyone else who had been affected by the tragedy.

And then there was Molly's sharing of how hurt and upset she'd been about her paralysis. Though, of course, he'd known she wasn't glad to be in a wheelchair, he realized that he and the rest of the family had stopped talking about it, thinking she was fine, or that at the very least, she'd come to terms with it.

Now he realized that all their silence had done was make her feel like she couldn't share her feelings. Feeling more confused than ever, John knew if he stayed at home and kept silent, he would feel like his head was going to explode.

Needing to be around any one of the Eight, he quickly told his parents that Molly and Danny were fine, then walked out the back door, grabbed his bike, and rode down to Will's house.

He discovered Will sitting by the fire pit on the side of his parents' house. And he wasn't alone. Logan, Katie, Kendra, and Harley were there. And, to his surprise, so was Marie.

They looked as surprised to see him as he was to see them all gathered together—without his knowledge.

Even though he shouldn't, he felt a little hurt. "Did we have something planned that I forgot about?"

"*Nee,*" Katie said. "Kendra and I were bored so we came over here to see what Will and his sister were doing."

"I had just come over," Logan said.

"And I was over here doing some work for Mr. Kurtz," Harley explained.

Marie shrugged. "I was driving home and saw Kendra's bike in the front, so I took a chance and stopped over. Being with them seemed better than being alone."

Walking to her side, he said, "I feel much the same way."

When she smiled up at him, John's turbulent emotions finally eased. Being with her was right. Planning a future with her felt right, too.

"You okay?" she whispered.

"*Jah.*" Needing some kind of connection, he stared at her lips. Would Marie get mad if he bent down and lightly kissed her? Surely not.

Now, the others might be shocked or even tease them. But did that really matter? Maybe . . .

"John B., now that you know all about us, tell us what's going on with you," Will called out, dispelling his train of thought. "Why are you here?"

He stood up and looked at the lot of them, gathered round. Harley and Will were sitting on closed coolers with Kendra. Katie was sprawled on a lounge chair next to Marie.

"What is going on?" she whispered to him.

How could he put into words everything that was going through his head?

When he hesitated, Katie shifted on her lounge chair and smiled up at him. "Will, it could be he's only here because of Marie." She winked at the others. "Word is out that John is now a mini-*Englischer* and only has thoughts of Marie these days."

Looking down at his jeans and T-shirt, he laughed. "I *canna* deny that."

As he'd hoped, Marie's expression softened, and the rest of them chuckled.

Harley stood up and opened the large Igloo cooler he'd been sitting on. "You want something to drink? I've got some water bottles inside. A couple of sodas, too."

"I'm all right. *Danke*."

Even in the dim light, he could tell that Kendra was eyeing him closely. "If you don't want to tell us, I understand. But talking about it might make you feel better."

He knew enough about Kendra to know that she kept quite a bit to herself. He hoped one of these days she would trust one of them enough to let her guard down. Realizing that he actually did trust these people more than anyone else in the world, he spoke. "I overheard something this evening. I was . . . well, I was eavesdropping on my little sister."

"Amanda or Molly?" Marie asked.

"Molly."

Kendra winced. "Oh, John."

"I didn't say I was proud of it. Anyway, I overheard the boy she has been seeing talk about Andy's death."

Harley frowned. "What was Danny saying?"

John paused. "How did you know my sister was seeing Danny?"

"It wasn't hard to see. They were together at the Fall Festival, remember?"

"What did Danny say?" Will asked.

John chose his words with care, wanting to do justice to Danny's words. "He's worried about his brother, Sam. I guess their home life ain't so good, and while Danny has dealt with it by being outgoing and taking on extra work, his little brother has been holding all his hurt and anger inside. Danny said his brother is only biding his time until he is old enough to leave. When Molly questioned that, he said . . ." John paused, gathered himself, and then blurted, "Danny said that Sam doesn't want to end up like Andy. So unhappy that he takes his own life."

He could practically feel the hurt float off of each person surrounding him.

"That was pretty harsh of Danny to say," Katie said.

"I would agree, except I started thinking that maybe all of us, or maybe some of us, have been hurting but keeping all that pain inside because we didn't think the others wanted to see us fall apart."

New tension filled the air, making him uneasy. He started talking faster. "All I meant is that I've really missed Andy. I can't think of the number of times I've started to go by his house and then stopped myself. Or thought of a joke that he would like. His death has created a gap in my world. A fissure. And sometimes? Well, sometimes, I feel like crying."

"We all do," Harley said.

"*Nee*, I'm not done. I'm trying to tell ya that sometimes I just feel angry. I feel like yelling at Andy. I feel like telling him that he shouldn't have kept everything inside. That I would have listened. That any of us would have helped him. That . . . that he didn't have to kill himself."

Shocked that he'd said those words, shocked that he'd actually talked about being angry, he felt his cheeks flush and a hard knot form in his throat. He inhaled several times, trying to catch his breath.

He kept waiting for one of them to say that he wasn't the only one feeling that way. But the only sound he heard was the faint chirp of crickets from the field nearby.

As the silence continued, John lowered his head. "I'm sorry. I guess I was imagining things. I mean, let's just forget about—"

"Marie's crying," Kendra said, her own voice thick with emotion.

He stepped toward her. "Marie?"

She held up a hand, as if trying to act like she was okay, but then that hand flew up to her face as she cried harder.

Just as he knelt by her side, a hundred recriminations filled him. What had he just done?

THIRTY-THREE

"I remember everything that happened that day, too," Marie said, standing up. Glancing at her mother, she smiled. "Of course, I do have a pretty good scar from that surgery on my ankle as a reminder."

Kneeling by Marie's side, John felt his eyes fill with tears as he rubbed her back. Seeing her this way was almost physically painful for him.

Their Marie Hartman, the girl who had always seemed to have control, the woman who usually took everything in stride, was now crying uncontrollably. Her usual posture, so confident, so poised, was crumbled. She didn't even seem to notice the tears that were falling down her cheeks in thick rivulets.

He glanced at Kendra, Katie, and the other men. Kendra and Katie were now standing next to Harley and Will. All four of them looked as surprised as he was about Marie's tears. They were also holding on to each other, too.

As hard as it had been to share what he had, John was glad he did. He now realized all of them had felt the same thing.

Looking at Marie, at the woman he knew he loved, John also knew he couldn't remain apart from her any longer.

"Ah, Marie," he murmured as he reached for her, sliding both of his hands along her arms, then shoulders, then gently pulling her closer. After a few seconds, she knelt down next to him. He responded by holding her even closer, practically positioning her in his lap.

She lifted her head, looking at him with an almost apologetic expression. "John?"

"Shh. Cry all you want, Marie," he murmured as he ran a hand down her back. "It's okay."

She relaxed against him and sniffed. A minute or two after, she placed her palms on his shoulders and looked into his eyes. "How did you know how I felt?"

"It was just like I said. I tried not to hurt, then I tried not to burden anyone else." Unable to help himself, he brushed back a chunk of her golden hair that had fallen over her eyes. The strands felt silky-soft. "I left my house, not even sure where I was headed. All I knew was that I wanted, no, *needed* someone to help me." He glanced at the others. "I guess God knew it was time, because he brought me to all of you."

Marie gave him a watery smile before slipping off

his lap and turning to the others. "Andy is gone, and it hurts so bad."

Will walked to her side and sat down next to her on the bench. "He still comes to my dreams almost every night. I both love the sight of him and dread it, too. Every time I see that smile of his, I feel like I'm losing Andy all over again."

Kendra and Harley returned to their places. Katie returned to her lounge chair and gestured to an empty chair for John. He sat down, too, completing their circle.

"I started crying at the grocery store the other day," Katie whispered. "There I was, minding my own business, when I turned the corner and saw a display of those dumb Twizzlers."

Harley cleared his throat. "John, I've had questions, too. Over and over I asked myself why he felt he had no other options but death. Why didn't Andy talk to us? Why didn't he trust me?" he continued, his voice strained. "Did he not realize I would have dropped everything in order to help him? I wish I could have been a better friend."

Kendra was sitting with her hands wrapped around her middle. "My thoughts are always more selfish. I always want to yell at him. To make him understand that I needed him."

"I thought Andy knew all that." John swallowed,

forcing himself to utter words he'd only admitted to himself. "But maybe there was more going on with him that he never shared with anyone. Maybe our friendship wasn't enough. Maybe even our love for him wasn't enough."

"I wish it would have been," Marie whispered.

John tried to think of the right words to say. Tried to think of anything to help ease Marie's pain.

To ease all of their sorrow.

But he couldn't. Weeks ago, he'd told himself that his sadness didn't really matter. That his feelings of loss could never compare to Andy's parents' grief, or to his sister Tricia's pain.

And because of that, he'd persuaded himself that he didn't deserve to feel so left out and left behind.

But perhaps, like so many things, he'd been wrong.

He licked his lips, trying to generate some moisture in his mouth. Anything to help make the words come more easily. "Andy was our leader. That is true. I always saw him as something bright and shiny, like a new penny."

Half speaking to himself because he really had no idea if he was making any sense, he said, "Have you ever seen those bright, shiny pennies? The ones where the copper is so light that you hate to even put your fingers on it because you know you'll tarnish it right away? But then you take hold of it anyway because you justify it, saying to yourself that it wasn't worth much anyway. So it don't really matter?"

He didn't look to see if the others understood, because he wasn't even sure if he understood where his words were coming from.

"To me, that was what Andy was like. Better than I imagined. Shiny, new . . . so perfect. Someone I always wanted to be around." John swallowed. "Now I realize that he was just as fragile as one of those shiny new pennies. He wasn't meant to stay shiny and perfect, because none of us are. As the years pass, we begin to look a little worn, a little tarnished by life and age and hurts."

Katie squinted, almost as if she was trying to picture a slightly tarnished Andy Warner. "Perhaps he didn't like how life had changed him."

"Maybe. I don't really know. I do know that all our marks and tarnishes and luster make us better on the inside. But sometimes those improvements aren't any easier to see."

"Even if he wasn't the same, I still wanted him in my life," Will said.

"I did, too," Harley murmured. "All of us did."

After a moment, Marie swiped her eyes. Let out a ragged sigh. Looked at him in the eye and kind of smiled. "Yeah, for all the tarnish of this situation, he still left a beautiful mark on us, didn't he?" She tucked her chin and swiped beneath her eyes again.

John knew what she was doing—attempting to clean up the mascara that had run under her eyes. He wished she hadn't been brought up to be so aware of herself. He knew he'd spend the rest of his life showing her that she was always beautiful to him no matter what. Even now, it wasn't her tear-stained cheeks that drew his eye but her vulnerability.

That was what was so dear to him. That was why she was his Marie.

"I saw Mrs. Warner at the drugstore a couple of days ago," Will said. "She . . . well, I think she was picking up some prescriptions for herself. I don't think she's been sleeping."

"What did you say to her?" Marie asked.

"When she saw me, she ducked her head, like she was embarrassed not to be all put together. But when I hugged her, she started crying, saying that she missed Andy." His voice lowered. "And she misses how things used to be."

John felt the back of his throat clench. He realized then that tears were threatening him, too. "I haven't gone to see Mr. and Mrs. Warner in weeks. I probably should."

"As soon as I got home, I told my *mamm*," Will added. "She said she was going to call on Mrs. Warner as soon as she was able."

"We can remind everyone else to visit, too," Katie said. "Maybe those visits will help Andy's parents remember that they're not alone." Suddenly looking stricken, she added, "Or maybe it won't."

Will shrugged. "But at least we'll have tried."

John nodded. When he noticed that Harley was wiping his eyes and looking embarrassed about his tears, he said, "I think it's all right for us to still be sad and to still be angry and missing him, too. We aren't shiny pennies, either."

"Not by a long shot," Will said.

As more thoughts bubbled to the surface, John forced himself to share. "I've also been thinking some about how much guilt I've placed upon myself."

"You've felt guilty, too?" Katie asked.

He nodded. "I kept thinking that I should have tried harder to stay in touch with Andy. That I should have known that he was different, that he was suffering. But it would have been impossible to read his mind."

"Every time we talked, he sounded like he was fine." Katie bent her head. "The last time we had any kind of lengthy conversation, it was all about Tricia and Logan."

Harley smiled softly. "Andy wasn't real pleased with one of his best friends spending so much time with his little sister."

"It even caught me off guard," Will said. "When

we talked, I told Andy that, then we both agreed that Logan's intentions were good and that it was out of our hands. We ended the conversation kind of laughing because we realized we sounded like doting parents."

"Maybe that's our answer then," John said.

"What is?" Katie asked.

"That even though we all miss Andy terribly, we can't change how things were . . . or turn back time. Even though we're all good friends, none of us are the same people we used to be. And I might be wrong, but I think Andy would have been the first person to agree with me."

Marie slowly smiled. "No, he would have said you would have been foolish to even try to make things the way they used to be."

"*Nee*, he would've said you were stupid as a bag of rocks for wanting that," Will corrected with a low laugh. "Andy never said words like *foolish* a day in his life."

Two tears slipped out of Marie's eyes as she started laughing again.

Next thing he knew, all of them were laughing. Minutes later, Harley was passing around sodas and Will was adding wood to the fire.

Marie got up and moved next to John. She relaxed against him as they all started sharing stories about things that had happened back when they were just kids.

As the sky got darker and filled with stars, John wrapped an arm around Marie's shoulders. Held her close.

And simply gave thanks for the moment. Even in the darkest of times, there was always a glimmer of light.

THIRTY-FOUR

John stood up and joined Marie. Then Logan, Elizabeth Anne, and Harley. Will walked right to Katie's side and threw an arm over her shoulders.

"Andy was a lot of things," he said quietly. "But what I can promise each of you is that Andy will never be just a memory to us. He'll always be our leader and our friend. Because of Andy, we'll never really be a group of seven. No matter what happens in our futures, we will always be Eight."

Thanks to the recent rain, the ground was soft. Too soft for her heels. Every time she stopped, the tips of her heels sank in, and then she'd kind of have to pull them out before taking another step.

Shaking her head at herself, Marie walked down the line of headstones on the balls of her feet, hoping that she didn't look ridiculous.

When they were about halfway to Andy's marker, John looked down at her. "What are you doing?"

"Trying not to sink my heels into the ground."

"Oh."

It was another one of those moments when their different cultures showed loud and bright. Of course, John didn't have any experience dealing with women navigating surfaces in high heels. Well, not until they had become a couple. "I wish I would have thought about how soft the ground was. I would've worn flats."

"Why don't you take them off?"

"John, I can't."

"Why not? Andy wouldn't care." She hesitated another couple of steps before an image of Andy, one from long ago, ran in her mind. The two of them had been juniors in high school, looking for all the world like two stars of the place. Andy, with his classic good looks and easy smile, she with her mother's ambitions and polish. Both living the consequences of their parents' hard work.

So they'd looked like every other teenager in the building, though maybe a little better off socially than some of the others. They'd still been close, too, but not as much.

Not as close as they used to be.

The day she was thinking of she'd been coming out of some class—chemistry maybe—and he'd been coming out of speech, and he'd grabbed her hand.

"Let's skip," he'd said, with a gleam in his eye that she hadn't seen in years.

"Andy." She'd pretended she was scandalized, but the truth was that it was the end of the day and near the end of the school year. Nothing was going to happen to them, nothing that really mattered anyway.

He'd played along, though it had been obvious from the start that he'd been onto her game. "The blueberries are out in Will's farm."

"Blueberries?" Warm from the sun. Growing wild near the woods. "Your car or mine?"

"Mine. It was my idea."

Less than an hour later, they'd changed clothes. Andy had grabbed a pair of shorts from his ball bag. She had on one of his worn baseball tees and another pair of his shorts, cinched tight at her waist.

And, just like in the past, they'd pulled off their shoes and were walking along the thickets barefoot.

She still remembered the feel of the weeds underfoot, the sun on her shoulders, the smell of dirt and decayed leaves, and the taste of warm blueberries on her lips.

But most of all, she remembered Andy's smile when he'd held out his hands and they'd been stained blue. It had been a little wicked, a little mischievous. Genuinely happy. He'd loved that day.

She had, too.

Before John could say another word, she pulled off

her shoes. Her toes curled against the closely mowed grass underfoot. Whereas before the grass had felt like only an inconvenience, now it felt perfect. Cold and soft. Almost familiar.

"Better?" John asked.

"Much."

"Want me to hold your shoes?"

"I've got it." She opened her purse and slipped her black patent sling backs inside. They vanished into the black hole that was otherwise known as her blue and tan Coach purse. She'd had it for years. It had proved to be both durable and perfect for holding just about anything and everything she'd needed to have with her over the years.

"Some things never change, hmm?"

Thinking about the two of them and the things they'd promised to each other the night before, she looked up at him and smiled. "Some things don't, but some things do."

He grinned, just as they met up with Will, Harley, Elizabeth Anne, Logan, Tricia, and Katie.

"Going barefoot, Marie?" E.A. asked.

"My heels were sticking in the dirt." She shrugged. "I wasn't going to take them off, but then John reminded me that Andy wouldn't have cared."

Logan held up a cooler. "He would have told us to get a move on."

"No, he would have already started walking," Tricia said. "He hated standing around and waiting."

Marie knew Andy's sister wasn't wrong.

Maybe because the reality of what they were doing was hitting them hard, or maybe it was simply because there was nothing left to say, they walked in silence the rest of the way. Beyond the statue of the lamb, to the left of a fountain, and finally to a space at the end of a row, right next to a wide open space that hadn't been claimed yet.

Looking at Andy's headstone, with ANDREW BEST WARNER carved in solemn, perfectly formed letters, Marie swallowed hard. She hadn't been here since she'd eaten Twizzlers next to his headstone.

John noticed and held out his hand. "You all right?"

She nodded as she took his hand and gripped it. "I'm good enough."

"I think here's a good spot," Katie said as she tossed her backpack on the ground and unzipped it. Then, with little fanfare, she pulled out a thin blue blanket and shook it out.

Will grabbed an end and helped pull it tight, then spread it out neatly on the ground. "This thing is massive, Katie," he said.

Katie looked pleased. "It was the biggest blanket I could find at the Walmart. It's soft, too. Everybody take off your shoes and get settled," she said as she tossed her flats off to the side.

There was a little bit of good-natured grumbling, but all of them did as she asked. Then, when Will opened the cooler, Logan started passing out brown sacks, each with a name on it.

"Your mother is *wunderbaar*," Katie said.

"She is," Logan agreed. "She liked the idea of us eating all together again. She liked the idea of that a lot."

Taking the sack with MARIE neatly labeled across its front, Marie held it on her lap.

"Want a soda?" John asked.

She nodded and took the Sprite he handed her before grabbing one for himself.

At last, they all were situated. Armed with food and drinks, each of them sitting haphazardly on the fabric, almost like a litter of puppies, it was almost perfect.

Almost.

She bit her lip. Again, the tears threatened to fall but she didn't want to spoil the moment. She took a drink of her soda instead.

Looking around, she realized the rest of them were all feeling the same sense of awkward loss that she did. Deciding that this time, at least, she could be the person to break the silence and say something meaningful, she opened her mouth to speak, to volunteer to lead everyone in prayer.

But Katie spoke first. "So, what do you think, Andy?" A new silence stretched out among them. Awkward and tense.

She continued. "I've got a turkey and Swiss on rye, which was never your favorite, I know. But I couldn't bring myself to make a peanut butter and jelly."

"I still can't eat them," E.A. whispered.

"None of us can except for Logan," Will teased.

"That's okay." Logan stared at Andy's stone. "I've got your back, buddy. Even though you left to begin your own adventure, you've still got us doing what we did best . . . following you."

"We've even brought the party to you," Marie said as she raised her can of Sprite.

"Andy, I hope you are sitting up in Heaven watching this, because yet again, you got your way. We're all together again," Harley murmured. "Just like we used to be. We're older and different and maybe even a little wiser."

E.A. wrinkled her nose. "Or stupider."

Katie laughed. "Or stupider. But no matter what, I'd like to think we're better."

"I'd like to think I am," Will said quietly as he reached out and pressed a palm on the side of the headstone. "Andy, all you had to do was be patient. If you would have given us a little bit longer, we would have come around. We just weren't quite ready yet."

"It doesn't really matter anymore," Katie said. "All that does is that we're all together now. *Danke*, Andy," she whispered. "Thank you."

Marie swallowed hard but didn't say a word. Neither did anyone else. Because really, nothing more needed to be said. They were all together, and they had Andy to thank for it. Andy and God.

And that, Marie realized, was why sitting on a blanket next to his grave didn't feel wrong at all.

For the first time in a long time, everything felt exactly right. Almost like they'd finally all come home. At long last.

Don't miss the next heartwarming installment
in The Walnut Creek Series

The

LOYAL ONE

Available now from Gallery Books!

PROLOGUE

MARCH

It was really too early in the season for a campfire near the Kurtzes' old cabin in the woods, but not a one of them had wanted to be anywhere else. The remainder of the Eight, along with a couple of new additions, had arrived just before sundown, each prepared to spend the night. An outsider would probably think they'd brought way too much.

Harley Lambright reckoned such a thing wasn't possible.

Though he was usually the first to arrive, Harley had gotten a late start. Therefore, he was still trying to shake off the stress of his workday. He remodeled homes and buildings around the area. It was a good job, and he often had more offers than he had time to do them—it wasn't always easy, attempting to make something old look new again.

Sometimes he just wanted to ask his customers to tear everything down and start from scratch. This had been one of those days. The house he was working on had been built in the 1930s and had already been through multiple remodels. Because of that, it was hard to make heads or tails of some of the plumbing and electrical work. His budget-conscious customers were having a difficult time understanding why he was insisting that everything needed to be brought up to code. After one such conversation, he'd actually considered walking off the worksite.

While the driver he'd hired slowly turned around on the narrow dirt road and headed back to town, Harley gave himself a moment to collect his thoughts and watch the activity around him.

Everyone was so busy, they would put a colony of bees to shame.

Will Kurtz was pulling out old folding chairs from a rickety storage shed just behind the cabin. Marie and John B. were carting over a cooler of soft drinks and a large straw basket filled with snacks. Logan Clark had his arms full with all the fixings for s'mores. Katie Steury was sitting on a rock, untwisting wire hangers.

The others? Well, the others did as they always did. They pitched in where they could and stacked wood. It was going to be a great night. A wonderful, *gut* one.

But then again, when had they not had a good time when they were all together?

With a bright smile on her face, Marie Hartman walked to his side. "So, what do you think, Harley? Are we ready?"

"I'd say so." Finally lifting the cooler he'd been carrying, he said, "I brought a mess of sandwiches."

She laughed. "While the rest of us brought soda, chips, and everything for s'mores, you are making sure we eat something healthy." Looping a hand through his arm, she tugged him forward. "What would we do without you?"

"I don't ever want to know." He smiled so she wouldn't realize how serious he was. This wasn't the night for that.

When they reached the fire pit, he spent the next ten minutes saying hello and finishing the final preparations.

And then, with a feeling of accomplishment, Harley pulled out a match, scraped it against one of the rocks surrounding the fire pit, and lit the kindling. Seconds later, a fire roared to life.

Logan clapped. "Look at that! We did it. And in spite of our jobs and family obligations, we all got here."

Elizabeth Anne raised her can of Sprite. "Amen to that."

"My boss asked me to stay late tonight, but I told him I had plans I couldn't miss," John B. said. "I've been looking forward to tonight for weeks."

"Me, too," Harley said. Looking around at all of his best friends, some Amish, some Mennonite, some English—most of whom he'd known for almost his entire life—he felt his body relax at last.

By the time the sun had completely slid down the sky and the first of the stars had begun to appear, the fire was crackling merrily and flavoring the air with the scents of fresh pine, old memories, and anticipation.

Looking at the flames, feeling the comfort and sense of contentment among all of them, Harley knew this was the perfect place to have a celebration. The evening was cool and crisp, the fire bright, the blankets surrounding them all were cozy . . . and the company even better.

But that was always how it had been. From the first summer the Eight had met, they'd felt an instant connection. Even though they all led very different lives, some firmly entrenched in the modern world, others steadfastly following the traditions and rules that so many generations had before, they'd stayed connected.

Over the years, they'd grown up together. They'd suffered hardships by one another's sides, and had commemorated everything from new kittens to first kisses to graduations in one another's company.

All that was why they'd come together to celebrate their group's first engagement. Logan had recently proposed to Tricia Warner, Andy's little sister, and few things had ever seemed like such a blessing.

But even though they all loved Logan and Tricia, it didn't mean that they couldn't resist doing a little bit of teasing and good-natured ribbing.

Or maybe even a lot of it.

"Come on, Logan!" Will Kurtz called out. "Kiss your bride-to-be one more time."

"All right. If I have to," Logan joked before pulling Tricia into his arms. Just as she placed her hands on his arms with a gasp, Logan gently kissed her cheek.

Groans abounded, along with someone tossing a paper cup at Logan.

"What kind of kiss is that?" John B. teased. "I kissed my first girl in the back of our barn with more enthusiasm than that."

"You probably kissed your aunt with more enthusiasm than that," Will quipped.

"Only on New Year's," John countered, quick as lightning.

Laughter filled the air as Tricia slapped a hand over her face in embarrassment. As for Logan? Well, he simply rested an arm around her shoulders and grinned. "It's the only kind of kiss you're gonna see, buddy. Now stop before you go and embarrass Trish."

"Too late!" Tricia called out, her face still covered.

As laughter erupted again, Kendra Troyer smiled at them all. "Isn't tonight perfectly perfect?"

Looking as contented as a cat at a dairy farm, E.A. nodded. "It's better than that."

Harley reckoned it was. Well, almost. Sometimes seeing Tricia Warner reminded him of the hole that Andy's death had created in their lives. Even though it had been almost a year since he'd taken his life,

Harley still missed him tremendously. Andy had been brash, loud, and a little spoiled. He'd also been loyal, kind, and sensitive.

Andy had been everything Harley had never been. And, in his worst, most insecure moments, everything that Harley wished he could have been.

With force, he pushed the first tinges of the depression he'd been battling away. He wasn't going to go there tonight. Not when there were so many other things to concentrate on.

As everyone around him started talking quietly, Harley allowed himself to glance at each one. Next to him were Logan and Tricia. On Tricia's other side was Will Kurtz. Will was Amish and worked at the trailer factory with John B., who was on Will's other side. Will's mother used to watch them all from time to time when they were young.

Sitting next to John B. was his sweetheart, Marie. John had grown up Amish but had recently jumped the fence for a variety of reasons, the main one being that he and Marie had fallen in love, and she was as English as a girl could be. Next in the circle sat Elizabeth Anne, all red hair, properness, and smiles. She was Mennonite and was best friends with Katie Steury, who was Amish like him.

Against his will, Harley let his gaze settle on Katie, thinking of how she looked so like the heroine in one of the more recent *Star Wars* movies. Back during his *rumspringa*, they'd all gone to the movies and thought Katie looked so much like a blond version of the actress Natalie Portman that they'd called her that for days.

Last but not least was Kendra Troyer, who was sitting on his left. Kendra was shy and a little awkward, and all of them were protective of her. He'd been glad that she'd become part of their extended group when they were teenagers.

"Harley?" Will called out. "You okay?"

"Hmm? Oh, *jah*. Just sitting here thinking."

"About what?" E.A. asked. "You look so serious."

Not wanting to admit that he'd been silently struggling with Andy's loss, Harley thought quickly. "Nothing much. I was only thinking about the night Marie and Andy graduated high school and we all went out together."

"Boy, I haven't thought about that night in ages," Marie said with a grin. "Hey, did any of your parents ever find out everything that we did?"

Will shuddered. "No way. *Mei daed* would have tanned my backside."

"You were lucky. My brothers found out," John B. said. "I had to do both James's and Anton's chores for a month in order for them to keep the secret."

Kendra waved a hand. "What actually did happen that night? I remember hearing that something had occurred, but I never heard the details."

"Believe me, you don't want to know," Marie said.

"I do," Tricia called out. "Come on, you Eight, don't be a tease. Andy never whispered a word about his graduation night."

"I ain't sure tonight's the best time to share it," Harley hedged. "I mean, it's a long story."

"Go ahead and tell it, Harley," Katie prodded. "It's Friday night, and none of us have anywhere else to be."

"All right. But don't say I didn't warn ya. It for sure doesn't show any of us in the best light."

"I'll try not to be too shocked," Kendra murmured, sarcasm thick in her voice.

Tricia reached for Logan's hand. "I am getting a little worried about what I'm about to find out."

"Don't get too worried," John B. said. "We didn't do anything that bad. I mean, we could have been a whole lot worse." Chuckling, he added, "As much as the story embarrasses me, I wouldn't change a bit of it."

"It ain't like we could ever change the past anyway," Will said.

Harley guffawed. "I do love it when you try to act all pious and perfect, William."

Looking sheepish, Will picked up his can of soda and sipped. "You're right. We were all once young and stupid. And for the record, I wouldn't have it any other way. Start talking, Harley. And don't leave anything out."

Feeling some of the pressure that had been weighing on him lighten at last, Harley stood up.

And, after mentally raising a toast to Andy, he began.

ACKNOWLEDGMENTS

The publication of this novel is quite a celebration for me, and I have many people to thank for helping *The Patient One* come to life. First, I owe a great deal of thanks to both my friends Clara and Celesta, for graciously allowing me to use their long friendship as the backbone for this series. I'm also very grateful for their smiles and patience with me as I continually ask questions for my books.

I am also forever grateful for my amazing agent, Nicole Resciniti, who agreed that I had an idea for a series that needed telling and navigated the tricky process of finding a home for it. Every writer should have an agent who cares so much.

Along those same lines, I'm indebted to my editor, Marla Daniels, and the whole Gallery team for taking a chance on me and my Amish novels. From the moment I joined Gallery Books, Marla and her team made me feel like a member of their extended family. That's been such a gift that I don't take for granted.

I'd also like to take this time to thank my readers, my Buggy Bunch, both current and "alumni," and for the many librarians and booksellers who've shared my novels. It's because of y'all that I can still write full-time, and I'm very grateful for that.

Finally, this note wouldn't be complete without acknowledging that I, like so many other people, have lost someone I loved to suicide. Making the choice to include this loss in a book did not come lightly or easily. I am grateful for my family and my faith for gifting me with the ability to now write about some of the pain that I experienced. If you, too, have lost someone you loved, I hope you will one day find a measure of peace as well.

6. The following verse from Proverbs guided me while I wrote this book. "Some friends may ruin you, but a real friend will be more loyal than a brother." How does this verse resonate with you?

7. I thought the following Amish Proverb could be good advice for many of the characters in the novel. "Our eyes are placed in front because it is more important to look forward than to look back." How might you or someone you love put this advice to good use?

8. Which characters are you hoping to read more about in an upcoming book?

READER QUESTIONS

1. What do you think about The Eight? Who are your lifelong friends? What do you think makes some friendships last years and years while others fade over time?

2. Much of the novel is about how different characters struggle with their friend Andy's death. What has helped you recover from a loved one's passing?

3. At first glance, one might determine that John B. and Marie have nothing in common. I happened to disagree! What do you think made their relationship work?

4. What did you think about John's choices? Did you agree, or do you think he made the wrong decision? How did you feel about his parents' and grandparents' reactions?

5. One of my favorite characters was Molly. What do you think will happen in her future?